The one he kept

Jill Norris

First edition

Editing by Lynn Smith & Susan Geary

Other books by Jill Norris:

Room 1210 -

Some doors should never be opened.

When two podcast hosts arrive at The Davidson House searching for answers behind its haunted past, they uncover something far sinister than ghost stories. Room 1210 has been waiting for them.

Whispers echo through the halls, shadows move where no one stands, and the deeper they dig into the hotel's history, the more they realize some spirits don't want to be remembered…

They want to be fed.

A chilling paranormal horror novel filled with ancient creatures, cursed tarot readings, and the terrifying hidden inside The Davidson House.

This is not a love story.

This story contains explicit sexual content, graphic violence, and disturbing themes involving control, obsession, and manipulation. Some scenes may be unsettling or triggering for certain readers.

Reader discretion is advised.

This book is dedicated to my amazing husband. You are my biggest cheerleader and constant source of support. Thank you for believing in me so wholeheartedly, for proudly sharing my dreams with the world, and always listening to me ramble about my books as I wrote them.

In loving memory of Diane, whose encouragement gave me the courage to write without fear. You were a beautiful part of my journey; this book carries a piece of you with it.

Chapter 1 Nick

He sat at the counter, methodically wiping the blade clean. Each slow swipe of the knife, a memory of what had just occurred. Sharp, vivid, and intoxicating. The fabric in his hand was warm now, damp with blood that had dried at the edges and sticky in the middle. He took his time, savoring the process.

The blade caught the light for a moment, and he noticed a stinging sensation pulsing at the tip of his finger. He looked down. Crimson beads had begun to rise and spill over his skin, and for a moment, he blinked in fascination. He had not even felt the knife slice through his finger. He watched as the blood swirled onto the blade, mixing with the small amount of blood from someone else.

He tilted his head, watching the mixture swirl, the two shades of red becoming one.

"Huh," he murmured, head tilting slightly. "Does that make us blood siblings now?"

A quiet chuckle escaped from him. "I'm a riot."

Still, the blood kept coming. Every swipe of the towel only smeared it further. He sighed, more irritated now than wounded, and finally laid the knife on the counter with a metallic clink.

He lifted his finger to his mouth, sucking the blood away with slow, deliberate intent, like it was a delicacy. His eyes fluttered shut for half a second, relishing the copper taste that grounded him in the moment.

"Not bad," he mumbled to himself.

He reached for the duct tape nearby and tore off a piece with his teeth, wrapping the finger in tight, sloppy circles. "That'll have to do for now."

Without hesitation, he picked the knife back up, wiped the last streaks of blood onto his pant leg like it was nothing more than engine grease, then slid it back into the sheath.

The snap of the button on the sheath clicked into place, and with it, the stillness in the cabin settled again like dust. Outside, the early morning sun began to bleed through the trees, stretching thin beams of light across the hardwood floor. Birds chirped in the distance; nature's little distractions, blissfully unaware of the horror nestled in the ranger's quaint, government-issued cabin.

He stood, stretching his back with a grunt as if he had simply finished a long night of paperwork. His boots creaked against the floorboards as he walked to the sink, washing his hands with a deliberate rhythm. The water turned pink, then red, then clear. He stared at the drain as the evidence swirled away into the pipes, gone like it had never existed.

The scent of pine and copper lingered in the air.

Across the room, a small radio crackled to life with the morning police dispatch, routine chatter about hikers on Trail 3 and a family of deer near the hatchery. He listened, amused, wiping his hands on a faded towel with a park logo stitched in the corner.

"Business as usual," he muttered.

He moved to the closet and pulled on his uniform, pressed, neat, and spotless. The badge gleamed. He adjusted his collar, checked his reflection in the mirror, and gave himself a small, approving nod. No one would question him. No one ever did. He was a fixture here. The friendly ranger.

One last glance around the cabin. Neat. Sterile. Deceptively ordinary.

He grabbed his hat, placed it on his head, and stepped out into the daylight. The forest greeted him with the scent of earth and wildflowers, hiding the rot beneath its roots. With every step he took down the porch, the wooden planks groaned softly, as if they too were tired of keeping his secrets.

Chapter 2 Danielle

The gravel crunched beneath Danielle's sneakers as she rounded the bend near the hatchery trail.

She slowed, then stopped.

Wind threaded softly through the trees. Birds chirped somewhere high above. Far off, the stream gurgled steadily over stone. It should have been peaceful. It always had been.

Instead, her stomach tightened. Danielle glanced over her shoulder.

Nothing.

She had passed two fishermen earlier and a woman walking a golden retriever. Now the trail stretched behind her empty, unnaturally still, like it had swallowed everything that had been there moments before.

Her fingers drifted to her chest, brushing the small body cam clipped to her shirt. A recent habit. It was for her ASMR content. It consisted of nature walks and ambient sounds. The videos seemed to be taking off. She did not realize how many people enjoyed watching her walk the trails.

She started walking again, forcing her legs to move.

The sensation returned almost immediately. A crawling awareness along her spine, intimate and wrong, like someone standing just close enough that she could feel the warmth of their breath without hearing it.

"It's just in your head," she whispered, barely louder than the crunch of her steps.

It did not help.

The trail narrowed as it curved deeper into the woods. The trees pressed closer here; their shadows were darker and thicker. Danielle tugged her ponytail tighter, pulse ticking faster. She hated how small the path suddenly felt.

That was when she saw him.

The forest ranger stood ahead near the fork in the trail, half-shadowed by the trees. His uniform was immaculate, green and brown blending seamlessly into the forest, like he belonged to it. When he noticed her, his mouth curved into an easy smile, dimples creasing his cheeks in a way that felt disarming despite itself. He lifted his hand in a slow, casual wave.

"Morning," he called.

Danielle forced a smile and slowed her pace. "Morning."

"You're out early again," he said. His eyes moved over her, not hurried, not openly rude, but with a deliberate attention that made her skin prickle. He was very tall, towering over her. His sleeves were snug around his arms, muscles shifting beneath the fabric when he moved. Dark ink peeked out from under the edge of his shirt, tattoos she could not quite make out, but just enough showed to suggest there was more beneath the uniform than the town's clean-cut hero image.

"Yeah," she said, shifting her weight. "I like the peacefulness of the early mornings."

As she stepped closer, she caught his scent, pine, and clean soap. Something warm and distinctly masculine beneath it. Her mouth went dry without warning. The reaction startled her, heat flickering low in her stomach before she could stop it.

That bothered her a lot.

He intrigued her in a way she did not know how to explain. In a way that felt dangerous.

She walked these trails every morning and seemed to run into him. Most days he never said anything, he would just tilt his hat at her and keep on going but he always watched her. Not in the forest ranger, I'm just trying to keep the park safe type of way, more of stalking her with his eyes.

He was friendly, approachable, and extremely handsome. The kind of man women noticed and the kind she instinctively assumed would use them up and discard them without a second thought. Bad news wrapped in a charming smile.

Still, standing there under his gaze, Danielle felt exposed, like the trees had leaned back to give him a better look.

She hated that her body reacted anyway.

"Name's Nick Chambers," he said. "If you ever need anything, I'm usually around."

"Thanks," Danielle replied.

Of course, she knew his name. Everyone did. Ranger Chambers, the town's quiet hero. The one who had pulled a drowning boy from the river years back. She doubted he knew her, though. She was no one special. Just a small-town girl who followed the rules, kept her head down, and never gave anyone a reason to remember her.

"You be careful," Nick added, gesturing toward the deeper stretch of trail. "Not many people come out this far this early. Easy to slip near the rocks by the hatchery pool."

"I'll stay on the path," she said quickly.

"Smart girl."

The words settled strangely in her chest. He held her gaze a beat too long, dimples fading as his expression shifted into something harder to read. Then his brow creased faintly.

"I didn't catch your name."

Danielle hesitated. Every instinct told her not to say it but she was online. Easy to find. And refusing to tell him would feel rude.

"Danielle," she said.

Something unreadable flickered across his face before the smile returned.

"Nice to meet you, Danielle," he said softly.

She smiled back, tight and polite, then stepped past him. She could feel his eyes on her back as she walked away, steady, unblinking. It was not until the trail bent again that she finally slowed, breath shallow, pulse racing.

By the time she reached her car, relief washed over her so strongly it left her weak.

She climbed inside, locked the doors, and pulled out her phone. With a tap, she stopped the recording on the hidden cam app. Her reflection stared back at her from the darkened screen, eyes bright and unsettled.

He makes my skin crawl, she thought. So why can't I stop thinking about him?

The question followed her long after she drove away.

Chapter 3 Nick

The percolator screamed on the stove top, but he didn't move.

He sat at the small table in the center of the cabin, staring at nothing and everything all at once. The chair creaked beneath him as he leaned back slightly.

Danielle.

That name tasted better than the drink ever would. He whispered it aloud just to feel it leave his mouth.

"Danielle."

It lingered in the air like smoke.

She had smiled at him again today. Not a real one. Tight lipped. But still… it was a start. She was polite and sweet, but a little too careful. She was cautious; he could see it in her body language. That made it even better.

It meant she was thinking about him, too. And he was becoming obsessed. He had watched her for a very long time, though she didn't know that. He had watched how her body moved, her smile when she saw a deer or moose in the distance, the way she would greet other hikers with her sweet personality. He wanted to know everything about her. What she liked, what made her giggle, what made her sad, and what made her excited.

He rose slowly, walked to the kettle, and turned off the burner. The room fell into silence again, save for the slow tick of the wall clock and the chirp of birds outside his window. He poured the coffee, black and steaming, into the mug and took a long, steady sip. Still thinking of her.

He moved to the sink, rinsing out a blood-speckled rag from earlier, scrubbing it clean like he was baptizing it, as red water spun down the drain. He smiled at the swirl. Everything came full circle eventually.

She was perfect, really. So full of life, and she seemed so innocent like everything in the world was new to her. It would be different with her. Not quick. Not messy like the others. No, she deserved a masterpiece.

He turned on the radio. Country music hummed softly through the static. He cleaned the cabin, even though it was always meticulously clean. He swept the floors, humming along. Then he folded the towels and took out the trash. And all the while, her name played on a loop in his head.

Danielle.

He wasn't just going to kill her. He was going to slowly take her life, enjoy every moment, stare right into her eyes as she took her last breath.

***

The next day Nick smiled as he walked through the forest thinking of Danielle. The leaves crunched beneath his boots as he stepped carefully through the underbrush, just far enough off the trail to remain hidden. Years of walking in this forest had made him a ghost in it. The land obeyed him. The trees cloaked him. The animals scattered when they sensed him coming.

Danielle was ahead, no more than fifty feet, walking with that same rhythmic bounce he had memorized over the past month. She was alone today. No dog walkers, no chatty couples with trail maps. Just her. She moved slowly, enjoying the beautiful scenery and the birds that sang near her.

He watched her crouch down to tie her shoe, the muscles in her legs flexing beneath her black leggings. She was close now. His breath slowed, his eyes tracking every movement like a predator zeroed in on prey. She stood back up and turned, heading deeper into the trail. That small offshoot trail. The one not marked on the visitor maps.

Perfect.

He moved with her. One step for every five of hers. He knew which branches to duck, which brush wouldn't crack beneath him. His breath fogged slightly in the cold air, but he didn't feel it. All he felt was the surge of excitement thrumming just beneath the surface of his skin. She had no idea someone was watching her, and he was absolutely sure that she would never suspect him. Not the friendly ranger. The helpful one. The one who gave her trail tips. The one who waved.

She was just so… naive. He had looked into her name. She was an only child to Jonathon and Wanda Ashford. They were a devout Christian family. Danielle worked at the community center and volunteered a lot. She was a quiet girl in town and kept to herself unless she was with her friend Emily. He knew she was quite different from the girls he usually attracted, which is why he had never run into her.

Nick had moved here from Georgia four years ago. Most women fawned over him, first when they saw him, and even more when they heard his voice. He could not stand women like that. They had no respect for themselves. They saw a fit, 6'4" man in a uniform and their minds turned to jelly. Their spot between their thighs clearly making all their decisions for them.

It made him want to drag it out, maybe really screw with her mind. What if she fell for him? That would really make the shock of what was happening even better. To watch the exact moment she realized who he really was. The moment that smile of hers would falter, and the forest would finally swallow her whole.

He licked his lips, then slowly pulled back, retreating deeper into the trees, circling around to a spot where the path narrowed and visibility vanished.

He was going to take his time with her.

And she wouldn't see it coming.

Chapter 4 Danielle

The shower ran too hot, fogging the mirror as Danielle scrubbed trail dust from her skin. She stayed under the spray longer than usual, letting the scalding water pound against her shoulders, trying to wash the anxious feeling out of her body.

It didn't work.

The walk hadn't helped. Not today. Her legs still felt unsteady, like she had walked farther than she remembered, and her thoughts kept circling in the same place no matter how hard she tried to steer them away.

The ranger.

She clenched her jaw, annoyed with herself and angry that her body reacted every time she thought about him. Angry that it remembered details she wished it wouldn't.

The way he had looked at her yesterday didn't feel friendly. It had not felt protective or polite or harmless.

It had felt like ownership.

The memory crept in uninvited: the way his eyes darkened when they moved over her, slow and deliberate, like he was measuring her. Like she was something he intended to take. The thought made her shudder, but not entirely from fear and that annoyed her even more.

By the time she dried off and curled up on her bed in an oversized sweatshirt, the unease had settled heavy in her stomach, a dull, constant weight. She pulled her laptop onto her knees, unclipped the tiny camera from her sports bra, and plugged it in.

Just check, she told herself. *Prove to yourself you're not imagining things.*

The footage loaded. The screen bobbed gently with each step she had taken; audio filled with birdsong, wind, and the faint rhythm of her breathing. It all looked so normal. Peaceful and safe.

She fast-forwarded and stopped quickly. There he was. He stood at the bend in the trail, right before it split. His uniform was immaculate, like the woods hadn't dared touch him. He smiled and waved, and she heard herself say morning in a voice tighter than she remembered.

Danielle leaned closer, her finger hovering over the pause button.

Something about the way he was standing. No. It was the way he was watching her. She rewound and played it again, slower this time. The moment she entered the frame, his posture changed. His body went still. The easy, friendly demeanor dropped away like a mask slipping loose. His smile was completely different.

And his eyes… they weren't meeting hers. They were consuming her.

Danielle's hand froze on the track pad as her throat tightened. That look wasn't friendly. It wasn't curiosity. It was hunger. As if she already belonged to him, and he was simply waiting for the right moment to claim what he had decided was his. Her breath hitched.

She rewound again and paused the frame the instant she came into view. His gaze was locked on her with unsettling intensity. His jaw was tight. His chest rose and fell slowly in the cool air. And for half a second, so brief she almost missed it, his tongue brushed across his lips.

Danielle snapped the laptop closed, heart pounding. Her bedroom felt darker than it had moments ago. Smaller. This wasn't just in her head. That look, that moment, it was real. The warning her body had screamed at her hadn't been imagination or paranoia. She just sat there, staring at the paused image that burned into her mind. The ranger stood tall and solid and composed, watching her like she was the only thing he wanted on earth.

For the first time in her adult life, Danielle felt truly hunted. Her gut told her he was not to be trusted, that there was something wrong with him. She thought about calling someone to ask about him, but she knew what the townsfolk would say and that would not ease the gut feeling she was having.

Everyone loved Nick and trusted him. He was very close to the detectives and the rest of the police department. The women in town fell all over him and even the women at church acted as if he was sent by God himself. She had overheard the married women at church one day in the kitchen all talking about him. How they would devour him if they had the chance and talking very explicitly about what they would do to him. They would say how God made him perfect and how he was such a sweet guy with the biggest heart and even bigger things in other places. One of the women had said they needed to find a way to convert him to the church so they could see him even more. At that point Danielle had left, not wanting to hear *good* Christian married women talking about Nick as if he was a piece of meat and they were going hunting.

Yet she understood their feelings towards him and that terrified her almost as much as the way she hated how her body betrayed her when she thought about him, the authority in his stance, the dimples when he smiled, his ice blue eyes, and the memory of pine and clean soap clinging to him. Heat pooled low despite her fear, confusion tightening in her chest.

The Christian girl in her knew better. Knew she should stay far away, yet even though her gut screamed at her, the rest of her body thrummed to life, wanting him.

Chapter 5 Nick

Nick could not sit still. His hands were shaking as he thought about Danielle. The fireplace wood had burned low, casting flickering shadows that danced along the cabin walls.

His skin itched; he needed a release. He wanted her blood wrapped around his knife badly. He needed to feel her take her last breath because of him, needing to feel the release of air from her lungs. Feel her blood, warm on his hands and see her eyes full of fear.

Nick ground his teeth, squeezing his hands into fists to stop the shaking. It wasn't helping. The thoughts of her kept playing in his head, her tight ponytail, the curve of her back, the rise and fall of her chest as he made her nervous.

He grabbed his uniform, slipping it on like he was wearing armor; it made him an invisible threat. He buckled his belt and holstered his knife, the familiar weight comforting at his hip. He needed someone to quiet his thoughts, even if only for a moment so he could think clearly. He wanted to enjoy Danielle's death and right now with the way he felt, he knew he would go too quickly with her, or he would slip up and make a mistake.

He hopped in the truck and it rumbled to life. As he drove through the woods, he saw a flicker of light, as if someone was having a fire. He killed the lights so he would not scare them off.

The sound reached him before the sight of them. Soft laughter echoed through the trees.

Nick stepped out of his truck and let the door close without a sound, the forest swallowing the noise. The giggling drifted through the trees like a lure, light and reckless in a place that fed on silence. He followed it toward the stream, boots sinking into damp soil, every step he took was calculated and careful.

Two girls stood knee-deep in the water, moonlight sliding over bare skin, their laughter bouncing off the trees as they splashed each other. They were young… too young to be this far out, too stupid to understand where they were. The night polished them with silver moonlight and made them look majestic.

Nick stopped just beyond the glow and watched them. They were both small, with narrow shoulders, and thin wrists that he knew would make them very easy to overtake. He pictured how easily the sound would leave them. How fast the forest would take them.

They were in mid laugh when Nick saw the blonde look up. Her smile faltered, the sound of her laugh breaking into a sharp, panicked squeak before she clapped a hand over her mouth. The brunette followed her gaze, eyes widening.

Nick stepped forward slowly, letting the firelight crawl up his frame, letting them really see him. Tall and broad, with his hands resting on his hips. His gaze stayed flat and unreadable.

"You girls supposed to be camping out here?" He asked. His voice was calm but official.

The brunette wiped water from her eyes, forcing a laugh that didn't land. "Chief Braider said it was okay. He told us this was, like… an approved spot."

Nick's jaw tightened almost imperceptibly.

He took another step closer, boots crunching softly on gravel. "Really?" he said quietly. "I don't believe you."

They exchanged a frightened look, their eyes widening.

"This isn't a designated camping area," he continued, tone dropping. "Not even close."

He let the silence stretch, watching it sink in.

Then he smiled. It wasn't warm. It never was.

"But" he said, glancing over them slowly, deliberately, "looks like you're havin' yourselves a good time." He stepped closer again, his shadow spilling over the water, swallowing their reflections. "You're not supposed to be out here past dusk. So, keep it down."

The girls seemed to relax as the blonde spoke. "Yes, sir," she said, lifting two fingers in a mock salute.

The disrespect tightened something deep in Nick's chest. He felt the anticipation flow through his body, slow and familiar, and he smirked before dropping his face back into place quickly.

"Alright… out of the water," he snapped, curling his fingers once in a lazy come-here motion.

They obeyed quickly, scrambling out of the water and grabbing their towels hanging from a low branch. Up close, they were even smaller than he had thought. Fragile and breakable. Nick kept his breathing steady. He needed to stay cool and calculated.

He lifted his flashlight and let the beam sweep their faces. They were pretty, and very unaware of what he was about to do. The kind of girls who thought bad things only happened to other people.

The blonde stepped forward, her smile sweet and practiced. "We'll be quiet," she said softly. "Promise."

Her gaze dragged over him. His height, his arms, the set of his shoulders. Her cheeks flushed. Then her tongue flicked out, slow, and intentional.

Nick almost sighed. He hated that. He knew exactly what she saw: six-foot-four, ice-blue eyes; authority stitched into his uniform. He had watched that look bloom on faces too many times to count.

The blonde let her towel slip.

"Oops."

She bent to retrieve it, movements exaggerated and deliberate. Nick didn't move. In his mind, her hair was already tangled in his fist, pulling her close to him. The sound she would make when her throat opened was sharp and brief.

She straightened and stepped closer.

Nick rested his hands on his belt, fingers brushing the knife clipped there. The familiar weight steadied him. With two girls, he needed to be patient and needed to stay in control.

He stepped closer, pretending to admire her. But in his mind, he saw Danielle's face, saw her begging, and choking on her own fear. His cock throbbed for a second, but he pushed the thought away. If he got too excited he would slip up.

"Ma'am, you're beautiful," he murmured. "So, you might want to be careful out here. Woods like these… they're quiet. Perfect place for people to disappear, there's a lot of creepy people out here."

She blushed harder. "Oh, I can handle myself." She placed a finger on her lip, trying to act seductive. "But I wouldn't mind if you handled me."

He gave her his best smile, the one he knew melted women and stepped closer to her.

"Well, ma'am… maybe this is your lucky night."

He leaned in, whispering warm against her ear, "Why don't you tell your friend you'll be right back? My cabin is just down the road. I'll show you a real good time."

She hesitated, glancing toward the tent where her friend poked at the fire. "I don't know. She won't want me leaving her alone."

Nick straightened, letting disappointment darken his face. "That's a shame, sweetie."

He turned and walked toward the truck. He didn't need to look back. He knew exactly how this game played out.

Sure enough, her footsteps followed moments later. He smirked. The cat and mouse chase always ended the same way. He reached for the truck door, pretending not to notice her. Then her hand touched his back.

"I mean…" she teased, "maybe we could just have some fun here. All three of us."

He turned slowly, letting his gaze lock into hers.

"Oh honey," he said softly, "I don't share."

Nick smirked and took her hand, his grip firm and possessive. He led her to the back of his truck; the metal of the tailgate cold and unforgiving as he bent her over it. His hand slid up the smooth column of her thigh; her skin chilled by the night air, a stark contrast to the heat that was building under his own skin. She giggled, a light, breathy sound, and pressed back against him, a foolish, trusting gesture. In a single, brutal motion, he fisted a handful of her hair and yanked her head back, exposing the delicate line of her throat. A soft moan escaped her lips. She had no idea she had just willingly stepped into the grip of something primal, something she should have fled from the moment she saw him.

His hand continued its ascent, his fingers tracing the edge of her bikini bottom before they stopped. He let the anticipation hang in the air for a heartbeat, a silent, savoring moment. His thoughts went to how good it will feel to hear her last breath, the one where he can hear and feel their soul leave their body. The thought of her blood sliding down his hand, warm and thick. His cock hardened as his hand slid to the knife. Then, with the fluid grace of a predator, he drew the knife from its sheath. It was a whisper of steel against leather. He drew the blade in a single, swift, horizontal line across her throat, before she could even register the sound, before a gasp could even form on her lips. The sound wasn't a scream, but a wet, ragged gurgle as her breath tried and failed to escape through the severed opening. Her hands flew to her neck, a useless, instinctual gesture; her fingers clawing at the mortal wound. It was too late. Within seconds, the fight drained out of her, and her body went limp, a dead weight resting against the cold metal. He tossed her into the truck bed with a dull thud, the finality of the sound sending a jolt of pure, unadulterated satisfaction through him. He closed his eyes, breathing in the scent of night air and coppery blood, forcing his own body's eager reaction down. Not yet. He still had to take care of the other girl. He grabbed a rag and quickly cleaned the knife off and slid it back into its sheath.

He turned away from the truck and walked back toward the fire pit, where the brunette stood alone, her face illuminated by the shifting, orange glow. She was a portrait of innocence, completely oblivious.

"Where's Lucy?" she asked, her eyes darting around nervously.

"Bathroom," his voice smooth as polished glass, not missing a beat. "Told me she'd be right back."

The girl hesitated for a moment, then seemed to accept the lie, nodding before resuming her task of poking the fire with a stick. Embers swirled upward like tiny, desperate sparks trying to escape the blaze. He watched her, a dark part of him imagining shoving her straight into the flames, just to hear that first blistering, inhuman scream. But fire was loud, and it drew attention.

He stepped closer, his boots crunching softly in the dry leaves. "Make sure you put that fire out completely before you go to sleep," he said, his tone casual, almost fatherly. "Don't need a wildfire out here."

"Yes, sir," she murmured; her eyes fixed on the hypnotic dance of the flames.

He moved closer still, standing just beside her, close enough to feel the heat radiating from her body. "I love fires," he said quietly, his voice a low murmur. "Amazing, isn't it? How one tiny spark can swallow a whole log in minutes." He looked at her, waiting for a reaction, but she barely seemed to hear him, mesmerized by the blaze, lulled by its warmth into a state of blissful oblivion. Perfect.

His hand drifted to the knife on his belt, his fingers curling around the familiar, worn handle. He needed to do this without a sound, without a scream that could carry on the night air. He shifted behind her, his shadow falling over her, eclipsing the firelight as he spoke again. "Stream's movin' fast tonight," he said lightly, his gaze fixed on the dark, glistening water just beyond the firelight. "Crazy how much rain we've had."

The girl still didn't turn. She had no idea she was standing on the very edge of her last moment alive. The utter dismissal, the way she didn't even acknowledge his presence, ignited a cold fury within him.

He unsheathed the knife in a silent, fluid motion. Before she could poke the fire again, he lunged, his arm hooking around her chest to pull her flush against him in a brutal, final embrace. He held her tight, feeling the frantic beat of her heart against his arm for a split second before he slid the razor-sharp edge of the knife across her throat. She didn't have time to fight. She gurgled, just like the other girl, a pathetic, wet sound. And with a hard shove, he sent her toppling forward into the fire. The flames leaped up to greet her, her hair igniting with a whoosh; the smell of burning flesh quickly overpowering the scent of pine and wood smoke. He watched, transfixed, as the fire consumed her, its orange glow painting a gruesome masterpiece on her skin. Nick didn't move. He watched as her blood hissed and curled into the flames, dark streaks vanishing into orange and red.

The sight was a primal trigger, a key turning deep within his gut. His climax began to build, not as a wave, but as a slow, tightening coil of pure, electric pleasure. He slammed his palm against the rough bark of a nearby pine tree, the sharp bite of the wood a grounding point as his body began to surrender. A deep, guttural groan tore from his throat as the tension finally snapped. Warmth flooded his boxers, a thick, undeniable release that pulsed through him in rhythmic, shuddering waves.

His eyes fluttered closed, and the scene before him dissolved into a perfect, visceral memory. He could feel the phantom warmth of her blood dripping onto his hands, the slick, coppery heat coating his skin. He could hear her last, choked gasp echoing in his ears, the sound of her life extinguishing as her body went limp and heavy in his arms. It was the perfect blend of power and finality; the absolute control he held over her last breath. That excited him in a way nothing else ever could. It was a pleasure that was so profound, so all-consuming. It left him trembling and utterly sated in the flickering firelight.

The first girl was still where he had left her, warmth lingering despite the cold night air. He lifted her easily, draping her over his shoulder like she weighed nothing at all.

At the fire pit, he didn't hesitate. He threw her onto the flames, right on top of her friend and used a stick to force their legs into the fire as well. The smell hit instantly, burning wood, scorched fabric, and flesh surrendering to heat. Nick closed his eyes and inhaled slowly, committing it to memory. His pulse slowed. The itch receded. Balance restored.

By morning, there would be nothing left but ash and blackened stones.

Nick walked back to his truck, hands steady, mind already shifting forward. Tomorrow, during his morning patrol, he would make the call. He would be calm, professional, and concerned. Another tragedy discovered, and no one would ever suspect the truth.

Chapter 6 Nick

Nick woke up that morning and poured coffee grounds into the percolator and set it on the stove. He stood in the kitchen, bare feet on the cold wooden floor, listening to the familiar rumble of the water heating up.

As he sat at the table, smelling the aroma of the coffee brewing, the smell of it brought back the smell of the campfire. Flashes of the night before ran through his mind as he reveled in the memories. He remembered the feeling of taking their last breath, especially when they thought they were going to get something much more fun. The feeling of their blood running down his hand. He had touched these girls in a way no one else ever could and made them gasp in a way no one else ever would. He remembered the way their bodies twitched and then gave out like a wind-up toy.

Bringing people into this world was a miracle, people said, but taking them out, that was a privilege many would never know, and he got to take it away. He remembered how the blonde had pushed back into him harder as the knife sliced through her neck like butter, the first gasp of pain. Most girls liked a little pain, and he knew that the first little bit had excited her, and the rest had come too quick for her to realize what was happening. She had welcomed death without knowing it.

The whistle from the percolator brought him back to reality. He stood up and grabbed a plain black mug, and poured the coffee to the rim. Steam curled towards his face and for a moment he closed his eyes and inhaled.

The smell reminded him of the dirt beneath his boots last night, the crunch of leaves as he moved behind the brunette. She clearly couldn't stand the fact that he had just had fun with her best friend. She probably figured if she ignored him, he would leave. If anything, it made him more intrigued to know how close he could get to her without her even realizing what was about to happen. She never had a second to wonder what he was doing. He had grabbed her so quickly and sliced so perfectly she died with the thoughts of being mad at her friend. She died pissed off and would never be at peace.

He loved how one had gone out giggling and the other burning with rage. Balance and harmony. Yin and Yang, he thought with a smirk. He had given them that gift.

As the first taste of coffee hit his tongue, his mind came back to the present. The heat scalded his tongue slightly, anchoring him. He had work to do. He knew he needed to wash out the bed of his truck and get to the campsite. He needed to rake the site, knowing the blonde probably left behind a blood trail and then he needed to call it in. He needed it to look like a complete accident, and that he was stumbling across it for the first time, disturbed by the scene.

He chugged the last bit of coffee in his mug, placed it in the sink, and then walked outside to wash the bed of his truck. As he hosed down the bed, he watched as the water mixed with the blood, making the water pink as it rushed out of the truck's bed. As it hit the dirt, red mud formed. He now had parts of this girl on his land, forever swirled into the earth. He could walk outside every day and know that she would always be here.

His thoughts went to Danielle. He could not wait until she was here as well. He needed her so badly, and even though these girls had helped calm the itch, he knew he really needed her. She might even calm the itch forever. Maybe her blood would run sweeter. Maybe she would scream the way he kept imagining she would, or maybe she wouldn't scream at all. The thought nearly made his knees buckle.

He finished cleaning up the truck and washing down his shoes. He dried his hands on a rag and hopped into the driver's seat. The truck purred to life. He loved his '92 Ford pickup. The square manly body that they no longer made, the steel that could hit anything without denting, this truck could take a beating and keep on going. He put the truck in drive and heard the familiar rumble of her telling him she was ready to go.

"Let's go make a discovery." He whispered to himself.

The tires rolled across the dirt as he pulled out of the driveway. Time to play the part.

Nick's truck rumbled low as he pulled off the trail and crept towards the clearing. Smoke still swirled from coals near the fire pit. The campsite looked quiet, peaceful even. Parts of the girls were still scattered near the fire pit, parts that didn't make it into the fire. The edge of a melted flip flop lay half submerged in the damp ground. He looked up to the sky as he heard the screech of a vulture flying in circles overhead.

"They always know." He muttered to himself.

As he walked closer to the pit, he could hear his shoes squeaking from the dew in the grass, the wetness clinging to the leather. Birds chirped in the distance, and a squirrel rustled in the underbrush nearby. He checked to make sure there were no signs of him being here last night and as he scoped the entire campsite. If anything was found it wouldn't lead back to him being the murderer; it would only solidify the story that he discovered the scene during his routine check of the grounds.

When he was satisfied, he returned to the truck and pulled out his radio.

"Ravensburg dispatch, this is Ranger Nick. I have a situation. It looks like a campsite incident. Requesting police and coroner to my location, east side of Hickory trail."

He leaned back in his seat and waited for his friends from the Ravensburg police station. He loved living here, Ravensburg was a small town, quaint stores lined main street, a cute antique store, bakeries, and the mom-and-pop diner where the waitress knew your order by heart. The kind of place where you waved at your neighbors and trusted the man in uniform without hesitation.

Broad Mountain State Park was a jewel in New Hampshire's wilderness. Towering evergreens, beautiful wildlife, and the ever-flowing Suncook River, where he patrolled and kept things safe. The view was amazing here. The mountains seemed to surround you and mirrored right into the gorgeous clear river. He loved watching people fly fish here or hearing kids with their parents running through the hiking trails. This was a great place to raise a family.

Nick's smile faded slightly as his thoughts shifted. He would not have a family here, nor did he want one. His childhood had been tainted. He had been on his own since he was 14. His parents had died in a horrible car crash from a drunk driving incident on I-95. He had been forced to live with his chain smoking, angry and bitter old aunt until he turned 18. She clearly hated that she had been forced to take him in. His parents had deemed her the guardian, God forbid anything happen to them. She left him alone a lot while she gambled and smoked her life away. She had been married, but Uncle Walter had left her after she had an affair. That was when she had become bitter. By the time Nick had come to live with her she was angry, yet she had done this. After that he enlisted in the Coast Guard and did four years in the fisheries division. It had given his life order and discipline. He had lost a few good friends. One had fallen overboard and was never recovered, and they had never explained what happened. Another had gotten pneumonia on the ship, and it had taken him down. Once he had finished his four years, he got out and he had gone to the White Mountains Community College for forestry. He wanted out of that lifestyle and area. He had lost so much and didn't want the memories anymore. After that he went to the Academy for Police Standards. He wanted nothing more than to become a Forest Ranger. He had been hired as the Forest Ranger in Ravensburg four years ago. He loved his job, the freedom, the open forest, and being one with nature. But his favorite part was the late night strolls of poor unsuspecting women who clearly needed saving if they were strolling the woods at night.

Danielle was different; there was something about her that kept him thinking about her. She pulled him in, and he was becoming obsessed with her. He needed to touch her, take her, and make her his. She was not like the others, and he did not want a quick moment with her; he wanted a long, slow, memorable time with her.

As he sat there thinking about her, daydreaming about what he could do, he heard tires on gravel. He turned to see the familiar police cruiser rolling to a stop behind his truck. Nick jumped out of the truck and raised a hand in greeting.

"Hey, Chuck."

"Hey, Nick, whatcha' got today?" The Chief asked, squinting at the fire pit.

"Two bodies, far as I can tell. Looks like girls, judging by the shoe and well… what's left. They must have snuck out here after I did my final pass at seven last night."

Chuck let out a low whistle, eyes scanning the area. "Jesus. After the last two murders, you think people would be smart enough not to come out here at night. How many times do we have to warn people."

Nick shrugged, "Clearly they like the rush of saying they outlived the murderer." Nick chuckled in his mind, knowing they did not outlive him.

Chuck shook his head. "Well, thanks, Nick, for calling it in. The coroner will be here soon to look at what's left of the girls. And the other detectives should be here soon. Hopefully, we can figure out what happened and catch this person."

Nick tipped his hat to Chuck before walking back to his truck. "Have a good day Chuck, hopefully you find the guy, so you don't have to keep coming out here and bothering me."

Chuck laughed and waved back. "See ya, Nick."

Nick chuckled to himself as he drove back to his cabin, knowing very well that their killer would not be caught today. Or ever.

Chapter 7 Danielle

Danielle stepped onto the familiar path, the crunch of leaves and gravel under her shoes a welcome rhythm. As she walked, all her thoughts melted away. She loved getting on the trail and losing herself to nature. She loved the peace of it. The chirping birds, the wind brushing past her face, the squirrels leaping from tree to tree with their frantic squeaks. And sometimes, if you were really lucky, you might even catch a glimpse of a moose.

Her pace quickened as she fell into her normal workout. She felt like she knew every step of this trail; she never tripped over a root or stumbled on a rock, never lost her footing in a hole or whacked her head on a low-hanging branch. This was her sanctuary.

As she got closer to the pond, the quiet place where she always stopped to breathe and enjoy the breathtaking view, she noticed something was wrong. She could see blue lights flashing and the glint of metal up ahead. As she got closer, she saw the police cars, there had to be at least four, all blocking the trail. An officer approached and stopped her.

"Hello, ma'am," the officer said, tipping his hat. "Sorry, but the trail is closed today."

"Closed? What happened?"

He hesitated. "We can't say much yet, but there was a terrible accident. I would urge you to not walk through here by yourself."

Her stomach flipped. "Oh… okay, thank you officer," Danielle said wearily. "I hope everyone is alright."

The officer gave her a tight smile and a nod before returning to the others. Danielle turned around to head back to her car. The words made her nervous. She loved it here; she didn't want it tainted. She hoped whoever had been hurt was alright.

The walk back to the car felt slower than usual. Her eyes scanned the woods, trailing the tree line, watching for movement. It was the same forest she had come to love, but it did not feel the same today. She felt like she was being watched.

As she got to her car, she saw a ranger's truck pulling up. Her throat felt dry as she tried to swallow, realizing who it was. She didn't know why this guy made her nervous, but something about him felt off.

Nick stepped out of his truck casually, tall and broad-shouldered, his uniform perfectly crisp. His smile was easy and charming. "Morning, darlin'," Nick said, closing his door. "The trails should be open again tomorrow."

She hesitated, then forced a polite smile. "Thanks… Do you know what happened?"

Nick stepped closer, his boots crunching softly in the dirt. "Yeah, a girl fell into her fire last night. Not sure what happened to get her there, but it's awful."

"Oh my gosh!" Danielle said, aghast. "That's horrible."

"I know. Poor girl was just trying to enjoy a nice night by the water."

"Poor thing," Danielle said as she walked to her driver's side door. As her hand wrapped around the handle, she heard Ranger Nick clear his throat. She only turned her head, wondering if the clearing of his throat was his way of getting her attention, but something about the sound made her skin crawl.

"Danielle," he said, his voice a little too soft. "Make sure you don't come here at night. It hasn't been safe here lately. I wouldn't want something to happen to you."

She turned fully now, facing him. His blue eyes were locked on her with unnerving intensity. "Thanks, Ranger Chambers. I'll be careful."

"Just call me Nick," he said, flashing that charming, too-perfect smile. "Have a good day, darlin'."

She gave him a polite nod and opened her door. As she slid into her seat, she turned to take one last look at Nick. Even though something in her gut told her there was something wrong with him, she couldn't help the small amount of intrigue. He was extremely good-looking, and she loved how he smelled, the scent of pine and cedar wood still lingering. If he was taking time out of his day just to speak to her, maybe she should enjoy it.

She wasn't sure if this new thought was curiosity, loneliness, or maybe a little of both. She hadn't had the best luck with dating. She was only hit on by guys online, and they only wanted her because she was popular on social media, and they just wanted to use her for clout. Thankfully, no one in town knew she was an influencer. She was the quiet Christian girl and that is all they ever saw. No guy wanted to be with the innocent, naive girl in town who dressed like she was eighty. They wanted the easy, sexy girl.

The fact that Nick clearly did not know her made her stomach flutter. She had a guy who seemed interested and did not know her enough to be bored with her. This was the new start she needed.

She rolled down her window and stuck her head out. “Nick,” she shouted.

He turned around with that smooth confidence, grinning like he had been waiting for her to say something more. “You gonna be patrolling tomorrow?”

“Every day, darlin’.”

Danielle smiled, even as her stomach turned. “Good. See you tomorrow, Nick.”

He smiled and tipped his hat. “Looking forward to it.”

Her gut was screaming this was wrong, but she didn’t care. She was not going to listen. Even if she only had a little fun and then tossed him aside, she deserved some fun. She turned on the car and heard the Banshee Seekers podcast from the speakers. She loved these girls and was sad that they weren’t making any new episodes. Their voices calmed her nerves as she gripped the steering wheel and pulled out of the park.

Chapter 8 Chuck

Chuck walked into the precinct feeling numb. His thoughts going back to the fire pit. The girls' charcoaled bodies flashed in his mind and the smell of burning flesh still clung to him. The lone flip flop hanging off of one girl's foot.

He walked past the receptionist without even saying hello. He always greeted Darla, but today he knew he could not put a smile on, even a fake one, and try to act like everything was fine, so he just tipped his hat.

He badged into the detectives' room, walked past the other detectives without even looking at them, and slammed the door of his office. His thoughts went back to the call from the forensics lab stating that the small bits of DNA they had recovered showed it was Carly and Tina. He had known those girls since they were born. He had watched those girls go from learning to walk, to going to kindergarten, to being Girl Scouts that he helped keep safe in the park. He remembered them going to prom and having bonfires in the campground. He had adored those girls and loved their families. Now he would have to explain to their families what had happened and promise them that he would solve the case and find their killer.

A single tear streamed down his cheek, and he wiped it away quickly. He could not believe these girls were gone, he would never see them around town again, driving down the road with the top down, laughing and singing in their cars, two carefree kids enjoying life. He took his hat off and hurled it across the room. This was a safe town, he thought to himself. Why would someone come to Ravensburg of all places and do something so heinous?

Chuck's thoughts were interrupted by a knock at the door. He looked up to see Parker standing in the doorway, a nervous look on his face.

"What's up, Parker?"

"We need to debrief the others so that we can start combing the area further and start asking questions around town."

Chuck nodded and stood up. He did not want to talk about these girls as if they were just victims in a town crime. They were special girls, girls who he had thought of as family, and now he was going to have to talk about them as if they were just exhibits A and B. His stomach twisted and he felt bile rise up his throat. He choked it down and grabbed his hat off the floor. He needed to get this debriefing done so he could find this damn killer and lock him up for good.

He walked into the main room and saw his detectives standing there along with other officers. "Good morning, everyone. We had a horrible incident happen last night. Two girls, both were of the same age, around 19 years old. Names are Carly Louis and Tina Hinkle. So far no evidence has been found at the crime scene, but I want a couple of you to really scour the area. Go farther than just the surrounding camp site.

"Whoever did this may have left evidence farther away. We are also going to need a couple of you to go with Ranger Chambers into a boat, we need the river scoured for evidence. We need others to ask family and friends close to these girls if they have had any interactions with people who may have made them feel nervous or threatened them in any way. Parker and Henry, you both are going to come with me, we need to notify the parents of these two girls. Calvin, make up the groups for me of where you want everyone to go. Let's find this son of a bitch before he hurts anyone else."

Chuck watched as all the officers nodded and then heard Calvin clapping his hands and getting everyone's attention so he could make up the groups. Parker and Henry walked over to Chuck with their heads hanging low.

"I'm so sorry. I know how close you were to these girls." Henry said in a low tone.

Chuck shook his head. "The part that bothers me the most is I feel responsible."

Parker touched Chuck's shoulder firmly. "You can't blame yourself. This is the doing of some sick bastard. You didn't know this was happening."

Chuck rubbed his temples. "The girls came to me asking for a place to camp but didn't want to go to the campground. They wanted to camp like they had before when they were in Girl Scouts. I told them to go to that spot by the river. Told them how beautiful it was and that they would be safe."

"Chuck," Henry said in a comforting tone, "that doesn't make you responsible. Ravensburg has always been a safe place and Broad Mountain is one of the safest parks ever. You didn't know."

Chuck just shook his head. He still felt responsible. They never would have been by the river and died if he had not told them to go there. Chuck watched as the officers started filing out of the room, everyone's face serious and ready to find the truth. As the last officer walked out, he saw Darla walk in.

"Hey Chuck." Darla said. She looked nervous and was fidgeting with her hands. "I know this is not a good time, but Jenny is here. She seems really nervous. States that she feels her safety is being compromised."

Chuck's eyebrows scrunched together, and his heart skipped a beat. *Same guy? Would they find this son of a bitch quicker than they thought?*

"Alright, I'll be right there."

He watched Darla walk out of the room and turned to the boys. "Let's talk to Jenny first and see what she has to say. Maybe it will help us in this investigation if it's the same guy after his newest victim."

Jenny sat on a blue folding chair near Officer Mendez's desk, her hands rubbing together nervously, her face pale.

"Hey, Jenny." Chuck said. He watched as her head shot up, her eyes brimmed with tears.

"Chuck." She said, her word clipped. He assumed if she said any more at the moment, she would probably just start sobbing.

"Follow me back to my office. I'm going to talk to you there."

Chuck walked Jenny into his office and her head swiveled from Parker to Henry. She looked back at Chuck with a confused look.

"I need them here. Something happened last night that we can't talk about yet, but whatever you are dealing with may help us."

Jenny nodded and without saying a word, she sat down in the brown leather chair across from Chuck's desk.

"Alright, Jenny. Darla said you feel you're not safe. What's going on?"

Chuck watched as Jenny took a deep breath and closed her eyes. She held each side of the chair, her hands turning white from how hard she was gripping them.

"Every night there is a dark colored car outside my house. It feels as if I am being watched. Two nights ago, I was walking into my living room and saw a shadow of a man looking into my window. As I got closer, thinking maybe it was just a tree playing tricks on my eyes, it darted away quickly. Sometimes when I go out, I feel as if someone is watching me. I have heard knocking on my door and my windows. I know whoever it is, they are trying to coax me out of the house." Jenny's eyes filled with tears, and Chuck noticed her arms were trembling. "I'm so scared, Chuck."

"When you see the car, what make and model is it?"

"I… I don't know. It's so dark outside I can't get a good view."

"Could you describe it for me?"

Jenny sat there for a second, eyes closed and eyebrows scrunched together. "It's a four door, dark vehicle. Older model, I think. Square shaped." She opened her eyes, but her face said she felt defeated. "That's all I can make out."

"Ok, well, that's a start. Thank you. Can you tell me what the person in the window looked like?"

Jenny shook her head. "No. It was so dark. It looked like he was wearing a hoodie. It covered a lot of his face. By the time I realized it was a person and not a tree or something else, he had turned and all I saw was a blur of someone running away. The person was in dark clothes, it looked like a blurred shadow running."

"Alright Jenny. I will come over later and see if I can make anything of this. Maybe he left tracks or clues behind."

"Thank you, Chuck."

Chuck stood up and walked her out of his office and to the door that led out of the detectives' room. He held her arm lightly and stared intently into her eyes. "We will make sure you are safe, Jenny. I won't let anything happen to you." Then he pulled her in and hugged her tightly.

"Thank you Chuck. I always feel safe with you."

Chuck watched as Jenny walked down the hallway towards the exit of the precinct.

"Alright, boys, let's go talk to the parents and get this over with."

Chapter 9 Nick

Nick leaned back in his chair, boots crossed at the ankle, a cold beer sweating on the table beside him. The late afternoon sun stretched long shadows across the floor of his cabin, golden light flickering through the pines outside. He had just finished cleaning his knife again, ritual more than necessity, but the steel gleamed beneath the low light. His thoughts, as always lately, were consumed by *her*. Danielle. She had said his name. Smiled at him. Called out to him from her car window like she *wanted* him to look at her. He could still hear her voice, still see the way her eyes danced with that delicious mix of curiosity and caution. She was close. So close to stepping into his world completely. She was coming around, and he could feel it. The way she hesitated, the way her hand lingered on the door handle like she was deciding whether to stay or go. Soon, she would start trusting him. She would start asking questions. Maybe she would ask for a tour of the trails. Maybe she would even accept a drink on his porch. And that's when he would know it was time.

But not yet. He wanted to take his time with her. He wanted her to get comfortable. To believe in him, to laugh with him, maybe even if he played it right, to crave him. He would make her feel like she mattered. Like she was the only thing on earth he cared about. He could tell she was shy, and inexperienced, and that only enticed him more. Then, when she felt safest… he would show her who he really was. He would watch the realization bloom across her face. Shock, betrayal, fear. Like a slow-moving flower opening under moonlight. He wanted to taste her screams. To hold her tight and feel her pulse fade against his skin. The last gasp, and that final look in her eyes when she understood everything too late. He grinned wide, chest rising with excitement.

"You're gonna be so beautiful in those last seconds," he whispered to no one.

A sharp rap on the door took him away from the daydream. Nick's body stiffened with annoyance. He turned slowly, placing the knife gently down on the towel-covered table. The knock came again, followed by a familiar voice outside.

"Nick? You in there?"

Chuck.

He wiped the grin from his face like smudging paint off glass and stood up. He opened the door with a lazy swing and leaned casually against the frame.

"Chuck," he said with a nod, "what can I do for you?"

The officer tipped his hat, face lined with exhaustion. "Sorry to bother you at home. Just had a few follow-up questions. Mind if I come in?"

Nick opened the door wider. "Not at all."

Chuck stepped inside, glancing around the rustic interior. Fishing gear on one wall, ranger maps pinned to another, everything clean and in its place. A picture-perfect cabin, just like the man who lived in it.

"Just wanted to ask if you heard anything strange last night," Chuck said, adjusting his utility belt. "Any unusual activity around the hatchery after your final sweep?"

Nick shook his head, keeping his expression neutral. "Nah, it was dead quiet. I did my pass around seven, like usual. Didn't see a soul."

Chuck nodded slowly, eyes scanning the room again before settling back on Nick. "You think it could have been foul play? Or just some drunk kids being reckless?"

Nick furrowed his brow thoughtfully, as if truly considering it. "Hard to say. You think it was foul play?"

Chuck sighed and ran a hand through his thinning hair. "It's lookin' that way. We found evidence of a second victim. Two girls. Burned pretty badly. Still need the coroner's full report, but it's not looking accidental."

Nick tilted his head. "Damn. That's awful. Two more? What the hell's goin' on out here?"

"Wish I knew," Chuck muttered. "Town's gettin' nervous. Two girls dead before this, now these two. People are scared. We've got folks canceling hikes; schools warning kids not to go into the woods. It's bad, Nick."

Nick crossed his arms, playing the part of the frustrated protector. "It's a damn shame. This used to be the safest place in New Hampshire. Families used to camp out here for weeks. You could leave your car doors unlocked, hike alone for hours without thinking twice."

Chuck nodded. "Miss those days."

"So do I," Nick said, voice low. "No one should be afraid to enjoy nature. Whoever is doing this… they do not deserve a trial. They deserve the same fate as those girls."

Chuck gave him a hard look. "You ask me, people like that shouldn't breathe another day."

Nick held his gaze, letting just the right amount of anger flicker in his eyes. "Couldn't agree more."

There was a beat of silence between them. Then Chuck exhaled, stepping toward the door.

"Well, that's all I had. I've gotta get back to the office and file the report. We will know more once the lab's done with the scene."

Nick followed him to the door, offering a friendly smile. "If I see anything suspicious, I'll call it in right away."

Chuck gave him a grateful nod. "I know you will. We trust you out here."

Nick tipped his hat. "Stop by for a beer sometime, huh?"

Chuck laughed, already heading down the steps. "Might just take you up on that. Take care, Nick."

"You too, buddy."

Nick stood in the doorway and watched the cruiser reverse, tires grinding softly over the dirt path. As the car disappeared into the trees, he leaned against the doorframe and smiled to himself. *You're looking for a monster… and you don't even realize that you're shaking his damn hand.*

Chapter 10 Danielle

Danielle sat at her computer desk, one leg tucked under her as she edited her "come take a walk with me" video. Her headphones were sitting snugly on her head, shutting out the rest of the world. It was an ASMR video where you just watched her walk through the forest while you heard the sounds of the birds, the crunching of leaves and twigs underneath her feet, her low breathing, it was all supposed to be a calming experience that people would put on in the background. A quiet escape from the chaos of the world.

She was only trimming out the parts where she may have tripped or started breathing too loudly. Her listeners liked it when these types of videos stayed consistent. Danielle watched the screen, getting lost in the walk all over again. Then she froze as she stared at the video. Standing a bit away, watching her, was Nick.

He stood there confidently, his hand casually leaning against a tree, his legs crossed at the ankle, with this serious look on his face. His posture looked almost staged, like something out of a commercial for forest rangers. She wasn't sure if he was serious because he was patrolling the area, especially with everything happening or if he was intently watching her.

The day this had been filmed she was nervous, her legs shaky, as she had seen him. Her gut had flipped, and her brain had yelled at her to scream and run, but now… she saw those eyes that drew you in, his tall built body, the way he stood showing everyone that came across him that he was not someone to mess with. His presence filled the entire background of the shot, silently dominating it. There was something magnetic about him.

Danielle could not understand why he seemed so keen that morning to talk to her. She wasn't gorgeous by any standards. She was your girl next door cute. She was five foot one, long wavy blonde hair, a narrow frame with no curves, her mother had not blessed her with boobs, granted she knew she had been blessed with a cute round butt. Yet she knew she had features that worked well on camera. She had been blessed with piercing green eyes with a fleck of gold in them, plump lips, and cheek bones to die for that made her make-up tutorials easy and flawless. If she couldn't have the body, at least she had the face. It made great content for YouTube since she usually filmed from the neck up.

She mostly did get-ready-with-me type of content and skin care routines. She also loved her walks and figured maybe other people did, too. She was very right. She had more likes on her silent walk videos than any other. She was quite popular with the YouTube community, with 1.5 million followers. Although she wanted to broaden her videos to explore all kinds of parks, different scenery, different animals, yet her fear kept her here. She was grounded to this place. Her parents were loving but very strict. They knew what the world had to offer and did not want their baby girl to ever see that side. They had put the fear of the world being horrible into her and now just leaving town made her stomach twist. She wanted to break free so badly but the what ifs always swirled in her mind. She did not want to be the next victim on TV, and her parents had painted a terrifying image of what strangers outside of this town were like.

So, her social life was the safety of YouTube. People could see her, but they couldn't touch her, hurt her physically or anything else. People could sometimes be mean with their words, but her parents always told her, "Words like that are for the insecure, they want what you have, crave your beauty and intellect, and because they can't see their own beauty, they want to take yours away."

Danielle always hoped that those people would get help so they, too, could love themselves the way her parents had instilled her securities about herself, and she also knew if they found God, they would learn to love themselves the way God loved them. She loved people and loved helping others. She volunteered whenever she could at the Ravensburg community center. She loved the people there so much, especially Emily Scag. She and Emily had been best friends since first grade, and Danielle adored her. Emily helped widen her thoughts on things and pushed her to go to other towns' events and fundraisers. That was the only time she really left the town, even then, it terrified her. The farthest she would go was two towns over and they were always church events, so she felt a little safer knowing she was around people who thought like her.

Her focus came back to the computer, getting one more look at Nick. She was intrigued by him. Why had he looked at her that way? Why had he seemed so interested in talking to her? He had even called her by name. Nick did not know she was famous and that's what made him different. He was not trying to gain her attention for his own personal gain. Even though her body was warning her, she couldn't wait to see him tomorrow and see that smile. She finished processing the video and uploaded it with the title *In the forest with a cute guide: Gentle ASMR Journey.*

She shut her computer off, walked to her bed and opened the book she had been reading for a couple of days, *Burn Our Bodies Down.* It was such a different type of creepy book, and she was loving it, a story about mystery and murder. But as she read, her head kept drifting to the woods and of him.

Chapter 11 Danielle

The morning sun filtered through sheer curtains, casting pale gold across Danielle's bedroom walls. Danielle sat at her computer table, which doubled as her vanity. With a stretch and a sleepy yawn, she powered up her computer and positioned the camera. She decided she would film a get ready with me, hiking edition.

She started her video with the same cute introduction, "Hey, fellow beauties. My name is Danielle and today you're going to get ready with me to go hiking. I'm going to show you how to wear just enough makeup to look natural while staying safe in the sun and looking cute!"

She started applying her skin care as she trailed on about the book she was reading and the town carnival coming up, interjecting about how important SPF was to wear and to make sure to reapply.

"Ladies, SPF is not optional. We protect our peace and our pores."

She held up her favorite brand, Naturium. "This one gives you that soft healthy glow without making you feel greasy. And here's a tip, mix in just a pea sized amount of your favorite foundation. Boom. You have got lightweight coverage without looking like you've tried."

She applied her holy grail mascara and eyebrow pencil that she talked about all the time to finish the look, then tied it all together by showing them how she did her adorable ponytail, high, sleek, and effortlessly bouncy. "Perfect for showing off your cheekbones and looking adorable for those cute hikers and rangers."

Her cheeks instantly warmed at her own words and she tried to play it off with a laugh. She ended the video by talking about the hike she would be going on in a little bit and to catch that video later today as well. She said her goodbyes and shut the computer down.

Danielle rummaged through her clothes to find the perfect matching workout outfit. She pulled out her favorite black shorts with a thin sky-blue stripe down the sides that hugged her thighs perfectly, and then she grabbed the same color tank top to match. Her sports bra had the amazing effect on the girls that gave them an extra lift, thankfully, since she was not working with much.

She checked herself in the mirror multiple times before lacing up her sneakers. She absolutely loved these sneakers and how her feet never hurt, it was like walking on clouds. She pulled her ponytail tight one last time and smiled before walking to her car. She couldn't wait to take to the trails and see Nick.

When she made it to the park, she pulled her car into the usual spot and sat there for a second just taking in the beautiful scenery. She had been coming here her entire life and had so many good memories of this park. From fishing with her dad, tiny pole in hand, excited even when she caught a fish the size of a sardine. She had hiked here with her mom, as her mom explained about the animals that lived there, and taught her about tracks and wildflowers that bloomed throughout, she was like a walking encyclopedia. And she remembered the many times she had gone swimming with her friends from the community center on summer days when the world felt big and safe. She knew her childhood had been great, even if it was limited to Ravensburg.

She opened her center console and grabbed her camera. She didn't want people to get uncomfortable thinking she was filming them, so she made sure it looked inconspicuous. It was a cute sunflower pin with the camera part in the middle. She pinned it to her shirt strap and got out.

As she made her way to the trail, her eyes scanned the area, but she didn't see him or his truck. Her stomach twisted thinking maybe he was just being polite and didn't actually want to see her. She was foolish to think he would be waiting for her, why would a guy like *him* want a girl like *her*?

As she rounded the first bend in the trail, she heard a twig snap next to her. She turned and smiled, but it was a squirrel hopping along the ground. It paused to eye her with a twitchy little nose before disappearing into the underbrush. She laughed at herself. *Focus, Danielle. You're here for the hike, and the view. Not him.* She came here because she could turn her mind off and just enjoy the walk and she was determined to do that and forget about him. She got to where the stream was, where all the police cars had been sitting. It had been a week since she had come down this path and it just looked like it always had, as if that person had never been hurt there, wiped clean from people's memories. She walked further and could see the gorgeous mountain views up ahead. This was exactly why she filmed, how could anyone not enjoy this view. She stood on the side of the cliff, staring at the forest below that stretched for what seemed like forever, and mountains that seemed to touch the sky and surround the forest in a hug.

"WOW," Danielle heard a voice from behind her. "What a beautiful view."

"I know. Isn't it breath-". Her sentence broke as she turned and stared at Nick. He stood there, tall and effortlessly composed, and that perfect smile that made her knees go weak.

"Yes," he said. "You are breathtaking."

Danielle's cheeks reddened and her head bowed a little at the compliment, yet she couldn't help the small smile.

"Oh, come on, this isn't even fair." Nick said, crossing his arms.

"What isn't fair?" Danielle asked, glancing up shyly.

"You're even cuter when you blush."

Danielle knew her cheeks were so red now that clowns would be jealous. Her dermatologist would be throwing topicals on her face, worried she was having a rosacea flare.

Nick stepped closer, his arms dropping to his sides, his eyes scanning every inch of her. She could feel his eyes devouring her, and his smile turned into a smirk that made her legs shake, and her pulse quickened.

"I'm glad to see you out here. It gives me something to look forward to. I can only talk to the squirrels for so long before they get bored."

Danielle giggled like a schoolgirl, annoyed at herself for sounding like that. She wanted that sultry giggle that women did in the movies that made men want to lean in closer.

Nick's eyes lit up at the sound. "I could listen to that laugh all day and night. You are something." He said in that deep, smoky voice.

Her mind went blank. She was so nervous around him; she wanted to bolt. She was not good at being sexy or knowing what to say in these situations. She had never been put into a predicament like this in her twenty-five years on earth. She blurted out the first thing she could think of. "I'd like that."

I'd like that. She smacked herself in her mind. What were you thinking, Danielle? *That's the best you could come up with? He's going to know you are naïve and not well versed in this. He's going to run when he realizes how boring you are.*

Nick smiled wider. "I'd like that, too, Danielle." He said smoothly. "Maybe over coffee tomorrow?"

Her heart was going so fast she thought she was going to have a heart attack. She knew she was sweaty and not in a cute, I just did a couple sit ups and now my face is glistening way. *Say something, Danielle*! She screamed to herself. "I'd like that… a lot."

"Great. Roasted Bean Cafe at eight? Before I have to start my day."

Danielle's mind yelled at her again not to say I'd like that one more time. "Sure, sounds great."

"Great. I'll let you get back to your hike." Nick tipped his hat and turned to walk down the path.

As soon as he was out of her line of sight, she finally let out her breath. She bent over, her hands on her knees, her body shaking from excitement. She knew her video would be horrible, and she was not sure it would even be usable since her legs were shaking, and she was breathing so heavily. She started walking back to her car. She tripped over countless branches, and she was pretty sure she even swore once, which she would definitely have to cut out of the video.

When she got back to her car her hands were shaking so badly, it took her three tries to unlock her door. Once she did, she quickly opened the door, and her body slumped very ungracefully into the seat. She sat there for what seemed like hours, playing those minutes back in her head. She was going to be getting coffee with Nick Chambers.

Wait until everyone in town saw who she was with, people loved Nick and really loved gossip. She was excited on a different level, too, because maybe this would show them that she was more grown up than they thought and would give her more responsibility at the center. She smiled as she slid into her seat fully and turned the car on. Her radio came on with Kesha's song "Blow," telling everyone to dance. The beat made her smile even bigger as she reversed her vehicle and started driving toward the community center.

Chapter 12 Nick

Nick felt lighter than he had in weeks. He seemed to walk taller today, his energy lighter, he felt giddy with anticipation. He even smiled at the occasional hiker without thinking twice. Underneath it all was a tremor of pure adrenaline.

Danielle. She had said yes.

He could still see her face when she had agreed to coffee. Those wide, innocent eyes lighting up, and the way her voice stuttered like she didn't quite believe he had asked her. And when she blushed? Jesus. He could have kissed her right there and then, tasted her fear, the excitement, the trust forming. The thought of taking her last breath made his heart quicken and his hands shake. He wanted her to fall for the fantasy, to lean into the comfort of his attention, to start thinking she might even be special, because for him, she was.

His nerves were tingling with excitement and the only way he knew to calm his nerves was to "kill" them. Just a quick, quiet, clean kill.

Nick was not sure it was smart to bring more attention to the park by killing another person so quickly, usually he waited a couple of weeks. He couldn't afford a mistake. But he needed this, he needed to calm himself down before tomorrow, so he didn't screw up and kill her before he was ready. He wanted to enjoy this slowly and unlike others he had murdered, Danielle made him crazy with excitement and made that itch to kill stronger than normal.

If he was careful, people would just think there was a serial killer near the park. But what if he didn't kill at the park? No… too dangerous, he could be spotted. At least being at the park people assumed he was at the cabin at night; no one would spot his truck out and about, and he usually used the same excuse that he was at home and that he had done patrol at seven and everything was quiet. He would have to hide this kill. He wouldn't be able to keep this one out in the open to be found. By the time she was found, people would have already forgotten about the two girls who had been murdered. They would have already settled back into denial.

He plotted where he would do it as he walked through the park. He watched people at the beach with their kids swimming, smelt the meat on the grills cooking with charcoal, and laughter from other kids running around the beach playing tag. This wouldn't be a good place to throw a body. Sand was soft, a kid would be digging for a sandcastle, and a nose would poke out of the sand. The kid would scream, parents running, patrol cars swarming. He returned to his truck and drove slowly around the park further. He drove past the stream area where he had just had fun with the girls the other night. Then he passed the swamp. He could place the person in the swamp; he was sure animals would eat her, snapping turtles, foxes, and even crows would strip the flesh off the bones. But animals were unpredictable, with that they may leave an important body part that the authorities could use to figure out who it was and when they were killed.

He turned down the path towards the campground. The main cabins were full, tourists everywhere. But there was one cabin, way in the back that people stopped using. Cabin 6. The roof had caved in where the bathroom was after a blizzard a couple of years ago. A moose had slammed into the front door during rut season chasing a raccoon, knocking the door partially off the hinges, and one of the kids staying here had accidentally thrown a rock through one of the windows. Vines now grew into the window, and up through the roof. It was being taken by the forest. None of the cabins sat near it, so no one would even notice if a dead body was in there.

He parked the truck near the maintenance gate and hiked the short trail to the cabin. The door creaked open as he pushed it, the heavy scent of mildew thick in the air. Light filtered through that shattered window, illuminating the dust that floated lazily.

He stepped inside. This would work perfectly. He would stash the body here. A tarp lay crumbled in the corner of the cabin, a rotted couch still sat against a wall. He could easily hide a cooler in here without it being found. Nick smiled, that's what he would do. He would stash the body in the cabin for a while. And with his plan ready to go, now he just needed a body. He would scout out the park tonight, and tomorrow he would be ready to see Danielle, his itch scratched again for the moment.

Chapter 13 Nick

Nick did his normal patrol at seven that night, a familiar rhythm, comforting and methodical. The sun had just begun to dip below the treetops, casting shadows on the forest floor. The soft whir of insects filled the air as he slowly rode the trails.

He drove through the campground, windows down, enjoying the fall breeze. People sat around their campfires, laughing and talking. Kids ran around kicking up dust as they played tag, and others zipped by on their bikes. Classic country music played softly in the distance. He loved hearing those noises and the amazing smells from the food. A couple of people waved at him as he drove past, and he tipped his hat at them. He was well known in the area and was very loved. People knew with him around they were safe.

He stopped his truck at one of the campsites, noticing Lenny Wellington sitting around the fire. "Lenny, how's it going?" Nick said, leaning his forearm on the truck's window edge.

"Hey, Nick! Things are good. I got dogs… hot dogs. Want one?" Lenny said, wobbling slightly as he stood, holding up a hotdog in one hand and a beer in the other.

Nick smiled and shook his head. "No thanks, Lenny. I'm going home to make dinner now. Gotta have a beer with my dog and don't wanna drink and drive."

Lenny raised his beer like he was toasting. "Nice, buddy! I'll be drinking, too. Cheers me from your place." Lenny said, laughing.

Lenny had clearly already had quite a few beers, and he probably didn't need another one. The best part about campers were that they drank and when they drank, they were oblivious to anything going on around them. Lenny wouldn't remember much tomorrow, but if he was asked, Lenny would swear up and down that Nick had headed home for the night. So would half the people at the site. He had laid the groundwork for his alibi without even trying.

He pulled into his dirt spot next to the cabin and sat there for a minute. He grinned, if everything lined up tonight, he would purge the buzzing underneath his skin. His heart was racing with anticipation; he needed someone to be foolish enough to be out here after dark. Someone who thought they could outrun death.

Later that night, he sat on the couch watching the news. Photos of two girls filled the screen; people wept as they asked about information for their beloved girls who had gone missing the other night. The news anchor's voice returned, somber. "No suspects, no witnesses. Police urge residents to avoid Broad Mountain State Park after sundown. Authorities believe a serial predator may be responsible." The eleven o'clock news ended with their music and Nick shut the tv off. It was time.

He slid into the driver's seat of his truck and started driving towards the hiking trail. He had made it a mile down the path when he noticed a small flicker of light around the corner. He knew this flicker well, it was a flashlight.

Nick eased off the gas and coasted onward until the beam of headlights caught a figure walking along the trail. A tall, skinny woman came around the corner, her hair tied back, leash in hand, a medium sized dog trotting beside her. As she saw the truck, she froze, and he saw her face get tight with worry. In order to keep her calm and not scream, he needed to identify himself.

"Evening, darlin'," Nick said as he stepped out of the truck. "It's Ranger Chambers. Just patrolling the area."

At the sound of his voice, he watched her shoulders slump, and a smile appeared on her face. "Oh, goodness, you scared me for a second."

"You really shouldn't be out here, ma'am." He walked closer to her as he spoke. "It's not safe this late."

"I know." She said, sighing. "But Henry insists on his walks, and it's been too hot during the day."

Nick looked down at the dog, some sort of retriever mix. "That's for sure. Can't wait til this heat wave is over." He questioned if he should do anything, he didn't hurt animals and if he tried anything that dog would do what they do best and protect her. Worse, this wasn't just anybody; this was *Jenny McGrath.* She was well known in town, the only dermatologist in the area, and everyone loved her. She was a very nice lady and had helped him out in the past with a bad sunburn.

He smiled and gave the dog a gentle pat along its back. "Well, Jenny, you be careful, and Henry, you keep her safe." He ruffled the dog's back fur and started to walk back to the truck when he heard the dog growl.

Nick stiffened, hand already going to his belt. He turned towards the dog who was looking into the forest. As Nick turned to see what was in the woods, he saw the buck. His antlers were huge, ten-point buck for sure. The dog was getting riled up and Jenny tried to shush him, but it wasn't working well.

The buck bolted in the opposite direction which made Henry go crazy. He leapt onto his hind legs, barking.

Jenny fumbled with the leash and when Henry dropped to all fours, she lost control. Henry bolted into the woods.

"HENRY!" Jenny screamed, but he was adamant about getting that buck. Jenny went to run after him, but Nick grabbed her arm.

"Hey, running ain't going to fix this. That dog is on a mission. Let's just walk in that direction. We are bound to find him."

Jenny's head bowed slightly, and she wiped her eyes. "You're right. I just love him so much. I wouldn't want anything to happen to him."

Nick offered a warm, practiced smile. "Don't you worry, darlin'. We will get him back."

They started walking into the woods, flashlights bouncing off the trees, hearing the rushed footsteps from the dog in the distance and the occasional bark. As they got about a quarter of a mile into the woods, Nick grabbed the knife from his sheath and gripped it tight.

"Hold on." Nick said, grabbing her arm. "Just listen for a second so we can track where he's running."

Jenny held her breath, straining to hear. He needed this badly, to feel her blood pour onto his hands. To feel her body become heavy in his arms. They stood there listening intently for twigs cracking or barking; she was so focused on listening she never saw it coming.

The blade crossed her throat in one smooth, practiced motion. It was so clean she didn't even have time to understand what was happening. Nick caught her at the waist as her strength gave out, holding her upright as warmth spilled between his fingers. Her body trembled once, twice, then sagged against him like she was giving herself over to him.

The reaction hit him instantly. His body reacted with a violent, shuddering force that had nothing to do with horror and everything to do with soul-shattering ecstasy. His stomach clenched into a knot of pure, white-hot pleasure, and his head swam. The world tilted on its axis as a dizzying wave of lust washed over him. He felt the heat bloom in his groin, a deep, pulsing throb that built with impossible speed. His knees buckled, a tremor wracking his entire frame as a thick, warm gush of liquid flooded his boxers. A powerful, uncontrollable release that left him breathless and trembling. The sheer, primal power of the moment, the feel of her life draining away in his arms, had shattered him completely. But even as his body shuddered in the aftershocks, a cold, rational part of his brain took over. He knew he needed to work quickly. The night was not over. He grabbed Jenny and threw her into the back of the truck and headed for his cabin.

Once there, he didn't waste time. Every movement was practiced and efficient. He retrieved two airtight Yeti coolers from the porch, their white plastic glowing faintly in the dark. He laid Jenny on the ground and took out the hand saw, forcing himself into a narrow focus where nothing else existed, no thoughts, no hesitation, only the work that needed to be done. It was ugly, exhausting, and precise, but he did not stop until it was finished.

When he was done, he packed what remained of her into the coolers, methodical as he filled the empty space with charcoal and baking soda, layers meant to smother scent. He snapped the lids shut and secured them with four numbered locks; the soft clicks sounding far too loud in the quiet night.

He quickly threw the two coolers into his truck's bed. He went inside to change his clothes and soak these. After he had cleaned himself up, he quietly drove back to the campground. He patrolled the area, making sure no one was up or stirring in their tent or cabin. No lights seemed to flicker on, and it was so dark in the park that you wouldn't be able to identify anything without a flashlight. No late-night guitar playing or kids laughing, just the hush of the wind in the trees. No one saw him carry the coolers into the cabin. He dumped them in the corner and covered them with the old tarp. He knew the coolers would at least help keep the smell away long enough for this group of campers to go home. Everyone would go back to their normal lives, completely forgetting anything odd they may have thought they saw.

As Nick hopped back into the truck, he knew he had made a mess at home and needed a cover for that. He went back to the area where Henry had run off. He rolled down the window, rifle in his lap and he waited quietly.

After a half hour of sitting quietly he saw the buck. Tall and proud, standing in the shadows. He quietly cocked the rifle and placed it right outside the window. He made sure his aim was perfect and pulled the trigger. The buck went down hard. He was such a big buck when he hit the ground it made a loud thump that shook the ground around the truck.

He grabbed his knife from his belt and started to gut the deer quickly and efficiently. After ripping the guts out, he dragged the deer along the ground back to the truck. By the time he got to his truck bed he was breathing heavily and sweating like crazy. With the small amount of energy he had left, he picked up the deer and threw it into the truck bed. When he got back to the cabin, he hung up the deer to bleed out right on the hook where Jenny had bled out. The blood swirled together perfectly and now no one would question why his grass was stained red.

After making sure there were no other signs of Jenny, he went inside to soak this uniform as well, then he hopped in the shower to make sure Jenny wasn't on him either. As her DNA swirled into the drain, his jitters were gone. He was calm, cool, and ready to see Danielle without any worry of a screw up.

Chapter 14 Nick

Nick sat back in the worn rocking chair on his porch, a steaming cup of black coffee resting loosely in his calloused hand. The wood creaked softly beneath him as he gently rocked back and forth. The porch overlooked the vast, undisturbed sweep of wilderness that stretched for miles in every direction. In front of him, the early morning sun climbed slowly over the distant ridge line, bathing the mountaintops in a warm, golden hue that bled down into the trees. The mist still clung low to the ground in soft ribbons, curling around the tree trunks and lifting off the field like breath rising from the earth.

The sky above was painted in soft strokes of orange, lavender, and blush, one of those rare, perfect mornings where the world looked too peaceful to be real. Birds chirped from hidden nests in the trees nearby, their songs bright and melodic. A breeze rolled through the valley, just enough to stir the tall grasses.

And then… movement.

A doe, slender and graceful, bounded from the tree line and into the open field. Her hooves barely made a sound against the damp earth as she paused to sniff the air, ears flicking, and alert. For a moment, Nick simply watched her, his face unreadable. To anyone passing by, he would have looked like a man completely at ease, lost in the serenity of nature.

But inside his mind, the calm was starting to shift, darkness slipping beneath the surface of the peace, tainting the quiet like a drop of ink in water.

As Nick took in the beauty of nature, his mind drifted back to the first time he killed, a memory etched into his psyche. He was twenty-six, a new forest ranger eager to explore the wilderness and the thrills it offered. One evening, he invited his girlfriend Nicole back to his secluded cabin, where the intimacy of the setting seemed to heighten every sensation.

They started making out on the couch, their bodies pressing against each other, the heat between them palpable. As Nick's hands roamed over her thigh, he felt a surge of excitement when her hand slid over his pants, feeling the hardness that had grown beneath the fabric. Their kissing became more passionate, fueled by the growing intensity of their desires. Nick grabbed a handful of her hair and pulled her in tighter, his grip firm and possessive. She responded with a moan, her hands gripping his thigh with equal fervor. As she pulled away to straddle him, the anticipation in the air was electric.

Nick pulled her tank top over her head, revealing her bra. With a swift motion, he pulled down the bra cup, exposing her perky breast. He swirled his tongue around her nipple, eliciting a loud moan from her. His hands gripped her ass, feeling the softness of her skin as she ground herself against him. He could feel her wetness seeping through his pants, a sensation that made him grip her even tighter, knowing the marks would linger as bruises.

Nick bit her nipple, and as she moaned loudly, he bit harder, her scream a mixture of pain and pleasure. She began to unbuckle his belt, her fingers fumbling with the clasp. Nick lifted her off himself and stood up, making it easier for her to finish undressing him. He ripped off his shirt and unbuttoned his pants, letting them fall to the floor along with his boxers. She gasped as she saw his hard, thick length, her face a mix of nervousness and anticipation, knowing he wouldn't fit easily.

Nick lay her down on the sofa, his eyes gleaming with a mix of lust and something darker. As he spread her legs apart, he slammed into her, his mouth capturing her scream. He didn't slow down, his thrusts powerful and relentless. Her fingernails dug into his back, leaving red marks as she moaned loudly, savoring every moment. Nick slid his hand around her throat, gripping it lightly at first. She smirked and pushed back against him, encouraging him to go further. He gripped her harder, feeling her hands tighten on his back, her nails digging deeper. The harder he gripped, the more he enjoyed the sensation of power and control. As her eyes shot open in panic, Nick realized she couldn't breathe. He gripped her throat tighter, feeling her nails dig into his back as she struggled to push him off with her legs. He thrust into her harder, his grip unyielding. After a few minutes, her legs and arms went limp, and in that moment, Nick came harder than he ever had before. The knowledge that he had taken her last breath was even more thrilling than the act itself. He kissed her lifeless lips as he pulled out and stared at her. His release oozed out of her still body, and he hardened again.

Nick blinked slowly as the morning sun stretched across the mountains, dragging him back from the memory that ignited it all. The warmth of the sunrise kissed his skin, but it couldn't match the fire crawling just beneath the surface of his nerves. That night, his first kill, had shown him the truth about himself, a truth deeper than desire, darker than pleasure. Sex had meant nothing in the end. It was fleeting and empty. What had truly awakened him; what had truly mattered, was the moment she stopped breathing. The moment her eyes widened in panic, her body bucked against him, and her hands clawed at his skin in a desperate plea to live. That was the moment he came alive. That was the moment he felt something real, powerful, and transcendent. Nicole had been special. Not only was she the first but the feelings he had for her only made the power of the kill that much stronger.

After that, he no longer chased lust. He didn't need the softness of skin or the sweetness of a moan. All of that was background noise. It was the kill that fulfilled him. Watching the life drain from someone's eyes, that was his ecstasy. That was his high, and his victims were always the easy ones, the ones who had no respect for themselves. In his eyes, they did not deserve to live. Nicole had been no different. He knew she only looked his way because of how he looked. He was arm candy, and she had a sweet tooth.

But lately… the kills were starting to feel stale. Slipping up behind someone and ending it quickly? It wasn't enough anymore. There was no spark, no tension, no terror. He missed the struggle, the moment when the victim knew. The moment when their trust shattered and pure fear took over. Nicole had looked him right in the eye as her lungs gave out. He could still see it, her confusion turning to horror, her body thrashing beneath him, the way her nails had dug into his back not in pleasure, but in desperation. That was what he wanted again, no, not want. He needed this.

Danielle was going to give that to him. She didn't even realize she was already his. Every smile she gave him, every awkward laugh, every time she blushed, he was embedding himself in her mind. He was shaping her reality, chipping away at her defenses like a sculptor with a chisel. And when she finally trusted him, when she let her guard down completely, that was when he would take everything from her.

But not yet. He needed to savor this, draw it out like a fine wine. He wanted to make her fall in love with him. Crave him. Need him. Only then would her betrayal feel like art. Only then would her final moments taste as sweet as the first one. Their coffee date was in just a few hours, and he could already picture the look in her eyes when he greeted her with that warm, charming smile. She would never see the devil behind it. Not until it was far too late.

And that was what made it perfect.

Chapter 15 Danielle

Danielle sat at her vanity, hands trembling slightly as she dabbed the last bit of blush onto her cheeks. Her stomach churned with anticipation, nerves fluttering so wildly it felt like a colony of butterflies was trying to escape. It had been years since she felt this kind of anxious excitement, the kind that clings to your skin and wraps around your ribs, making it hard to breathe but somehow even harder not to smile.

Today was the day.

She was going to get coffee with Nick Chambers. The forest ranger. The town's most talked about bachelor. And somehow, he had chosen her.

Yesterday at the community center, she had gushed to her best friend, Emily, about the chance encounter. Emily's reaction had been immediate and dramatic, screeching with delight loud enough to make the older volunteers glance their way from the food pantry table.

"Oh my *God,* Danielle," Emily had squealed, practically vibrating with excitement. "Nick *freaking* Chambers? Do you even realize what this means? He's like… the town's golden bachelor. Rugged, quiet, and mysterious. That man chose *you.* You lucky, lucky girl."

Danielle had giggled, cheeks turning pink, admitting in a whisper that she still couldn't get over how *good* he smelled. That musky, woodsy cologne with a hint of pine and cedar that lingered long after he left. But behind Emily's congratulations, Danielle had seen it, that faint shadow of jealousy behind her friend's eyes. The way her smile didn't fully reach one corner of her mouth. Not that Danielle blamed her. Nick was the kind of man women in town wrote diary entries about.

But now, as Danielle stared at her reflection, doubt started to creep in.

Was she really the kind of girl Nick would date?

Her classmates had never let her forget what they thought of her. The recluse. The quiet weirdo. Whispers followed her wherever she went, stories that ranged from bizarre to cruel. That she was a Skinwalker her parents kept locked away to protect the town. That she was a kidnapped child raised in secrecy. That she was some government experiment with plastic doll parts and no belly button, or that she was the crazy bible thumper. She had heard it all.

But today… today was her chance to flip the narrative. To show everyone that she *was* desirable. That she wasn't just the quiet girl with a camera, she was wanted. Desired by someone everyone else wanted.

She reached for her favorite tinted lip balm, giving her lips a subtle rosy hue before smiling into the mirror.

"All right, y'all," she said sweetly to the camera that had been recording her date-makeup tutorial. "That's how you do a soft day-date look that can be turned into a romantic night vibe with just a few simple tweaks. Have a beautiful day!"

She gave a wink, clicked the stop button, and turned her attention to the closet.

Most of her wardrobe was modest. Long dresses that went below her knee, and shirts that showed nothing. She was sick of her clothes that made showing skin a sin. The kind of wardrobe built out of years of overbearing parental modesty. But not today. Today, she reached toward the back of her closet, pulling out *that* dress, the one she had kept hidden behind an old winter coat, out of sight and out of her mother's reach.

It was light pink, soft, flowy, and scandalously short by her family's standards, skimming mid-thigh with a neckline just low enough to hint at cleavage. She paired it with the push-up bra she had bought during a secret trip to Manchester with Emily. The dress hugged her in all the right places, and her girls finally made an appearance with this bra. For the first time in a long time, she didn't feel like a child playing dress-up.

She looked like a woman.

She twirled once in front of the mirror, the skirt flaring around her legs. Her black and white low-top Converse gave the outfit a casual edge, cute, comfortable, and very *her*. She slung her purse over her shoulder, took a deep breath, and walked out the door with a grin that no one could wipe away.

***

The Roasted Bean Cafe came into view, and her confidence took a sharp turn into anxiety. She parked her car and sat for a moment, frozen, gripping the steering wheel.

What if I misread this? What if he's not even interested like that?

Her thoughts spiraled. But then she remembered the video footage. She had watched it several times. She had seen the way he looked at her, the things he said to her. The way he made her knees feel like they were made of air. She had seen it. She knew he wanted more than just a friendship with her.

She wasn't going to let old insecurities steal this from her. She was beautiful and worth Nick wanting. Even if she needed to remind herself constantly.

She pushed her breasts up just a touch, checked her reflection once more, reapplied her lip balm, and finally stepped out into the morning air.

She opened the doors, and the smell of breakfast hit her in the face. The sweet smells of pancakes, maple syrup, and sizzling bacon. Her mouth watered, thinking of all the delicious food the cafe made. She scanned the area looking for him, loving the hum of conversation that filled the cozy space.

As she scanned the cafe a little slower, she saw him. He was perched at the breakfast bar, talking casually to one of the waitresses, his uniform perfectly fitted to his tall, broad frame. One arm rested lazily on the counter, the other on his thigh; muscles taut beneath the fabric. He turned around after Gerald patted his shoulder in greeting as he passed by on the way to his table. When Nick's eyes met hers, his face lit up in that slow, confident smile that made everything else blur and her stomach flipped.

As he stood, it was like the entire room dimmed behind him. Danielle only saw *him.*

He walked toward her with the kind of ease only a man completely sure of himself could manage. Each step was steady and deliberate. Commanding. She could barely hear the buzz of chatter anymore. It was just Nick.

He stopped in front of her, smirking, his hands resting on his belt. He tipped his hat and said in that deep, smoky voice, "Hello there, darlin'."

Danielle's stomach fluttered with excitement as Nick placed his hand on the small of her back, guiding her toward their table. His touch was firm but respectful, and the warmth of it lingered as he pulled out a chair for her.

"Thank you," Danielle said with a smile she couldn't have put away if she tried. As he sat across from her, she could not quite understand why someone as handsome as Nick had asked her to coffee. His gorgeous, crystal-blue eyes were locked onto hers with a magnetic intensity, and she found it hard to breathe, let alone look away. His earthy pine scent filled the area, and she took a deep breath, committing it to memory.

"So, darlin'," he asked, his voice smooth and deep, "you going on your walk after this?"

"No," Danielle replied, brushing a strand of hair behind her ear. "I have to go help out at the community center."

Nick's gaze softened. "Well, that's very sweet of you. Do you help out there a lot?"

"As much as I can. I love working with the kids."

Before Nick could reply, the waitress arrived to take their order. They both ordered coffee, and Danielle asked for water as well. As she finished, she caught a glance at Nick watching her intensely. Not on her face, though. She watched as his eyes slowly scanned lower, stopping at the top of her dress, where the swell of her breasts peeked out slightly. She smirked as she finished the last word of the order and looked over at Nick.

"You trying to commit my looks to memory?" She teased, raising an eyebrow.

Nick's grin widened. "I can't help it. You are absolutely gorgeous."

Danielle's cheeks immediately turned bright red, and she knew no amount of foundation was going to cover that up. He chuckled softly. "So, what do you do for work?"

Danielle did not want to reveal that she was an online influencer. She knew she would not be able to handle it if he ended up acting like every other guy who knew, taking advantage of her for clout or only talking to her because she was popular in the YouTube community. She didn't think Nick was like that; he seemed more mature, refined, an older soul, but she didn't want to take that chance.

"I work at the community center. I do light work to help out. Still living with my parents helps a lot."

"Well, that's mighty nice of you to care about people that much. You've got a good heart, Dani."

"Thanks. It's a really rewarding job. Watching these kids grow up and do really well has been amazing. And helping out people who don't have much, wherever I can… you never know if it will be you next time, and someone might be taking care of you." Danielle shrugged, realizing her answer was kind of cliché, but she didn't care.

They talked more about the center. Danielle talked about how there were some people who had the world by the balls and then, with one misstep, were homeless, jobless, and completely lost. She brought up how she had seen kids who had everything, and when they lost it all, they started running with bad crowds or bullying kids who didn't want to live to see the next day. Danielle's voice grew steadier as she talked about how she helped all of them and had watched everyone flourish because she saw kindness in people.

"The community center has a lady who helps people find jobs again. We help people find cheaper living so they can move out of the shelter, and places where all kids are treated equally and there's no bullying. Kids can feel safe here. And they really thrive."

"I think it's very noble of you, Dani. I've watched some of these kids from the community center change dramatically. You being a part of that is amazing and a lot of hard work, mentally. You are quite something. I know those kids appreciate you a lot."

Danielle looked down shyly, overwhelmed by the praise. "Thank you, Nick. I'm just doing my part to keep Ravensburg a safe and happy place for everyone."

As she looked back up and into his eyes, something in his expression shifted. His eyes darkened, just briefly, and he smirked slightly before it vanished, as if it was never there.

"That's great. People should feel safe here."

Danielle decided to change the subject off of herself. "So, how is it being a ranger? Do you like what you do?"

"Love it. I get to keep people safe and be in nature every day." He chuckled in his head at the answer, knowing some people would never be safe from him.

Danielle smiled wide. "You must love seeing all the animals? I've lived here my whole life, and I've only seen a moose a couple of times, and I was awe-struck."

"Oh, all the time. They are beautiful creatures. And massive when you get close to them."

"Oh wow! How close have you come?"

"Well, we do have hunters who are allowed to hunt for moose if they hit the lottery. People get really excited about it."

"Oh, right. You've probably seen quite a few." Danielle felt like an idiot. Of course he had seen them up close; he probably helped hunters hoist them into the back of their trucks. "So, what's the scariest moment you've ever had as a ranger?"

She could see Nick's wheels turning at the question; it was probably a stupid question. This man didn't look like he would ever be scared of anything.

"I would have to say the day little Kenny almost drowned."

Danielle knew bits and pieces of the story from around town; people never stopped talking about Ravensburg's hero.

"He was swimming in the river with his family. They were keeping a really close eye on him, and he had floaters on his arms. Nothing should have gone wrong. His mom said she turned her back for one second to grab him a towel, and when she turned around, his floaters were on the beach, and he was gone. She was screaming frantically. I happened to be close by and heard the screaming. I came running, and everyone was just screaming and pointing at the water. It didn't take long for me to realize what had happened. I jumped into the water and looked around but couldn't see anyone. I dove into the deeper part of the river and looked around, but the water was murky now; I couldn't see very far. When I came up, I heard a quick scream. My eyes scanned the area, and I saw the bob of a head. He had made it about a quarter of a mile down the river and was being pushed under the water by the current. I swam as fast as I could. By the time I got to him, he was out of it. I rushed him onto land as fast as I could and did CPR for a couple of minutes. I had never been so relieved when that kid coughed. They rushed him to the hospital to be on the safe side, and he ended up in the hospital for a couple of days because of pneumonia, but he's doing good now."

Danielle could see the slight fear in his eyes as he retold the story, as if it were happening all over again. "Oh, my god. That's terrible. Did you ever find out how the floaters came off?"

"He said he wanted to be like his siblings, so he took them off to show them he could swim too."

"Oh, no. Poor thing. That must have scared him so much."

"He was pretty shaken up. He didn't go swimming for a couple of years, but I just saw him a couple of days ago, swimming again. Granted, he's a lot bigger now. He doesn't need the floaters anymore." Nick chuckled and smiled, and it made her heart melt, seeing him talk excitedly about this boy.

"Well, I'm really glad he had you to save him."

"I'm just glad I was around. The family is a really good family. I wouldn't have wanted to see what it would have done to them if he hadn't made it."

The waitress came back with the coffees and water. Danielle thanked her and picked up her mug. The smell of the coffee made her eyes roll back for a second. She loved the earthy scent, knowing how good it would taste. She took a sip and as she placed the mug down, her eyes caught on two older women talking and pointing in her direction. She chuckled and leaned in.

"I think we're being talked about, Nick," she said, nodding her head in their direction discreetly.

Nick chuckled. "I'm not surprised by that. Is it old lady Jenkins and her friend Lola?"

"Yup. And they are smiling and giggling like two schoolgirls."

Nick laughed a little harder. "They've been runnin' the Ravensburg rumor mill for fifty years."

Danielle grinned. "Well, I am pretty sure we just gave them their headline for the week."

Danielle's heart started racing and her breathing hitched as Nick reached across the table and took her hand, rubbing his thumb against the back of it.

"I'm sure now they will really have something to talk about," he said, smirking.

She hoped he had grabbed her hand more out of actually wanting to touch her and not just for their audience's benefit.

They continued talking about each other's hobbies and more about the community center and the park. After three cups of coffee and two hours had passed, Nick glanced at his watch.

"Pretty sure I'm a little late for patrol, but it was definitely worth it." He smiled that gorgeous smile, and his eyes twinkled a little, mesmerizing her.

Danielle stood up and smoothed out her dress. "It was really nice having coffee with you. I really enjoyed it."

"I did, too. We'll have to do this again sometime." Danielle watched as Nick put money on the table. Then he placed his hand on her back once again, leading her to the parking lot.

"Well," Danielle said, "I have to get to the center, and you definitely need to get to the park. Make sure everyone is safe in the water."

"Yes, ma'am. Have a good day, and hopefully I'll be seeing you soon."

"Oh, definitely. I can't stay out of the park."

Danielle watched as he tipped his hat and made his way to his truck. Her heart sank a little as she watched him get inside. She was hoping for a hug or a kiss on the cheek. Now she was mad at herself for not moving closer, for not making herself look inviting. She should have made a move or said something flirtatious.

When she got inside the center, she saw Emily standing by a table helping an older lady place a couple of shirts inside her bag. Danielle walked over and cleared her throat; a smile still plastered on her face. Emily looked up and smirked.

"Well, good morning, love. Heard you were up early this morning at the café with a handsome ranger."

Danielle rolled her eyes but couldn't help but smile. "How do you already know about that?"

"Old lady Jenkins has a faster network than the FBI. Everyone knows."

Danielle laughed, knowing how true that was. Mrs. Jenkins was the town's gossiper; she thrived on everyone else's business. Not that there was much to talk about here. In a town this small, even a decent cup of coffee with the wrong person became headline news.

"God," Emily sighed dramatically. "He is so damn handsome. I'm honestly jealous you got to sit there and stare into those eyes."

"I could've stared at him forever," Danielle admitted. "And his scent… I swear, I can still smell him."

"I'm shocked it ended at coffee."

"I wanted more," Danielle said softly. "I just didn't want to come on too strong right away."

"Why not? Hop on and enjoy the ride."

"Oh, my god, Emily." Danielle smacked her arm, and they both burst into giggles.

"So," Emily said, leaning in, "are you going to ask him to go with you to the Ravensburg fair?"

"I don't know. I don't want to seem pushy… or annoying."

"You're not being pushy. You're showing interest. Guys like that. They don't want to make the first move every time. Make the move, girl."

"You really think so?"

"I know so. Don't be shy, Dani. Let your wild side out, I know you've got one."

Danielle took a breath. "Okay. I'll ask him tomorrow when I go for my walk. I'm just… nervous he'll say no."

"Schrodinger's cat, babe. You'll never know if you don't ask."

She smiled. "You're right. I'm gonna ask."

"And think about it," Emily added with a grin, "you could end up on the Ferris wheel with him. All close. You could pretend you're scared, cling to him a little. Get real up close and personal. Maybe touch something… personal." Emily wiggled her eyebrows.

"Oh, my god, perv," Danielle laughed, smacking her arm again. Their laughter grew louder, drawing a few curious looks from around the room.

"Okay," Danielle said, wiping tears from her eyes. "Tomorrow. I'm definitely asking."

"That's my girl," Emily said proudly. "Let the town gossip all they want. You're finally living, Dani."

Danielle smiled softly. And for the first time in a long while, it actually felt true.

Chapter 16 Nick

Nick's ranger truck rumbled over the winding dirt trails of Broad Mountain State Park; the morning sun spilling golden light through the dense canopy above. Summer had the place alive, fishermen stood in the shallows casting lines with quiet patience, hikers disappeared into the dirt paths, and the air itself seemed heavy with the scent of pine, lake water, and warm earth.

He stopped his truck at the beach and watched as the little kids ran into the water, only getting their toes wet, then screamed and ran back out laughing. Then other kids sat on the sand making castles, so focused on patting areas to make the walls stronger and lightly fluffing sand off to perfect the turrets, completely entranced on the build.

He scanned the water, making sure no one was in distress, even though a lifeguard sat at his station watching intently. He smiled as he caught a glimpse of the Crawford boy that he had told Danielle about this morning. He was now about nine years old and swimming with the big kids, not a fear of the water at all. He was so proud of how that kid was doing.

But his mind didn't stay there long; it never did.

His thoughts drifted to Danielle. Watching her at the coffee shop, intently staring at her body. The girls she usually hid under a sports bra were peeking out, and he was pretty sure it was just for him. He was certain she didn't show off her body to anybody. He loved that he was having this effect on her. The thought that she might have done that for *him* sent a darker, more possessive satisfaction curling in his chest, yet part of him wanted to cover her up, her body was for his enjoyment alone.

Listening to her talk about the community center, the pride she had for that place. She was a very shy girl, so to see her talk with such conviction was amazing. Maybe she wouldn't be such an easy kill like he had thought. Maybe she had a good fight in her.

Then his thoughts went to her full lips, the thought of her lips on him, wrapping around his thick length, as he shoved her head deep onto it, making her gag and beg for air. He wanted to feel her nails dig into his legs, feel her hot breath on him, heavy and ragged as fear set in a little. He wanted to pull her ponytail, making her lips lift just enough off him so she could gasp before shoving her back down on it. He could feel himself hardening just thinking about it. The things he wanted to do to her, make her feel things she never felt before, and then end it before she could enjoy anything. He wanted to watch her eyes go from needing him, craving him, to then fearing him all in the same moment, and make her say god's name for a different reason.

He adjusted himself, the pressure of his pants not giving him much space as he hardened further. As he did, he pictured her hand around it. He wanted her dainty hands all over him. He wanted her body wrapped around him. He wanted to see her gorgeous face as she gave him that devilish smile. He wanted to see the dirty side of her, the side she didn't show people, he knew it was there, and he wanted it for himself. He needed her in so many ways, needed to feel himself inside of her. He wanted to hear her moan as he tugged on her breast and then feel her fear as he slid the knife along her throat.

His fingers tightened on the steering wheel, his jaw tight.

It was a dangerous game because, alongside the hunger, another thought crept in. He couldn't explain it if he tried, his mind betrayed him, replacing the knife with the slow drag of his hand sliding along her throat, not for pain but pleasure. He pictured his lips kissing her neck, gingerly with affection. Hearing her name come from his lips as he softly touched her skin, feeling her lips, soft and pouty as they touched his.

He shook his head to make that thought go away. He couldn't feel those feelings. He couldn't complicate what was going on. He needed to keep his mind on track, or he would slip up. Affection clouded judgment; she was a target, nothing more. There would never be more with Danielle.

As much as he tried to push her away, he was struggling. He saw her face in his mind again, that shy look she gave him after he had complimented her, her face flushing red, the twinkle in her eye, the way…

A rap on the window broke him from his thoughts. He turned his head to see Judith Johnson standing there. "Hey, Mrs. Johnson, what can I do for ya?"

"Just wanted to know if you'd like water?" She said, holding up the bottle in question.

He shifted in his seat, trying to make sure his arousal was concealed.

"Thanks, darlin', I'd love one." He grabbed the water bottle and smiled.

Her cheeks reddened and her smile widened. Judith was the kind of woman everyone in town had a story about. She had been married for fourteen years, yet everyone knew she cheated on her husband quite often. She loved to flirt with other men, and Nick wasn't sure if her husband Carl was oblivious or if he just didn't care, but it was embarrassing. He needed to do something about her. Keep her in line. She deserved to be punished for what she was doing, and he would love to be the one to do it.

But this wasn't his problem, Carl needed to be a man and set his woman straight. Maybe with a hand, or a belt. Women like that needed to be put in their place and told what to do. He smirked thinking about her bent over Carl's knee, her ass red as he explained how things were going to go from now on. Her whimpering as she repeated back what she would do. He would have her repeat the rules as her ass reddened further, then have her get on her knees and say them one more time before she finished him off like a good wife should.

"Well, Mrs. Johnson, I have to go back to patrolling. Enjoy the beach."

"Oh, I will. I'm sure you have a great view out here." She said, licking her lips seductively as she pushed her chest out just a little to show the girls off in her tight bikini top.

"I'm sure your husband appreciates the view more. But maybe it should just be for him."

That landed like a slap. Her chest went down, her eyes narrowed, and her body language immediately said she was not happy with that answer at all.

Before she could reply, he put the truck in drive and tapped on his door. "Well, gotta get back to my job."

Judith stepped back, hands on her hips, a sour look replacing her practiced charm. She clearly wasn't used to being rejected. It made him chuckle knowing he had somewhat put her in her place.

But the only person he really wanted to truly control was Danielle. And she wouldn't even need the sharp edge to bend. She struck him as someone who wanted to please, someone who would yield if guided firmly enough. The challenge would be breaking through that shyness and coaxing out whatever she kept hidden from the world.

She would be his. For a while. Until the game ended.

Chapter 17 Danielle

Danielle closed the door behind her, the familiar click echoing in the quiet entryway. She hung her purse on the wooden hook by the door and slid her keys into the small ceramic dish her father had made in high school shop class.

She could smell her mom's cooking wafting through the house. The smell of fresh basil and tomatoes mixed with the sweet smells of blueberry pie made her mouth salivate. Her mom was an amazing cook, and dinner was never simple at their house. The only time she could remember having something easy like a sandwich for dinner was when her mom would go out for book club night with her friends. Dad would have to cook, and ham sandwiches were his go to.

She smiled at the thought of her parents still deeply in love with each other. They had always been affectionate, from slow dancing in the kitchen, to the sweet hand holding during movies. Her dad would bring her coffee in bed every morning, and her mom would fuss over him in return. It wasn't just love, it was a partnership, and Danielle had grown up knowing that was what she wanted one day. She had lived a sheltered life, sure, but she was grateful for it. They showered Danielle with love, made her feel special and always told her she could do anything, nothing was too hard, and no job was unattainable. Granted, becoming a YouTuber was not what they were thinking and initially they weren't thrilled, but they saw her helping in the community and how she was home to help them out a lot, and they realized having her around more was a blessing.

Danielle and her mom were extremely close. She cherished the time they had because she knew so many people who didn't have that with their parents, like Emily. Emily had lost her mom when she was twelve, and it had always been really hard for her. Danielle's mom had stepped up and taken her under her wing and still does. Emily's dad is amazing when he's home, but he works a lot and travels, so most of the time it's just her in that big house. Danielle knew the life she had many would kill for, so she never took it for granted. Her family was her everything and nothing would come between that.

"Hey, Mom, I'm home." She called out.

She could hear the clattering of pots and pans in the kitchen, light country music wafting through the house from the Alexa device.

"Hey, sweetie, I'm in the kitchen."

Danielle chuckled, *no kidding.* With all the noise, it wasn't a hard clue to figure it out. Danielle walked into the kitchen, her mom's brunette hair sat in a perfect bun on her head, she was short like Danielle, long blue dress that almost hit the floor, a white apron covering most of it.

"Spaghetti tonight?" Danielle asked, guessing from the tomato ends and basil leaf pieces strewn on the counter. The pasta roller dusted in flour.

"How'd ya guess?" Her mom teased, grinning.

"YouTuber by day, detective by night." Danielle chuckled as she walked over to inspect the pie resting on the island. The smell of sweet blueberries and buttered crust swirled around her.

"There's another pie in the oven for Mrs. Jenkins," her mom said casually. "I talked to her a little while ago, you know."

Danielle froze mid-sniff. "Wow. News travels fast. Let me guess, you already know?"

"Oh my gosh, Danielle, I am so excited," her mom gushed. "Nick Chambers? He's gorgeous. And sweet. And did I mention gorgeous?"

Danielle laughed. "You might have."

"So," her mom said, turning to face her fully, "spill."

"There's not much to spill yet," Danielle admitted. "We went out for coffee. That's about as far as we've gotten."

"You didn't ask him to the fair as your date? He didn't kiss you on the cheek? Nothing?" Her mom asked, clearly disappointed.

"Nothing yet, Mom," Danielle said gently. "We've just started talking."

The truth was, Danielle had hoped for something last night, a kiss, a hug, some small sign she wasn't imagining the spark. Instead, it almost felt like he was keeping her at arm's length, like maybe he only wanted to be friends.

Her mom shrugged. "Well, I'm sure something will happen soon. Give it time. Slow and steady wins the race. Besides," she added with a smile, "who wouldn't want to say you were their date? You're a catch."

"You have to say that," Danielle said. "you're my mom."

"I absolutely do not," her mom shot back. "I'd know if you were a dud."

"Mom!" Danielle gasped.

They both burst out laughing, and Danielle felt that familiar warmth settle in her chest. She loved that she could talk to her mom like this, without judgment or lectures, just honesty and comfort, exactly when she needed it.

Danielle's tone softened. "Mom, how did you know Dad was the one?"

Danielle's mom's face lit up and a smile spread. "Your dad was perfect from the moment I met him. We locked eyes across the library table and I vowed to my friend Lucy that I would marry him. I asked him to the Sadie Hawkins dance that day, and we have been inseparable ever since. It has been a fairytale romance."

Danielle knew she didn't immediately feel that way about Nick. There was a nervousness that she couldn't shake. He watched her with an intensity that made her heart race, but she realized her nervousness was probably from her inexperience. She knew she was very inexperienced when it came to the women Nick was probably used to.

"What if I'm not enough for Nick? I'm not like the other girls he has probably dated."

Her mom's expression turned serious. "A real man will never think that. You're an amazing girl with a great heart. He would be stupid not to see you as enough. Remember that."

"Thanks, Mom."

"And know your worth. You'll know if he is right for you. Pray on the matter as well. God will always give you the right answer."

Danielle squeezed her mom tightly. "Alright. I'm going to go do some work. Let me know when you want me to bring that pie to old lady Jenkins."

Danielle headed up to her room and shut the door. She felt strongly that she wanted Nick to be the one. She wasn't sure if that was her naive side talking but at this point, she didn't care. She wanted Nick. She just hoped he felt the same way.

As she sat down at her vanity, pondering what kind of make-up tutorial she would do today, her mind floated to Nick. His gorgeous eyes, that smile that could melt every lady in the room, the way he stood, commanding everyone's attention without even trying. She pictured her arm wrapped around his, every girl staring at them, envy across the women's faces wondering how she was the lucky one. Her daydream softened, just the two of them in his cabin, nestled together on the couch. Nick lightly stroking her arm, and then his hand in her hair as he pulls her in for a soft romantic kiss. The thought made her breathing ragged, and her chest was beating rapidly. He was probably so sweet and gentle and caring. Making sure she was taken care of. Worrying about her needs. He always portrayed himself as this gentle giant who took care of everyone. She wanted that and wanted him. She was going to ask him to be her date tomorrow. She needed to make this happen so she could have the fairy tale ending like her parents.

Chapter 18 Nick

Nick sat on the porch, his favorite spot in the morning, the quiet sounds of nature and nothing else. His mug of coffee in his hand, swirls of steam wafting towards him, the earthy aroma putting his mind and body at ease. He loved these types of mornings. Fall was creeping in now that it was October. Nice chilly mornings, dew on the grass, and the smell of autumn slowly making its way, yet by noon it would be warm enough to swim, and shorts would replace sweatpants for the campers.

He took a sip of his coffee, the bitter taste of the black coffee swirling around his tongue, his eyes closed as he enjoyed the moment.

His eyes jolted open as the sound of tires rolling through the dirt came close. He looked in the direction of the sound and saw an officer's car coming towards him. He knew it was probably Chuck. He was the only one who usually paid him visits.

The car stopped right behind his truck, and a hand greeted him through the open window.

"Hey, Chuck." Nick said, holding his mug up in a greeting.

Chuck got out of the car and fixed his hat on his head. "Hey, Nick. Gorgeous out this morning. You can feel fall in the air."

"Can't wait. Favorite time of year. What brings you out here?"

Chuck shook his head slowly. "It ain't good, Nick. Dr. Jenny McGrath went missing. She's been gone for two days now. People are really worried."

"Oh shit. That's horrible. She's got family in New Jersey, doesn't she? Maybe she went up there?"

"They already checked and called everyone she knew. No sign of her."

"God. I hope she didn't make another house call to some creep. You know she's been known to do that."

"Yeah, it's in the back of our minds. We're tracing her phone calls now and hoping we can get a ping from her last whereabouts. She had made remarks that she didn't feel safe. I really hope nothing happened."

"Shit. I hope so, too. She's really loved around here. She's helped me out of a jam a couple of times."

"Just came out here to let ya know. Keep your eyes and ears out. We're hoping someone is stupid enough to talk thinking they're alone in the woods. Or maybe even drop a body."

"I'll make sure to listen and watch everything a little closer. She deserves to be found safe and alive. She's a great woman."

"I feel that. She saved my life. Caught that melanoma last year on my back. I'd be a goner if it wasn't for her."

Nick shook his head, making sure to show pure concern and sorrow for the woman who was missing. "There's a great team on it. You guys will find her."

Chuck tipped his hat. "Thanks, Nick."

"You want a coffee? I could slip something harder into it." Nick said, chuckling. Hoping to lighten the mood a little.

"No, thanks. Gotta get back to the station. I need to do some more digging and make a couple more calls."

"Alright. Offer stands when you need it."

Chuck put his hand in the air, "See ya, Nick."

Nick sat back down and slowly rocked in his chair. He watched as Chuck backed out of the dirt driveway and slowly started down the trail. The mug came back up to his lips and as he took another sip, a sly smirk came across his face.

People came to him for help, asked him to keep an eye and ear out, wanted him to patrol the area and make it safer. Officers came to him for information on who could have done it. And the best part, not once did they ever second question his whereabouts. Not honest, caring, safety first Nick. He was the guy you ran to when you were scared, the man who you felt would make sure no harm ever came to you.

Jenny McGrath sure felt that way as they went into the woods looking for Henry. Nick wondered why the dog never came back, how had that not alerted people to her disappearance. Maybe he had been attacked and was injured or dead.

That made Nick's stomach turn. He hated dogs being hurt; they were loyal and caring and sweet. They never thought to undermine someone or hurt someone, they never wanted to make you feel stupid or worthless. They listened and did as they were told, every time.

Nick was going to keep watch of the woods a little closer, maybe Henry was out there. He could get the dog help. That would give him even more brownie points if he had to bring Jenny's hurt dog to the vet, completely concerned about Jenny and Henry.

As he took the last sip from his mug, he stood up. He needed to go inside and get ready to go see Danielle. He couldn't wait to see her today, her hair bouncing as she walked, the adorable smile she had with the dimples that made men weak in the knees, those gorgeous lips, and the cheeks that reddened anytime he made a comment. He was so excited to see her, and the thought of one day making her ass as red as her cheeks usually were made him even more excited.

***

Nick had just parked his truck near the river where the lovely campers had been that mysteriously fell into a fire. He walked over to the waters edge, looking at the view of the mountains that seemed to envelop the area. The water lightly moving down stream, every now and then he would see a bubble where a fish had come up to feed on a fly. A moose caught his attention as he scanned the riverbank. Not too far downstream the moose poked his head out from the tree line to get a sip of water. He was massive, his velvet antlers were at least six feet long.

Nick had been lost in the sight of the magnificent creature when footsteps approached too close behind him, snapping him out of the moment.

He spun around sharply, irritation flashing through him as his hand instinctively went to the knife at his side. The tension vanished just as quickly when he saw Danielle standing there.

She looked incredible. Her black shorts hugged her legs, paired with a simple crop tank that showed just enough skin to make his thoughts drift. Her long blonde hair was pulled back into a ponytail, exposing her soft and delicate neck. Those lips he had already grown far too fond of curved into a smile, dimples setting in perfectly.

She wore confidence well, but it didn't fool him. Her fingers twisted together without stopping, her foot dragging back and forth through the dirt. He liked knowing he still unsettled her just enough. He wanted her to be uncertain and nervous right up until the end.

He wondered what she would be like alone with him. Would she always be shy and hesitant, unsure where to put her hands? The thought tightened something low in his stomach, and he welcomed the pressure, knowing she was the cause of it.

Her gaze flicked downward for just a second, widened slightly, then snapped back to his face. A faint blush crept into her cheeks, like she hoped he hadn't noticed.

He smirked. God, he loved how nervous and embarrassed she seemed to be.

"Hey, darlin'," he said easily. "How's your walk going?"

Her shoulders relaxed a little. "It's good. It's beautiful out today."

"It is," he agreed. "Come here. You've gotta see this. It'll make your day even better."

He took her hand and led her to the water's edge, placing a finger on his lips before pointing ahead. The moose still stood there, unmoving, almost unreal.

Her reaction was immediate. Nick watched as her eyes widened, and her breath caught. She pointed excitedly, then pressed her hand to her chest as her smile grew brighter. Nick watched her closely, his grip on her hand tightening just a fraction. When she looked back at him, her eyes were full of gratitude, excitement, and something dangerously close to affection. Like it mattered to her that he had remembered something she had said in passing.

Then he watched as her nerves crept back in. Her foot began its slow swing through the dirt again.

"So…" she said softly. "Um… I have a question."

His brow lifted. "Alright. Shoot."

"The Ravensburg fair is this weekend," she said, stumbling slightly over the words. "Emily and I go every year… and I was wondering if… if you'd want to go with us?"

He let the silence stretch just long enough to make her squirm, enjoying the way her cheeks reddened further, her foot tracing nervous circles.

"Danielle," he said, voice teasing, "are you askin' me to go as *your* date?"

She looked down, then back up, cheeks burning now, teeth catching her bottom lip.

"Y-yes."

A slow smile spread across his face. "You're absolutely adorable when you're nervous."

Her head dipped again, eyes fixed on her shoes. The need to punish her for looking down crept in and he pushed the thought away. He needed to keep the facade up for now of being the sweet gentleman.

"I'd love to," he said finally. "I'd be honored to go as your date darlin'."

Her head snapped up, eyes bright, her smile wide and genuine.

"Really?"

"Of course, darlin'. I don't take just anyone out for coffee."

Nick watched as she stepped closer, but he could see her hesitation. He closed the distance for her, taking her hand again, his thumb brushing softly over her skin.

"I'll pick you up Saturday," he said. "Four o'clock, after patrol. Sound good?"

"That's perfect."

She leaned in, kissed his cheek quickly, then turned to retreat down the trail.

He didn't let her.

He tugged her back gently, cupped her face, and held her gaze. He watched as she searched his eyes, uncertain, and his breathing slowed.

Then he kissed her, slow at first, before deepening it just enough to make his meaning clear. He felt her press closer, felt her smile against his mouth before he tightened his grip briefly, rougher this time, then released her.

She stumbled back, lips flushed, eyes dazed.

"I'll see you Saturday," she said, nervous excitement threading her voice.

"And hopefully Thursday and Friday, too," he replied smoothly. "I look forward to our walks."

"So do I," she said, her eyes flicking briefly to his mouth as she licked her lips. "I love the view."

His smile sharpened. "Then I'll try not to disappoint."

"Never," she said softly, nerves creeping back in. "I'll see you later, Nick."

Nick watched as she turned toward the trail, hips swaying just enough to demand attention. As her feet hit the trail, she turned around for one last look. She smiled, and then went back to the trail, her ponytail swishing perfectly. He watched her until she disappeared into the tree line.

He could still picture her cute nervous face, the way she kept moving her foot, the way her breasts pushed up against his chest as she breathed heavily during their kiss. The excitement in her face when he said yes to the date.

He couldn't wait to see her, although anger poured into his mind. He hated that he was having these weird feelings for her. He wanted to kill her and keep her forever. He wanted to take her last breath but also feel every breath and catch them with his mouth as he made her excited. He hated these conflicting feelings he was having but as much as he tried, he couldn't push them away.

He realized that until he ended her, he would have a lot of fun with her. He knew it would make him feel even more powerful, and even though he may miss her presence for a little, the memory of her eyes large and terrified, her last breath, her blood covering him; he would have those memories forever.

The sound of a twig snapping made his neck turn in that direction. He saw Carrie, one of the women from the church, turning and walking quickly the other way. He rolled his eyes and chuckled. The whole world would know in about five minutes that he had kissed Danielle, yet for some reason he liked the fact that people would know she was his. Yet he would make sure Carrie was silenced if she ruined Danielle's reputation at church.

He got back into his truck, put it into gear, and started making his way down the trail, ready to start his day and patrol the area, making sure everyone was safe.

As he got to the camping area, he saw Larry and his group. They came here almost every weekend during the summer.

Larry looked up and waved towards Nick's truck. Nick pulled up to their campsite and put the truck in park. His arm resting on the window, he yelled out. "Hey Larry. How's it going this weekend?"

"Not bad. This is the most gorgeous day we've had yet."

Larry began walking over, beer can in hand, stumbling a tiny bit even though it was only eleven in the morning. "Still can't believe first the girls in the fire, then Dr. McGrath. Crazy, huh?"

"It really is. This town has always been such a safe place."

"Yeah," Larry said, shaking his head slowly. "Those… poor girls. It was Tina an' her best friend Carly. I've known those girls since they were born. It's crazy t'think they're gone."

"Oh man. I didn't know them too well, but I know they were loved in the community."

"Yeah," Larry said, bowing his head. "Their funeral services'r tomorrow. The whole town is takin' it pretty hard."

"God, poor girls." Nick said, clicking his tongue. "Still curious how it happened."

"I know, right. I'm sure they'll figure't out. Our station has a pretty great detective team."

"Yeah, hopefully they figure it out soon. Let's make this town safe again."

"I'll cheers to that!" Larry lifted his can and then took a long sip."

"Alright, Larry. Stay safe. Gotta keep patrolling."

"Have a good'n, Nick. I'll have a beer for ya."

Nick laughed and put the truck in drive. Larry went back to his camping chair and grabbed another beer.

Nick rolled his eyes. He couldn't stand the drunks that came into town every weekend. They had no idea what was going on right underneath their own noses. They were too busy drinking and acting like fools.

He could murder someone in the next campsite, and they would never realize it was happening because they were too busy chugging and singing badly to the music pumping loudly out of their speakers.

Although he did like the fact that because of them, he could basically get away with anything and the only thing they would remember was that Nick the ranger was on patrol. They would tell the police he showed his face a couple of times a day and made everyone feel safe.

He chuckled and shook his head. He couldn't wait for Saturday now as well. Not only would he be with the most beautiful girl, her hand in his, maybe they would go into the fun house so he could hold her even closer as she got nervous. But it would also show people that he couldn't be the one killing these women because he was too busy with this gorgeous girl, all his time would be with her, another perfect alibi.

Chapter 19 Danielle

Danielle sat cross-legged on her bed, her laptop balanced on her knees as she scrolled through the footage from her walks, checking her pacing, making sure each clip flowed the same way the others did. When she reached the opening by the river, she stopped.

Nick stood there with his back to the camera, completely unaware he was being filmed. He wasn't patrolling. Wasn't the town's dependable protector or the strong, capable ranger everyone relied on. He was just a man, quiet and still, taking in the view like it was his alone for a moment. She paused the video and stared at the screen. She still couldn't quite understand how someone like him wanted her. The sweet, shy, always-second-guessing Danielle. Part of her wanted to question it, to pick it apart until it didn't make sense anymore. Instead, she chose not to. She didn't want to jinx it. She wanted to stay right here in the feeling and enjoy it for as long as it lasted.

She reached to press play again just as her door flew open.

Danielle jumped and looked up to see Emily barreling into the room. Emily rushed over and flopped dramatically onto the bed beside her.

"Oh my god, Danielle," she said, breathless. "I just heard the juiciest gossip."

"Oh yeah?" Danielle raised a brow, already smiling. "Do tell."

"I'm pretty sure you know more than I do," Emily said. "Carrie told Marie, Marie told Jackie, Jackie told old Mrs. Jenkins, and you know what happens after that. Apparently, you were caught making out with Nick Chambers."

Heat rushed straight to Danielle's face. There was no hiding it, her cheeks had given her away.

"It's true," she admitted. "I asked him to go to the fair with me. And… he kissed me."

"Holy crap, Danielle!" Emily squealed. "That's huge!"

"I know," Danielle said, her smile refusing to fade. "I'm so excited. Although, we usually go together every year… wouldn't mind if you tagged along."

"Of course! I'll be your moral support." Emily said, chuckling. "I get to hang out with you and Nick freaking Chambers this weekend."

They stared at each other for half a second before both of them started squealing and bouncing on the bed like kids.

"I've never been this happy, Emily," Danielle said once they caught their breath. "He's so sweet. And chivalrous."

"Okay, okay… skip ahead," Emily said impatiently. "How was the kiss?"

Danielle grinned. "It was amazing. At first it was soft and sweet. But the last one…" She hesitated, then smiled wider. "It got a little more possessive. Like he was making sure I knew I was his."

"Fuuuuuck," Emily breathed, dragging the word out like she could feel it herself.

"I know," Danielle laughed. "It was… a lot, in the best way."

Emily snapped back to herself. "Just be careful, okay? Don't rush into anything you're not ready for."

Danielle smiled softly. "Aw. You care."

"Shut up," Emily said, smacking her leg playfully.

They both giggled, then went quiet for a beat just long enough to process it all, before erupting into laughter all over again.

"So whatcha watching?" Emily asked, nodding her head towards the laptop.

"Oh, just the walk I took today. I need to do some editing so I can post it."

"Oooh, so the kiss is on there." Emily went to grab the laptop. Danielle held onto the sides possessively. She didn't want Emily to see her stuttering like a child as she asked Nick to the fair.

"No, I already deleted that part. Can't have my subscribers getting a free show."

"Oh boo, you're no fun."

Danielle shrugged her shoulders. "Sorry."

Emily shrugged, "Eh, I'll get a front seat view this weekend, anyway… I'm gonna go see what your mom baked. I'm hungry."

Emily walked out the door to go rummage through the kitchen. "Grab me an iced tea while you're there." Danielle shouted.

Then she quickly took the piece of the video that had Nick in it and placed it in her Nick folder. Then she deleted it from the walking edits and kept watching to make sure there were no other distractions or loud noises.

Emily came back to the room with a plate piled high with pie, chocolate chip cookies, and a handful of strawberries.

"Glad to see you at least decided to be somewhat healthy." Danielle said, chuckling.

Emily threw her a sideways glance as she stuffed the cookie into her mouth. Then she handed Danielle her can of sweet tea and proceeded to devour the next cookie.

Danielle chuckled and popped the tea open. The first sip was her favorite. That sweet taste but with the cold crisp tea taste. It always brought her back to memories of them being on the beach, laying out on their towels, as they talked about their favorite celebrities of the week, the town drama going down, and the cute boys that never looked their way. They had been the odd balls in town, with the weird haircuts and clothes their moms had got from the church rummage sale. They were bland girls that no one looked twice at, but after they had graduated high school, they started playing with makeup and watching YouTube videos on how to dress and do your hair. Slowly they started to look more put together, then Emily went into cosmetology school and fixed both of their haircuts. Once Danielle started to gain more confidence, she didn't look frumpy, she decided to take a risk and make a YouTube video. She loved how make-up and hair had given her confidence she never knew she could obtain. She decided if there were girls like her out there, she could help them. She never expected to blow up so quickly and to have this as her full-time job. She loved what she did and loved that she would get messages from girls thanking her because now they had found their confidence.

Danielle finished editing the video and threw a cute title and description onto it and published the episode. She closed the laptop and grabbed a cookie off Emily's plate.

Emily smiled and placed the plate a little closer. The pie was completely gone, and one tiny strawberry slice was left, but there were still a couple of cookies.

She grabbed the newest People magazine. No matter how easy everything was to find on your phone, Danielle loved having a real magazine in her hands. Being able to flip the pages and smell the perfume samples they always shoved in them.

"You see Jennifer Aniston's gorgeous dress? She's so beautiful." Danielle said, shoving the magazine into Emily's face.

"God, I know. She's in her fifties and you would never know it."

They both sat in silence flipping through magazines and enjoying each other's company without having to make small talk. Danielle loved how comfortable they were with each other. She loved their friendship and was glad for Emily's pushing personality. If it wasn't for her, she would not have asked Nick to the fair. She couldn't wait to see Nick again. The thought of this gorgeous man, with his commanding presence, holding her hand through the fair, wanting her. She couldn't wait to see the girls in town drooling and annoyed as they saw Nick's arm wrapped around her, at some point his lips on hers, making everyone jealous.

Then Emily broke the silence. "So, what are you going to wear to the fair?"

"Honestly. I hadn't thought about it yet."

"What! Danielle, you have to look perfect."

Emily shot off the bed and ran to Danielle's closet, rummaging through her clothes.

"Ugh, everything is floor length and modest. Where's your hot clothes you hide?"

"In the way back of my closet."

Emily snuck into the back of the closet and all Danielle could hear was hangers sliding on the pole quickly. "That's it. None of these are Nick worthy. We need to go shopping. Get your shoes on, we have work to do."

Daniele rolled her eyes but couldn't help smiling at the same time. She guessed it was time to dress more like a wanted woman and less like the modest godly girl she was.

Emily threw Danielle's flip flops at her. "Let's go. We have got to find you something he will remember you in and want you out of at the same time."

***

They pulled up into town a few minutes later, parking in front of Jackie's Boutique. The moment Danielle opened the door, warm air scented with sweet perfume drifted out to greet them, pop music humming softly through the space.

"I love this store," Emily said, already pushing Danielle inside. "She just got in the cutest stuff."

Emily immediately darted toward the racks, flipping through hangers at lightning speed. Shirts were pulled free and tossed at Danielle as Emily moved on to the next rack without slowing down. Danielle glanced down at the growing pile curled over her arm. Pink, green, and red. Sparkles, loud patterns, sequins.

Sequins? Who even wore sequins anymore? This looks aggressively nineties.

"Come on," Emily said, piling on even more. "You've got a lot to try on."

They squeezed into the dressing room together. Privacy had never been their thing. They had done everything side by side for as long as Danielle could remember, this included. Honestly, it would have felt strange if Emily wasn't there. Danielle tried on the first top; a pink tank covered in silver sequins. It hung awkwardly, shapeless, turning her into a box.

"Oh god, no," Emily said immediately, shaking her head. "Take it off."

The next few weren't much better. Some were too tight, others too loose. One showed absolutely nothing; another showed way too much, bending over would be a gamble. Then Danielle pulled on a black crop top. It was longer than most, just brushing her belly button, but the neckline dipped just enough to make someone look twice. She paired it with a fitted jean skirt that hit mid-thigh.

Emily's eyes lit up. "Oh. Yeah. This is it. You look adorable and hot."

Danielle turned slowly in front of the mirror. She had to admit, it looked good. Really good.

"Okay, don't move," Emily said. "We just need shoes." She vanished from the dressing room.

Danielle turned back to the mirror, slower this time, letting her thoughts wander. She imagined Nick's gaze lingering on her neckline, his hand resting on her thigh, thumb tracing lazy circles as it crept closer to the hem of her skirt. Her breath caught just a little.

Emily burst back in, snapping her out of it, holding up a pair of brown cowboy boots.

"These would be perfect. Try them."

Danielle slipped them on, unsure. She studied her reflection.

"Oh my god, those are adorable," Emily said, clapping.

Danielle frowned slightly. "They're… cute. Just not me."

Emily tilted her head. "You don't like them."

"Not really. They don't feel like me."

"Okay, stay put." Emily grinned. "I grabbed another pair."

She returned with low-cut black Vans.

Danielle smiled instantly. "I don't even need to try these on. I love them."

Emily laughed. "I knew it. You'll look perfect."

As Danielle changed back, excitement fluttered low in her chest. Saturday couldn't come fast enough. Danielle couldn't wait to see Nick. She was going to look hot, and she was determined to be more confident and make a move on him that would end up with them alone doing more than just kissing.

Chapter 20 Chuck

The funeral home smelled faintly of lilies and old varnish. The kind of scent that clung to dark wood and whispered that this building had seen more than its fair share of tears. The air was thick with warmth from too many bodies packed into the main room; voices hushed to a murmur, footsteps muffled by worn carpet.

Two caskets, side by side, dominated the front of the room. Matching arrangements of white roses and pale blue hydrangeas framed each one, the colors blending so perfectly it almost looked like one seamless display. The girls would have liked that. Carly and Tina were inseparable since birth, best friends in a way that made "best" feel like an understatement, and now they were lying in rest together, as if the town refused to split them even in death.

Chuck stood near the front, his broad shoulders squared but his eyes soft, waiting for the right moment to approach the mothers. They stood together like sisters themselves, clutching tissues, their bodies swaying slightly toward each other as if bracing against the same wind.

When there was an opening, Chuck stepped forward. "I'm so sorry," he said, his voice low but steady. They both managed faint smiles, the kind that lasted only a heartbeat. "Thank you for coming, Chuck," Carly's mom said. "It means a lot."

"Of course. These girls…" He glanced toward the caskets. "…they were special to all of us."

Tina's mom dabbed her eyes. "You know, I was just telling Janet… remember when you brought them home in your cruiser that night?"

Chuck laughed despite the ache in his chest. "Seventeen years old, drunk as skunks. Standing on the roof of that house, swearing they were about to make internet history."

"Oh, God," Carly's mom laughed softly, the sound breaking on the edges. "Carly shouting about how it was going to be the best clip on the internet."

"They swore they'd be asked to be on that YouTube channel… what was it called?" Chuck paused to think.

"Two Crazy Dudes," Tina's mom supplied, shaking her head.

"That's it. And I told them if they jumped, they'd be making the news in a very different way." He smiled at the memory of the two giggling girls in sequined shorts and bare feet, swaying on the roof line, daring gravity to test them.

The women's laughter faded into the hum of the room. Chuck gave them each a warm hug. "I'm so sorry again. If you need anything, you know where to find me."

As he stepped back, his eyes drifted toward the rear of the room. Nick was standing there, hat in hand, the brim pressed against his chest. He was talking with Calvin. They chuckled lightly and then embraced, Calvin quickly tapping Nick's back before making his way to another crowd. Chuck felt a ripple of relief seeing Nick there. He had been a great addition to the park staff, dependable, easy to like. The kind of man you trusted without thinking.

It was hard to reconcile that trust with the brutality of what had been done to these girls. Chuck's mind caught for a moment on the impossibility of it. These weren't troublemakers. They weren't careless. They ran the Blissful Bakery, kept their heads down, and organized fundraisers for the community center. The whole damn town loved them.

He watched as Nick began making his way forward, stopping to clasp hands, pat shoulders, murmur condolences. He had that ability to blend into grief without making it about himself, a rare quality. When Nick reached him, Chuck gave him a light hug and a pat on the back. "Hey, Nick. Glad you could make it."

"I wouldn't miss it," Nick said. "I watched those girls start that bakery. The whole town was proud of them. Sweet girls."

"They really were. Families are going to have a tough time. At least they've got a town that'll step up."

Nick nodded. "We've got a pretty amazing town when tragedy strikes."

Chuck scanned the crowd, familiar faces from every corner of the community, plus strangers whose ties to the girls were a mystery. He cataloged each one, letting instinct do its quiet work. No one here set off alarms. The grief looked real, the eyes red, the smiles brittle. Some whispered and laughed softly, sharing stories to cut through the heaviness.

When Chuck glanced back, Nick was at the front, speaking to the families. He hugged each set of parents, and as he turned away, there was a flicker of something on his face, a small smirk. Chuck's stomach tightened.

"Hey, Nick," Chuck called, raising his hand.

Nick came over. "You okay, Nick?"

"Yeah. Carly's dad just told me he was glad to see me, and said my handsome face made his day. You know how he jokes. I just… smirked. Glad he can still joke a little, even now."

Chuck let out a breath he hadn't realized he had been holding. His gut quieted. "You wanna grab a beer?"

"I could use one. Meet you at The Drunken Raven in ten?"

"Sounds good." Chuck clapped him on the back and headed out.

Near the entrance, two detectives stood in a tight knot; their voices pitched low. Chuck joined them.

"Anything new?" he asked.

Detective Henry Mills shook his head. "We found their shoes, clothes, and phones near the riverbank. No signs of foul play. No DNA. No weird texts or calls."

"Like they just… walked away from everything?" Chuck frowned.

"Yeah, except we know they didn't. The coroner said the bones that were left showed no signs of foul play."

Detective Parker Rollins chimed in. "And now Dr. Jenny McGrath's missing. Whole different kind of red flag. Her dog is gone, too. She would never go anywhere without that dog unless she was working. Kids are beside themselves."

Chuck's frown deepened. "Phone ping?"

"Last ping was her house. She left it behind. Neighbors saw her around dinner, then nothing."

It was unlike Jenny. She was predictable and careful. This wasn't a woman who vanished without telling anyone.

"I don't get it," Chuck muttered. "I've had eyes on her since she came into the precinct all shaken up. She seemed safe. Settled."

Parker shook his head slowly. "We've got someone out there taking women. Quietly. Cleanly. We're running out of time to find him."

Mills and Parker exchanged a look that was grim and heavy.

Chuck felt the unease crawl back up his spine.

***

He thought of Jenny's kids again, the way they had clung to the porch railing when he had stopped by to ask questions. The older one tried not to cry. The younger one had not bothered.

Chuck took a slow drink, staring at the far wall but seeing only the puzzle. He tried to fit the pieces together. Timelines, last sightings, the geography of the disappearances. The lines refused to meet.

The door opened, letting in a gust of cool night air and the faint sound of crickets. Nick stepped inside, scanning the room until his eyes found Chuck. He smiled, and for a moment, Chuck felt the comfort of normalcy.

Chuck felt Nick slide onto the stool beside him. The faint scent of cold night air clinging to him, along with something woodsy, and pine, maybe cedar. He set his hat on the bar and signaled to the bartender with two fingers.

"Busy in there tonight," Nick said, his voice low, almost casual. "Feels like the whole town showed up."

"Yeah," Chuck replied, swirling his beer. "Small towns do that. We take care of our own."

The bartender placed a Samuel Adams in front of Nick, the golden foam lapping at the rim. "Thanks, Gary." He took a slow sip, like a man savoring his first drink in hours.

For a moment, they sat in silence, listening to the low hum of conversation from a booth in the back. Then Chuck leaned forward. "You knew the girls pretty well, didn't you?"

Nick tilted his head, his eyes narrowing just a fraction before softening again. "Well enough. I stopped in at the bakery a lot. I mean, who doesn't like warm cinnamon rolls on a cold morning?"

Chuck gave a faint smile but didn't look away. "I was thinking more… did you ever see them outside the shop? Around the park, maybe?"

Nick drummed his fingers lightly on the bar. "Sometimes. They liked walking along the trails, especially in spring. Carly always stopped to take pictures of flowers. Tina… she'd pick them and tuck them behind Carly's ear."

Chuck watched him closely. "That's a lot of detail."

Nick smirked faintly. "Guess I notice things."

"That you do," Chuck said. He took a sip, letting the silence stretch. "They ever seem worried to you? Like someone was bothering them?"

Nick shook his head. "Not that I saw. They were friendly, but… I don't know, maybe a little trusting. They talked to everyone."

Chuck thought about that. "Trusting gets you in trouble."

"Sometimes," Nick agreed, his eyes dipping to his beer.

The bartender passed by, dropping off another glass to Chuck. When he walked away again, Chuck leaned in a little. "You know, I keep thinking about how fast it happened. One day they're baking, raising money for the community center, making everyone's morning better… and then just gone. No struggle, no signs they even saw it coming."

Nick took another slow sip before answering. "Maybe that's better, don't you think? Not seeing it coming?"

Something in the way he said it; it was calm, almost gentle, and it made the hair on the back of Chuck's neck rise. But the man's face was unreadable, his voice without an edge.

"Depends on your point of view," Chuck said.

Nick chuckled quietly. "You sound like you've been talking to too many philosophers."

"Or too many suspects," Chuck countered, though there was a playful note in his voice.

Nick raised his glass in a mock salute. "Well, here's to hoping you find the right one."

The conversation drifted after that, memories of the girls' fundraiser for the high school football team, the time Tina tried to bake a triple-layer cake and collapsed the whole thing in the oven, the way Carly laughed so hard she couldn't breathe when it happened.

But beneath every anecdote, Chuck was listening for something else. Watching the way Nick's eyes lingered when he spoke about them, how sometimes his smile didn't quite reach the corners of his mouth.

When the clock above the bar ticked toward midnight, Chuck pushed his empty glass away. "Well, I should let you get home."

Nick nodded, finishing the last swallow of his beer. "Yeah. Long day tomorrow."

They stood, shaking hands briefly before parting.

As Chuck stepped into the cool night air, his mind was no closer to answers, but his gut wasn't quiet anymore. Something about Nick… it didn't fit neatly into the box he had put him in.

Chapter 21 Nick

The drive back to his cabin was quiet, the night air cool against the open window. The moonlight cut through the tree line in pale strips, flashing across the hood of Nick's truck as he wound down the mountain road. The two beers hadn't done much to him, he had been careful not to drink too much, but the conversations lingered, the voices from earlier still circling in his head.

Chuck had been in a talkative mood at the bar, leaning back on his stool with a beer in hand, reminiscing about the girls. They had swapped stories, some light, some heavier, and in between the laughter there had been questions.

"What do you make of it, Nick?" Chuck had asked at one point, leaning forward, voice low. "Those girls… out by the stream that night. I just keep running it through my head. It's not adding up."

Nick had shrugged, casual, careful. "What do you mean?"

Chuck had tipped his bottle toward him. "No footprints. No drag marks. No tire tracks. Nothing on the bank. It's like the whole place was wiped clean. Even the water… nothing floating. No clothes, no jewelry, nothing. Hell, their phones seemed to be wiped clean. Like someone wanted it that way."

Nick had kept his expression neutral, swirling his own beer. "Could be they went out there on their own, had too much to drink and lost control."

Chuck had studied him for a moment, eyes narrowing ever so slightly. "Maybe. But I've been on the force long enough to know when a scene feels… staged."

Nick had let a beat pass, then gave a small, understanding nod. "You're just doing your job. Looking at all the angles."

The conversation had shifted eventually, Chuck shaking off the unease like a man who knew better than to chase a gut feeling without evidence. They talked about better days and about the bakery the girls had opened, about the way they used to hand out leftover muffins to kids hanging around after school. Chuck had laughed remembering how, when the girls were barely out of their teens, he had caught them drunk at a party, perched on a stranger's roof ready to jump into a pool.

"Carly told me it was gonna be the best clip on the internet," Chuck said, letting out a small laugh.

"Said they were gonna be famous and get invited onto that 'Two Crazy Dudes' YouTube channel. I told 'em the only thing they were getting was a ride home in my cruiser."

They had laughed at that, the sound easy between them, and then the talk had drifted to Danielle.

Chuck's tone had softened. "I'm glad you found someone, Nick. Danielle's a sweet girl. She could be good for you, ya know? Fill your time with something other than work."

Nick had nodded, letting his smile reach his eyes. "I'm excited to see where this goes."

"Just…" Chuck hesitated, his gaze steady. "She's a sweet Christian girl and a little naive. Don't take that the wrong way, but I don't want to see her get hurt. Take things at her pace."

"I will," Nick had assured him, his voice calm and certain. "I'd never pressure her. I'll make sure she's happy."

Chuck had seemed satisfied with that, finishing his beer before clapping Nick on the shoulder and heading out into the night.

Now, the memory of that conversation hung in Nick's mind as he stepped into the stillness of his cabin. He shut the door behind him, the click of the lock sharp in the quiet, and walked over to the mantle.

On it sat a small tin, the Coast Guard emblem on top. Ordinary to anyone else, maybe a place for coins or paper clips. But to Nick, it was far from ordinary.

He sank into the couch with the tin in hand, the springs groaning softly under his weight, and pulled the tin into his lap. His fingers lingered on the cool surface for a moment before he lifted the lid.

Inside, cushioned by a folded piece of cloth, lay the necklace. The silver chain caught the lamplight, the small heart shaped charm gleaming faintly. He could smell it still, the faint trace of her perfume mingled with the metallic tang of blood; a scent etched into his memory.

She had been his first here. The first kill that had shown him what he really was.

He picked up the necklace, the chain cold against his skin. His thumb rubbed over the charm, back and forth, the motion slow and deliberate. He could see it dangling against her throat that night, feel it brushing his lips when he kissed her neck. He could feel it under his palms when he closed his hands around her throat.

The memory was vivid, her eyes wide at first, then softening into that glassy stare as her life ebbed away. The way her body went slack, the final tremor in her limbs. The sound of that last breath, ragged, desperate, then gone.

And him… finishing so hard it stole his own breath. The surge of power, the godlike control, the heat flooding through him. It had been the strongest orgasm of his life. In some twisted corner of his mind, he had thought she could have gotten pregnant from it if she had survived.

His jeans tightened, the pressure immediate and almost painful. He needed that again. Needed it badly.

Not with Danielle. Not yet. Danielle was something else. Something to keep.

This was different. This was about the hunger.

But he had to be careful. Killing in the park right now was a risk. The place was crawling with extra patrols after dark. His shift ended with too many eyes on him.

He needed someone no one cared about. Someone whose absence would barely register. Someone who could vanish without stirring the water.

And he would have to get rid of the body without leaving a trace.

His hands trembled as he thought about it, the images flooding in. He thought about how it would feel, how it would sound. His pulse pounded in his ears. His breathing quickened, shallow, and uneven. The ache in his jeans grew sharper, almost unbearable.

But he wouldn't touch himself. Not now. Not without a kill. That was the point. The waiting made the release so much more intense when it came.

He needed a plan, and he needed it soon. Before Saturday. That way he could see Danielle and play the role Chuck thought he was, the attentive, patient, and safe ranger. He couldn't risk letting the hunger show.

Nick stood, the movement sending a jolt of sensation through him. His hand twitched toward his crotch, adjusting himself, and a low groan slipped out before he could stop it. He was too close already; a few more touches, and it would be over.

He forced his hand away, focusing instead on the tin. He set it carefully back on the mantel above the fireplace. Just another bit of clutter to anyone else. But he knew it was there.

The air in the cabin felt heavy, pressing against his skin. He turned toward the bathroom, flicking on the light. The bulb hummed overhead, casting a cold, pale glow over the tiled walls. He twisted the shower knob all the way to cold. Water burst from the nozzle, icy and relentless.

Stepping in was like stepping into a wall of knives. The shock stole his breath, and made his muscles seize. He braced one arm against the tile, head bowed, water coursing over him, numbing him. It was the only thing that could strip his thoughts down to nothing, at least for a little while. He stayed there until his skin burned from the cold, until the ache dulled enough that he could think past it.

When he finally shut off the water, he wrapped a towel tight around his waist and padded down the hallway to his bedroom.

The bed was waiting; the quilt rumpled from earlier. He collapsed onto it, the mattress sagging under him, and let his head sink into the pillow. Sleep pulled at him almost instantly, but just before it claimed him, his mind wandered back, not to Danielle, but to Nicole, the girl with the heart charm.

The one who had shown him what he was capable of. And Nick smiled in the dark. Because it was only a matter of time before he felt that way again.

Chapter 22 Nick

Nick stood in the kitchen, staring out the window mindlessly as the coffee percolated. When he heard the whistle he grabbed his mug and poured, his mind doing it all without him even thinking about it. He was exhausted and had not slept well.

It had started with the dream of his first kill but it wasn't her. Danielle sat on his lap. Danielle was the one getting excited, feeling her wetness soaking into his pants. It was Danielle's neck his lips grazed as he grabbed her hips. It had been such an amazing dream, feeling himself getting close in his dream. Then, a loud boom came as his door was kicked in, Chuck standing in the threshold, handcuffs hanging from his hands, "Let's go, Nick. We've got the evidence we need. Grab the evidence, boys!" He woke up suddenly, his sheets soaked in sweat, his heart thumping in his chest so hard he felt it would leap right out of his chest.

Then came a crack and a loud boom. He heard the loud boom of the tree hitting the forest floor. He quickly pulled his jeans on and ran outside. The wind was whipping hard, his face getting pelted with rain as lightning and thunder rolled through making it impossible to see. He knew he needed to go check on the campers and make sure everyone was safe.

Nick's truck skidded to a stop at the entrance of the campground, windshield wipers fighting a losing battle against the wind and rain. Headlights cut through the storm just enough for him to see the pure chaos.

Families ran in every direction, shapes blurring in the downpour. A tent tore loose from the ground and slammed into a nearby tree, its fabric snapping violently in the wind like a wounded animal.

Larry sprinted through the campsite, flashlight swinging wildly as he shouted into the storm, "You guys, okay?" The words were ripped apart by the wind, meant for no one and everyone all at once.

Nick yanked the hood of his rain jacket over his head and jumped out of the truck. The wind hit him full force, nearly knocking him sideways. Rain lashed his face, stinging like needles, and he had to fight just to stay upright. He heard the snap of branches breaking off trees in the distance.

He spotted the first family huddled together and barreled toward them, flashlight bouncing.

"HEY… COME WITH ME!" He yelled, his voice raw as he waved them forward.

They stumbled after him toward the empty camping cabin. Nick fumbled with the key, hands slick, rain pouring so hard he could barely see the lock. One of the kids started crying, sobs sharp and terrified, while the mother pulled him close, whispering reassurances that sounded more desperate than comforting.

The door finally swung open. They rushed inside. Nick slammed it shut behind them.

Instant silence. The wind vanished, replaced by an eerie, unnatural quiet that rang in his ears.

"You guys okay?" He asked, breathless.

They nodded, shaken. The father straightened his shoulders, forcing calm. "Yeah. We're good. Thank you, Ranger Chambers. We didn't know if it was safe to drive… we didn't know what to do."

"You did the right thing," Nick said. "Stay here tonight. We'll clean everything up in the morning. I've got to get the rest of the families inside."

The man dipped his head in gratitude as Nick turned and went back into the storm.

Rain hammered his face again, relentless. He shielded his eyes with one hand and scanned the campsite, searching for movement, but all he could see was dark shapes against darker shadows.

One by one, he rounded them up. Shouting. Pointing. Herding soaked, frightened families into empty cabins. Thank God it was late in the season, every cabin stood vacant and ready.

At the final cabin, he ushered Larry's family inside and slammed the door. Water pooled at Nick's boots, his pants plastered to his legs.

"Alright," Nick said, chest heaving. "I've got to check the rest of the park. Make sure no one's out there stuck in this."

"Thank you, Nick," Larry said, shaking the rain from his jacket.

"No problem. Stay here. No matter what you hear… do not go back out. I need you all safe."

"Will do," Larry said, giving him a shaky salute before turning to his family. His daughter whimpered on the couch, soaked and shivering, while her mother disappeared into the bathroom for towels.

Nick didn't wait. He stepped back into the storm. The wind slammed into him again, rain coming down in sheets. Empty beer boxes tumbled across the ground like debris, tent hooks clawing at the earth, barely holding on before being ripped free.

He ran for his truck and slammed the door shut, hands numb, body frozen to the bone. The engine roared to life. Headlights flared—

A bear stood in the campsite, massive and unmoving, staring straight at him.

Nick revved the engine once. Twice. The bear growled loudly and then vanished into the trees.

"Jesus," Nick muttered.

He prayed and hoped with everything in him that the families listened and that no one stepped outside tonight. Not for anything.

He pulled out of the campground and patrolled the trails, headlights sweeping empty paths, rain-slicked dirt, nothing but wind and darkness.

After half an hour, exhaustion won. He headed home.

Back at his cabin, he sprinted for the door, barely keeping his footing in the mud. Inside, he kicked off his boots, peeled off his soaked shirt and jeans, dropped them in a sopping heap by the door. The socks followed.

Nick grabbed a Samuel Adams from the fridge and cracked it open. The first swallow tasted like bitter heaven. His body shuddered as it went down.

He turned the shower on full heat and stepped in, taking another swig. The water burned at first, fire against frozen skin, then slowly sank deeper into muscle, into bone.

He braced his arms against the tile wall and let the heat thaw him as images replayed in his mind, terrified faces, crying kids, tents flying like ghosts. He was grateful he had gotten them inside. Grateful he had woken up from that awful dream before it became something worse.

Steam rolled off him as his body finally loosened.

He finished the last of the beer, shut off the water, dried off, and stumbled to bed. He collapsed onto the mattress, naked and uncaring, sleep taking him instantly.

He shook off the memory and took another sip of coffee, the bitterness snapping him awake just enough to keep him from stumbling around the cabin. Mug in hand, he stepped out onto the porch.

Pine needles and twigs covered the floorboards. His rocking chair lay on its side, knocked over by the storm. Nick set it upright and sank into it, surveying the damage.

It wasn't terrible, mostly small branches and debris scattered across the porch. He knew better, though. The trails would tell a different story.

He took another sip and rocked slowly, his head still fuzzy, his brain begging him to crawl back into bed. For a moment, he considered calling out sick. The thought almost made him laugh. There was no one to call. He was the only ranger here.

The campers needed to be checked on. The park needed to be cleaned up.

When the mug was empty, he went back inside and got dressed. He paused in the bedroom, staring at the bed, soft, warm, and tempting. A nap sounded perfect. He knew better. It would never be just a nap.

He pulled on his uniform, brushed his teeth, fixed his hair, and headed out.

At the campground, branches littered the ground, but most of the tents were still standing, miraculously intact. He had helped the campers load their chairs and loose gear into their vehicles the night before, and he was grateful for the small mercy.

He walked toward the cabins as families stepped outside, gathering together and quietly taking in the destruction. One massive tree had come down, blocking a trail that led to another trail, something to deal with later.

Nick climbed out of his truck and approached the group.

"Hey… everyone alright?"

"Hey, Nick," someone said. "Yeah. We're all accounted for and unharmed. Thanks to you."

"Just glad we had empty cabins," Nick replied.

"Yeah, so are we," Larry said with a chuckle.

Nick spent the next two hours helping clean up, righting camping chairs, re-securing tents, and collecting litter. He and Larry wrestled the runaway tent out of the nearby tree. Nick noticed Larry was actually helpful when he wasn't drinking, clear-eyed, steady, able to hold a conversation without slurring his words.

Eventually, the campsite began to look normal again.

Nick tapped Larry on the shoulder. "Alright. Have a good morning. I'm going to go clear the trails."

"Thanks again, Nick," Larry said. "If you need any help, just holler."

"Will do."

Nick waved to the rest of the campers and climbed back into his truck.

As he drove the trails, he stopped to move fallen branches that could trip someone up, mentally noting spots he had to come back to later with the leaf blower. Farther in, the real damage revealed itself.

Two massive red oak trees lay across the trail, completely blocking it.

Nick sighed. That was going to take some work.

He turned the truck around and headed back to the cabin to grab his chainsaw and gear, then backed the truck up to the woodchipper, already planning out the long day ahead.

He made his way back to the site. He grabbed the yellow tape and taped up the area making sure to go down far enough so no one would bother him. Then he started working on getting everything cleared up. He knew Danielle walked this path, and he wanted to make sure she had her trails. He hoped he would still see her today at some point. He loved her cute walking outfits that showed her body off perfectly. She had a perfect butt, and in certain shorts showed it off perfectly. Her adorable tits that she would push up to give him a show.

Her assets were perfect for her tiny figure and stature. And then there was that face, those dimples, and those amazing green eyes. He was entranced by her. She was perfect, in more ways than one. He loved the shy little way about her, and her adorable personality; she was never fake. He was sure she didn't even know how to be anything but the sweet girl she was.

He cut off his chain saw and grabbed his water. As he drank, he thought about her hips swaying as she would walk away, his eyes glued to her. His head snapped up as he heard a rock being kicked up. He turned towards the sound and saw a blonde girl walking towards him. She had quite a figure. Huge chest, tiny waist, in this sports bra and shorts so short he wasn't quite sure they were shorts. She bounced towards him as if her tits bouncing would make him forget she was trespassing at the moment.

"Can I help you?" Nick said in an authoritative voice.

"Oh my gosh, so sorry. I'm not from around here. I came for a hike. Heard this was the most gorgeous park to hike. I was told to take this trail and that there's an amazing waterfall up here. Figured it was just taped off from a fallen tree. Took my chance."

"Yeah, well it's not open and you're trespassing."

The lady looked pissed off by that comment, her hands going to her hips, one foot in front of the other. "You can't just let me through? This isn't a crime scene, is it?"

Nick was annoyed. He just wanted to clean this up so Danielle could get through. The lady came closer, as she tugged her sports bra down, making the girls pop out even more.

"I clearly didn't make a good impression. My name is Kylie. I'm from Michigan. I came to New Hampshire on a self-help road trip. I really want to see this gorgeous view everyone posts about."

"So, is this how people from Michigan act? Yellow tape means nothing?"

She offered a tight, practiced smile and took another step toward him. A calculated movement meant to be alluring. She pushed her chest up, the silicone-filled mounds straining against the thin fabric of her shirt.

"I can make it worth your while," she purred, her voice a husky, seductive whisper. Her hand, which had been rubbing her neck, slid down slowly, tracing the exaggerated curve of her very fake tits until it reached the waistband of her shorts. Her fingers lingered there, hooking under the fabric and pushing it down just enough to be an invitation.

It hit him then, a crystal-clear realization. She wasn't from here. The confidence, the entitlement, the way she moved through the world as if it were a buffet laid out just for her. She was a tourist, and a ghost passing through. No one would immediately look for her here. She was an opportunity.

"Well, you are gorgeous, darlin'," he drawled, his voice a smooth, predatory hum. "If you want, I can show you where the waterfall is. But I'd like my payment before we make our way."

"Oooh," she said, her cheeks blushing.

Nick felt an annoyance bubbling up. The only person he wanted to see blushing was Danielle. "For you… anything," she breathed, her eyes gleaming.

He stalked towards her, his movements no longer those of a man, but of a predator closing in on its prey.

"Sit on the bed of the truck and don't move," he commanded, his tone leaving no room for negotiation. She scrambled to obey, her movements clumsy with sudden nerves. She jumped as the deafening roar of the woodchipper suddenly came to life; its mechanical shriek tearing through the quiet night.

"Why… why is that on?" She stammered, the seductive mask slipping to reveal the frightened girl beneath.

"I tend to make girls get very loud," he said, his voice casual, almost conversational. "Wouldn't want anyone to hear you." He closed the distance between them, grabbing her hand and sliding her over the hard, thick ridge straining against his jeans. Her eyes flew open, the realization of his size registering on her face in a wave of shock and a flicker of something that looked like fear, but also a dark, twisted curiosity. "Turn around. Hands on the truck bed."

She did as she was told; her movements swift and obedient. He moved behind her, looking down at the perfect, heart-shaped ass. Men must fawn over this, he thought. She had an amazing figure, and in another life, one where Danielle didn't exist, she might have been fun to break slowly. But this wasn't that life. The only one who got to play with him like that was Danielle.

He slowly slid his hand up the back of her thigh. She pushed back into his touch, a soft moan escaping her lips. She thought this was part of the game, an innocent, thrilling detour on her little journey of self-discovery. He knelt, and as his hand continued its path up her thigh, his other hand closed around the grip of the chainsaw resting on the truck bed. He slid his hand up over the swell of her ass to her waist, his touch possessive.

"You want me, sexy?" He asked, his voice a low, dangerous statement rather than a question.

"Yes," she moaned, her voice thick with desire.

He wanted to see her face as he killed her, to truly see that moment of dawning terror, but he knew it wouldn't be possible. He needed this to be fast. He pushed his hips forward, grinding the hard bulge of his erection against her, letting her feel exactly what she had provoked. She moaned louder, pushing back against him, and for a moment, he felt himself almost give in, the pleasure so intense he was on the very edge. He pushed against her again, his hand fisting in her ponytail, yanking her head back. Her moan was a sharp cry of pleasure-pain. He stepped back, the sudden loss of contact making her whimper. He undid his belt, the metallic click loud in the air, and slowly unzipped his pants. He pushed his body close to hers once again so she could feel him. His hardness rubbing between her thighs. Hearing her moan in pleasure made his heart race knowing the next moan that came from her would be from pain. He wanted to feel her body stiffen and tremble at the same time. The smell of fear that would permeate the air. He could feel his pre-cum beading onto the tip of his cock as he thought about it.

"You want this?" He asked, his voice thick with lust. "Tell me how bad you want this."

"I want…"

Before she could finish the pathetic, breathless sentence, he yanked the cord on the chainsaw. The engine roared to life, a monstrous, mechanical scream that devoured the night. As she turned, her face was a mask of confusion; he saw it. The exact moment the fear hit her, the instant she understood she had made a fatal mistake in crossing the yellow tape. The sight of her terror, pure and undiluted, sent him over the edge. He was right there.

As her mouth opened to emit a scream that would never be heard, he swung the chainsaw. The blade didn't just cut; it obliterated. Her head flew from her shoulders in a spray of blood and bone, landing with a wet thump near his feet. Her body, for a horrifying, surreal second, remained standing. A headless monument to her own folly, before it flopped over onto the truck's bed, a lifeless, broken doll.

He dropped the chainsaw, his finger releasing from the trigger. He let the heavy tool drop to the forest floor with a dull thud, his hand flying out to brace against the cold metal of the truck bed as a profound tremor wracked his body. She looked perfect laying there, a canvas of destruction. Her neck was a grotesque masterpiece; the ragged wound oozing a thick, dark river of blood that stained her skin and the metal beneath her in a growing, obscene pool. The sight was an aphrodisiac; a primal command his body was helpless to ignore. He needed to cum. It wasn't a want; it was a need as sharp and desperate as a hunger.

His cock was painfully hard, a rigid, throbbing testament to the horror that lay before him. He wrapped his hand around the shaft, his grip almost punishing, and began to stroke, his eyes fixed on her body. Every now and then, a nerve would fire, a muscle would spasm, and her leg would jerk, or a finger would curl. These were the final, useless echoes of a life he had extinguished, and each one sent a jolt of pure, unadulterated ecstasy straight through him. Every fresh ooze of blood from her neck made his mind fracture, his thoughts dissolving into a haze of pure, depraved lust.

He could feel the pressure building at the base of his spine, a tightening knot of pleasure that promised a devastating release. He rubbed the sensitive underside of the tip with his thumb, his gaze drifting from the twitching corpse to the absurd perfection of her fake tits, still defying gravity even in death. Then his eyes dropped to his own hand, to the blood. Her blood. It coated his fingers. That was the final, exquisite detail that sent him hurtling over the edge. He came with a strangled cry, his body arching as he spilled himself onto her, his hot, white release pulsing out in thick ropes. It landed on her stomach, her chest, swirling into the cooling blood in a grotesque, intimate masterpiece. His entire body shuddered, not just in pleasure, but in a profound, soul-deep relief as the last wave of his climax washed over him, leaving him breathless and trembling in the aftermath of his perfect art.

He forced his breathing to steady and adjusted his jeans with mechanical precision, as if correcting a uniform out of place. The moment had passed. Whatever his body had done was irrelevant now. What mattered was cleanup.

He turned the chainsaw back on and started slicing her body into pieces. He knew it would be a lot easier to chip her up after. He loved how easily the saw went through her body, the teeth so sharp they slid through her bone like butter. It slid through so easily that the blood didn't splatter. After she was chopped, he dragged the pieces closer to the mouth of the woodchipper. The machine waited where he had left it, the engine still running. He fed the machine piece by piece, methodically, and efficiently. The sound was harsh and industrial, metal and power doing exactly what it was designed to do. Nick kept his eyes forward. He didn't rush, didn't pause. When the machine finished its work, there was nothing left to identify, only matter reduced to waste, indistinguishable from the surrounding debris.

He shut the machine down, climbed into his truck, and drove back to the cabin without checking the mirrors. There was no need.

Inside, he moved quickly but calmly, taking his clothes off. He scrubbed his skin clean and put new clothes on. The stained ones went straight into the washer, detergent measured carefully, cycle set to soak. Routine. Familiar. He wiped down the sink, the counter, the doorknob, small details most people overlooked. Nick did not.

The leaf blower went into the truck bed. He locked the door behind him and returned to the site.

The taped-off area looked wrong at first, disturbed earth, and flattened leaves, but that was easily corrected. He worked the blower until everything blended back together, funneling it into a manageable pile. He shoveled it into the bin with the rest, careful not to scatter anything. When he finished, the ground looked ordinary again. Empty, and unremarkable. The kind of place no one remembered.

The last two fallen trees still blocked the trail. He approached them without irritation. Work was work. The chainsaw roared to life, chewing through wood as chips sprayed outward. His arms ached, his hands buzzed with vibration, but he didn't stop until the path was clear enough to walk through without obstruction.

That was all anyone would care about.

The chipper was reattached. The tools were loaded. He drove back to the cabin as the sky began to darken, the world pretending it was a normal night.

Behind the cabin, he shoveled the contents of the truck's bed onto a tarp and dragged it through the bulkhead doors into the basement. One load at a time, he fed the stove, the heat building. Flames swallowed everything without question. Evidence. DNA. All reduced to ash and smoke.

He worked steadily, relentlessly. No breaks. No sitting down. He hadn't slept during the storm, and he wasn't going to sleep now. Sleep came after the work was finished.

By the time the sun had fully hid behind the mountains, the truck bed was empty. He rinsed it out thoroughly. Bleach stung his nose as he wiped down the chainsaw, the handles, and the metal teeth. He checked the truck, the cab, and the floor mats. Then he checked everything again. Only when he was satisfied did he put the tools away.

Then he went inside and turned on the shower.

Hot water poured over him as he stood still; one arm braced against the wall. His head bowed, his eyes closed. Not relief. Not regret. Just fatigue. Heavy and absolute.

He needed to sleep. That was all.

Wrapped in a towel, he walked to the bedroom and lay down. The bed accepted his weight, and the moment his head touched the pillow, he was gone.

Chapter 23 Danielle

Danielle glanced out the window just as his truck pulled up to the curb… right on time. A flutter of nerves twisted in her stomach, excitement and disbelief tangling together. This wasn't just hanging out. This was a date.

Emily appeared from the kitchen. "Is he here yet?" She asked with a mouthful of food.

"What do you mean yet? It just hit four," Danielle said.

Emily rolled her eyes. "And? First dates mean early."

"Jeez, Em. Give the poor guy a break. He works a real job, one where you can't just leave whenever he wants."

Emily shrugged and swallowed whatever she had been chewing. A knock sounded at the door, sharp and sudden, and Danielle shot to her feet, heart pounding. She still couldn't quite believe this was happening.

She smoothed her hands down her skirt, brushing away imaginary wrinkles. She took a deep breath and opened the door, and then her mouth went dry.

Nick stood there looking unfairly good, somehow even more muscular out of uniform. He wore a dark gray T-shirt that hugged his chest and arms, faded blue jeans, and brown leather work boots. A dark gray ballcap sat low on his head, making his eyes stand out even more. For a moment, Danielle was convinced her legs had forgotten how to function.

"Hey, darlin'," he said, tipping his hat.

"Hey… Nick," she managed, her voice coming out embarrassingly small.

Emily appeared behind her, clearly immune to sudden muteness. "Hey Nick! How's it going?"

"Hey, Emily. Not too bad. You?"

"I'll be better once I'm shoving fair food into my face."

Nick chuckled, but his eyes never left Danielle. "You ready to go?"

Danielle nodded quickly, not trusting herself to speak.

"We'll be right back," Emily said, already rolling her eyes. "Bags and sweatshirts."

Nick smiled and headed back to his truck.

The second the door closed, Emily snapped her fingers in front of Danielle's face. "Hello? Earth to Dani. What happened to you?"

"I don't know," Danielle groaned. "He just looks so good and I panicked."

"Get it together. If you like him this much, acting like a malfunctioning robot is not the move."

"You're right," Danielle said, shaking her hands out. Get it together.

When they stepped back outside, Nick was leaning against the passenger door of his truck, looking effortlessly good doing absolutely nothing. Emily nudged Danielle forward. "Act normal," she whispered.

Nick opened Danielle's door for her. "Thank you," she said softly, instantly annoyed at herself for sounding shy.

He nodded and opened the back door for Emily. "Why thank you, sir," Emily said with a dramatic curtsy.

Nick laughed as he slid into the driver's seat. He glanced at Danielle and winked. Heat rushed to her cheeks, giving her away immediately. She was grateful when Emily started talking since Danielle had temporarily forgotten how conversations worked.

"So, Nick, how was work?" Emily asked.

"Good. Nice day. Quiet at the park."

"That's probably a good thing," Emily said. "Means no one's getting into trouble."

"I'll take those days anytime," Nick said.

Danielle saw him look over at her, and concern seemed to fill his face.

"You okay, Dani?" Nick asked.

She blinked and pulled out of her daze. "Yeah… just hungry, I think. Sometimes my blood sugar drops and I kinda… zone out."

"Well, we're almost there," he said easily. "I'll make sure you get fed."

She smiled at him, relieved by the excuse. The Ferris wheel came into view, lights blinking against the evening sky, kids screaming happily in the distance.

"Oh my god, I'm going to eat everything," Emily announced.

"Relax," Danielle laughed. "The food's not going anywhere."

"Shut up," Emily shot back. "Fair food is elite."

The smell of fried dough and grease drifted into the truck, making Danielle's stomach growl. "They better have good fried dough this year," she said. "Not those burnt little ones from last time."

Emily groaned. "Don't remind me. I complained to everyone."

Danielle laughed, remembering Emily's crusade over fried dough until a fried Oreo finally saved the night.

"Remember the year we ate like maniacs and then went on the Tilt-A-Whirl?" Danielle asked.

Emily burst out laughing. "You were screaming you were going to puke, and that kid next to you started crying because he thought you'd throw up on him. You scarred him for life."

"I did not scar him for life."

"Oh, you absolutely did."

Nick smirked from the driver's seat. "I'm with Emily. That kid's still haunted."

Danielle swatted his arm playfully. "Not you, too."

They parked, and Danielle waited as they circled the truck. Nick placed a hand on her back as they walked toward the entrance, sending another wave of nerves through her. After he paid, they stepped into the fair. Kids running with plastic swords, and stuffed animals bigger than their owners, while parents watching closely.

Danielle smiled. She had been coming to the Ravensburg Fair her whole life and always with Emily.

"I want everything," Emily declared. "What first?"

Danielle chuckled, ever since she had known Emily, that girl could eat all night here and never get full. Yet she was a stick figure, where she put it, Danielle would never know.

"Ooh, steak grinders are good here," Danielle said.

Nick lifted his hands. "I'm just here for the company. You decide."

Emily zeroed in on a food truck labeled Mac and Cheese and All the Things. "This is it. First stop of many."

She sprinted ahead. Nick reached for Danielle's hand, and her stomach flipped. She squeezed his fingers, heart racing.

The first tent they passed was a balloon dart game, the guy running it shouting at anyone who wandered by.

"No one leaves a loser! Everybody wins a prize! The more you pop, the bigger the prize!"

Emily didn't even slow down. They passed duck ponds, milk bottle tosses, basketball hoops, until she stopped short at the shooting gallery.

"Let's do this one, Danielle."

Danielle already knew how this would go. Her aim was terrible and always had been, but Emily looked way too excited to say no. Nick paid for all three of them, and as Danielle lifted the gun, she accepted her fate.

"You ready to be pulverized?" Emily asked, grinning.

Nick raised an eyebrow. "Bring it on, Emily."

Danielle chuckled at them, and then she watched as they lined up, guns propped, both of them staring straight ahead like this was life or death. Nick had turned his ballcap around, and her stomach flipped with how good he looked. Then she turned to her own lane and saw rows of little bunny targets waiting to be knocked down.

She missed. Every single one.

Halfway through, she glanced over. Nick hadn't missed once. Every bunny dropped cleanly. Emily missed a few but was still holding her own.

Danielle tried again. Focused harder. Missed again.

When the bell rang, Nick whooped. "So close!"

"Yeah, yeah," Emily laughed. "I almost had you."

"Not even close," Nick said, smirking. "I smoked you."

Then they looked at Danielle's score.

Emily squinted. "Did you even shoot?"

Danielle shot her a glare. "Yes, Emily. Unlike you two, I care about the bunnies."

Emily burst out laughing. "Okay, loser."

"Here," Nick said, already pulling out more money. "Let me help you this time."

"Oh please," Emily said. "Even with help, I'll still win."

Danielle lifted an eyebrow. "I bet you your stuffed animal I beat you this round."

Emily blinked. "You're on."

The bell rang again. Nick stepped in close, setting the gun against Danielle's shoulder. "Look straight down the sight," he murmured. "Picture the center of the bunny. Don't pull the trigger until you're sure."

He stood right behind her now, hands settling on her hips to guide her stance. "Tiny bit to the left, darlin'. Right there."

Danielle adjusted and squeezed the trigger, and the bunny dropped.

She squealed. "Did you see that, Emily?"

"One lucky shot," Emily scoffed. "Relax."

"Again," Nick said calmly. "Same way."

Danielle focused, fired, and the next bunny fell. Then another. And another.

By the time the bell rang, she stared at the scoreboard in disbelief. She had beaten Emily by five points.

"Well?" Danielle said, laughing. "What now, Emily?"

Emily shook her head, grinning. "I can't believe it. In all the years we've played these games, you've never even come close."

She handed over a pink stuffed bear. "For the champion."

Danielle hugged it in triumph and then realized Nick's hands were still on her hips.

Her legs instantly turned to jelly, her stomach flipping hard enough to make her worry she might lose everything she'd just eaten.

She took a steady breath and turned to face him. "Thank you. For the help."

"Anytime, darlin'," Nick said, smiling. That smile, the kind that made her look away before she did something embarrassing.

Emily was already scanning the booths for their next victim. After a few more games, she declared it time for another round of food.

Danielle was already painfully full. French fries, corn dogs, ice cream, and cotton candy, but Emily insisted they share a blooming onion anyway.

By the time the sun began to dip low in the sky, the concert area buzzed with anticipation. Danielle's excitement built with every passing minute. Lawrence Gardner, the newest country star, was about to take the stage. She had followed his music from the very beginning, back when he first started posting songs online. Seeing him live felt unreal.

Emily chattered nonstop beside her, barely containing her excitement. They had worn his songs out in the car, in their rooms, everywhere. They were obsessed.

Nick stepped up behind Danielle and wrapped his arms around her waist.

Emily caught it immediately and wiggled her eyebrows, making Danielle laugh nervously. Nick's arms were strong and warm, solid around her, and the way he held her made her feel protected and wanted. His breath brushed against her neck, sending a shiver down her spine.

She couldn't stop replaying the night in her head, the way he kept looking at her, the quiet smiles, the way his eyes always found hers. How he held her hand, made sure she ate, checked in to see if she was having fun. He was sweet and so much more than she had expected. She knew she was already falling for him.

Standing there with his arms around her, safe and wrapped in him. She no longer had that tinge of worry about him. Whatever gut feeling had made her feel that he was dangerous was gone.

The announcer took the stage, hyping the crowd, and asking if Ravensburg was ready. Cheers erupted, the energy electric. When his name was finally announced, the music blasted through the speakers and the curtain pulled back to reveal the band.

The crowd screamed.

Lawrence jogged onto the stage, waving. "How's everyone doing tonight in Ravensburg, New Hampshire? You ready for a show?"

The response was deafening. People whistled and screamed all around her.

The first song kicked off, and Danielle and Emily screamed the lyrics at the top of their lungs, laughing and dancing, bumping into each other as they sang. Danielle was so caught up in the moment, with the music, and with her best friend, that she almost forgot Nick was behind her.

That is, until Lawrence started playing a slower song, a song he had written for his girlfriend, and she felt Nick once again behind her. His arms enveloping her, her body tight against his. She could feel his body heat radiating onto her. Then she felt his lips caressing her neck. She froze, excited for this to be happening but so nervous, not knowing how to respond. He slowly kissed Danielle's neck, his arms tightening slightly around her. She could feel the palm of his hand on her stomach, and then felt his grip tighten. She pushed into him lightly, not wanting him to stop. He pushed right back, and then she felt him harden slightly, the bulge pushing on her lower back and her breath caught. The song came to an end, and everyone clapped. Except for her; she was so lost in this moment. Of him touching her, his lips on her, feeling how much he wanted her.

The next song started, and Danielle felt him retreat. Her heat sank as she felt a chill breeze between their bodies. Then Nick took her hand and spun her toward him, one arm sliding around her waist as he pulled her close again. The song was slow and romantic. A song Danielle loved, one she had played repeatedly in her room. Nick swayed with her gently, holding her like it was the most natural thing in the world.

"I'm really enjoying being here with you, Dani," he murmured, kissing her neck softly.

"Right back at ya," she replied, immediately cringing inwardly. *That's what you went with*? She scolded herself. She knew that she sounded naive and could not figure out how Nick could be interested in her.

Nick only smiled and tightened his hold. Danielle rested her head against his chest, his height enveloping her completely. She glanced up and noticed a few women nearby watching them, arms crossed, expressions tight. She had heard the rumors about how Nick turned women down, how no one ever saw him with anyone.

Well, Danielle thought, guess those rumors are officially dead.

When the song faded and the crowd erupted around them, Nick didn't pull away.

Danielle felt it immediately, the way he stayed close, his forehead resting against hers, his body angled just enough to shield her from the press of people around them. It wasn't accidental. It felt deliberate, like he was keeping her exactly where he wanted her.

The noise of the fair dulled, the world shrinking down to the warmth of his body and the steady way he held her.

His hand slid into her hair, fingers threading through it with quiet ownership, anchoring her there. There was nothing tentative about it now. When he kissed her, it was slow, his lips lingering like he already knew she wasn't going anywhere. Danielle's breath caught hard in her chest.

Then she kissed him back. His mouth moved against hers with purpose, deep and unhurried. One arm wrapped firmly around her waist, pulling her closer until there was no space left between them, until the world had narrowed down to just the two of them. Danielle's hands clutched the front of his shirt, grounding herself as her knees went weak.

Her heart wasn't racing from nerves. It was racing because of the way he held her, like he meant it. Like he wasn't sharing this moment with anyone else in the crowd.

Nick tilted his head, deepening the kiss just enough to leave her dizzy. It wasn't frantic or rushed. It was controlled. Claiming. When he finally pulled back, it was barely an inch. His thumb brushed her cheek, slow and deliberate, as if reminding her he was still there. Danielle opened her eyes and met his gaze, her chest rising and falling.

For a moment, neither of them spoke.

The fair surged back into existence. music, laughter, and shouting, but Danielle felt suspended in the circle of his arms, protected by the way he stood so close, so solid.

Nick leaned in again, brushing a softer kiss over her lips, then her cheek, then just beneath her ear. His voice was low, unmistakably possessive.

"I've wanted to do that all night," he murmured.

The words sent a shiver through her.

And then a scream tore through the air. Danielle turned just as a middle-aged woman stormed toward them, her face twisted with rage and grief, her finger pointing straight at Nick.

"How dare you!" the woman screamed. "I know what you did! She was my baby girl!"

Nick reacted instantly. He stepped in front of Danielle, completely blocking her from view, his body turning slightly so she was pressed behind him. One arm reached back without looking, settling firmly at her hip—an unmistakable signal to stay put. To stay with him.

"Ma'am," Nick said calmly, though his voice carried authority, "you need to stop."

"Oh, don't you play innocent with me!" the woman shrieked, jabbing her finger into his chest. "Nicole was my baby girl! She's gone because of you! You killed her!"

She shoved him again, sobbing now, screaming accusations through tears. Danielle watched Nick's shoulders tighten, his stance widening just slightly, and when the woman screamed the name Nicole, Danielle saw it.

Fear.

It flashed across his eyes for a fraction of a second before vanishing behind control.

The woman turned suddenly, trying to look past him.

"You," she snarled, pointing toward Danielle. "You had better stay away from him. Or you'll be next."

Nick didn't let her get another word out. "That's enough," he said sharply, shifting so Danielle was fully hidden behind him now. "You will not talk to her."

Before Danielle could react, Chuck stepped in.

"Ma'am, you need to leave."

"I shouldn't have to leave!" The woman fought, struggling as more officers arrived. "He did this!"

They escorted her away, her screams echoing until they disappeared into the noise of the fair.

When it was over, Danielle stood shaking slightly, adrenaline buzzing through her veins. Nick turned back to her immediately.

For just a heartbeat, she saw it again, that flash of fear, before it disappeared. His hand remained firm at her waist, grounding her.

"I'm sorry you had to see that," he said quietly. "She shouldn't have come near you."

"Nick… who was that?" Danielle asked. "And who's Nicole?"

He hesitated, then lowered his head slightly, but he didn't step away from her.

"When I first moved here, I started seeing someone. Her name was Nicole. I loved her, and we got serious fast."

Danielle's chest tightened.

"One night she was supposed to come over," he continued. "She never made it. I called her mom, and she thought Nicole was with me. Two days later, Chuck told me they'd found her body in the woods."

Danielle felt sick.

"They said she wasn't killed there," Nick said. "She was placed there."

"Oh my god," Danielle whispered. "Nick… I'm so sorry."

"The cops ruled me out," he said. "But her mother never did."

"That's horrible," Danielle said softly. "I understand grief, but she shouldn't keep doing this to you or threatening me."

His jaw tightened. "She doesn't know how to handle the grief."

Something heavy settled in Danielle's chest. She understood now why no one ever saw him on dates or being around girls. Yet it made her wonder why he had finally decided to try again and with her.

Nick lifted her chin, forcing her to meet his eyes. His grip was gentle, but firm. "The moment I saw you, I couldn't get you out of my head. I fought it. I didn't want to want you."

Danielle's stomach fluttered. How did he know what she was thinking?

Her breath caught. "You're not afraid I'll hurt you?"

"I was," he admitted. "But I'm more afraid of losing you."

Danielle stepped into him, wrapping her arms around his waist. "I'm not going anywhere."

Nick's arms closed around her immediately. Holding her tight, making her feel protected.

"Good," he murmured. "Because I won't let anything happen to you."

A throat cleared and brought Danielle out of her moment with Nick.

"Sorry to interrupt, guys." Chuck said. "Just wanted to apologize for Nicole's mom, she still has a hard time with Nicole's passing. She was told if she pulls a stunt like this we would have to get a restraining order on her and she will spend some time in jail."

"Thank you, Chuck, for helping out. I know this is hard on her, but she's not the only one who still grieves every day."

"I know, Nick. I know." Chuck lowered his head, he clearly was grieving the loss as well. "I'll let you guys get back to your night."

As Chuck walked away, Emily stood in his place.

Danielle watched as Emily came to her side, "Hey, you ok?"

"Yeah, a little shaken up, Nicole's poor mom. I feel horrible for her."

Emily rubbed Danielle's back. "I know… but to accuse Nick? Everyone knows him and knows he would never do anything like that."

Danielle looked at Emily and smiled. "I know. That's what is so weird. Thank God for Chuck deescalating the situation."

"Alright," Emily said. "I have had enough fun for now. I saw my dad in the crowd, gonna ask him for a ride home. Do you want to go with me?"

"No, I'm good. I'm gonna get a ride home with Nick… and before you say anything, don't. I'm going to be fine."

"Alright. I love you. I'll see you tomorrow at the center?"

"I'll be there." Danielle hugged her friend tight, and then Emily walked off to find her mom.

Danielle turned around to see Nick talking to Larry and a couple of his friends. She walked over and grabbed Nick's hand. He looked over at her, and she could see the worry etched on his face. "You ok, darlin'?"

"I'm good. Emily is getting a ride home with her mom. She's tired and has had enough excitement. Pretty sure she may have eaten too much as well."

Nick chuckled, "Glad you're ok. Hey, you wanna get out of here?"

"Sure." Nick grabbed Danielle's hand and brought her back to the truck.

The ride was a quiet, comfortable silence that settled deep in her bones. Light country music drifted from the radio, a soft soundtrack to the night. Nick held her hand the entire time, his thumb tracing slow, hypnotic circles on the back of her hand, a possessive yet gentle rhythm that claimed her without a word. They pulled into a lookout on Broad Mountain, a place she knew as lovers' lane, where the town below glittered like a fallen constellation, and the mountains stood as silent, sleeping giants in the background.

He killed the engine and was out of the truck before she had even registered the silence. He opened her door, his touch a firm, guiding pressure as he took her hand and led her to the back. In one fluid motion, he picked her up, his strength effortless as he settled her into the truck's bed before jumping in after her. He sat where the bed met the cab, his back resting against the cool glass of the window and patted the space beside him.

"Oh, forgot something," he said, hopping out again. He returned with a fluffy black blanket. "In case you're cold," he murmured, draping it over them both, creating a small, private world under the vast, starry sky.

Danielle stared out at the town she had grown up in, a tapestry of lights she knew by heart. She could almost hear the distant music of the fair, the laughter, and the squeals of children hopped up on sugar. It was a world away, a different reality from the one she was in now. Nick's fingers tangling in her hair pulled her back. Her eyes rolled back in her head, a soft sigh escaping her lips. His other hand rested on her mid-thigh, a warm, heavy weight under the cover of the blanket. She looked into his dark eyes, getting lost in his touch, and then his hand stilled. She felt him brush her hair aside, his lips finding the sensitive skin of her neck. He placed slow kisses along her throat, each one a brand. His other hand tightened on her thigh, a possessive grip that sent a jolt straight through her. Her entire body began to tingle, a low hum of awareness building under her skin.

He kissed her cheek, then her lips. It was soft and tender at first, but it quickly deepened into something hungry, something demanding. She felt his tongue trace the seam of her lips, an eager, silent command. She parted them willingly, desperate to know how he tasted. She could taste the sweet ghost of the cotton candy they had shared as his tongue swirled against hers, exploring, claiming. She felt a deep, insistent throb between her legs, and the feeling of the slick heat pooling there. She grabbed his shirt, pulling him closer, needing more of him.

She felt his hand on her thigh slide higher, disappearing under the hem of her skirt. Their kiss grew more frantic, more intense. He gripped her hair tightly, fisting it, pulling her into him as his other hand slid closer to the edge of her underwear. He broke the kiss, trailing his lips back down her neck, to her collarbone, then hovering just above the low-cut neckline of her shirt. With his free hand, he slowly pulled the fabric down, exposing her breast. His lips encircled her nipple, his tongue swirling around the hardened peak. Danielle moaned, arching into him. Emboldened, her hand slid under the blanket, and though a tremor of fear shot through her, she moved it forward, brushing over the hard, thick ridge straining against his pants.

A deep, guttural moan vibrated in his chest, and he slowly laid her down against the blanket. He propped himself on his elbow, his mouth finding hers again, hungrier this time. He bit her lower lip, a sharp, possessive sting, before shoving his tongue back into her mouth. She loved tasting him, needed more of him. She felt his hand return to her thigh, resting for only a second before sliding up to tease the edge of her thong. He rubbed his fingers along the lace, then over it, feeling the dampness that had soaked through. Danielle moaned and pushed against his fingers, a silent, desperate plea. Then she felt him slide the fabric aside, and his fingertips brushed against her slick, bare skin. A loud moan was caught by his mouth still on hers. She felt his fingers glide through her wetness before landing on her clit, rubbing softly, slowly. Her body vibrated, a feeling she had never experienced before, a tightening low in her stomach. His fingers slid lower, teasing her entrance before returning to her now-swollen clit. He swirled his fingertip faster, rougher, and her whole body tightened; her head growing fuzzy and her breath caught in her throat. And then it was like lightning striking her mind. Little stars exploded behind her eyes as a rush of pure ecstasy washed over her entire body. She felt herself pulsing around his fingers, her body twitching as he made slow, gentle circles, drawing out the sensation.

His fingers left her, slowly making their way back to her breasts. He pulled her shirt down further, exposing them both, her nipples hard and begging for his attention. His mouth immediately latched onto one while his hand teased the other. Her body pushed into his, a mindless, desperate motion. She didn't know it was possible to come that hard and still want more, to need more of him.

Then he pulled away. The sudden loss of his touch was jarring. Her lips missed his, her exposed nipple pebbling in the cool night air. He unbuttoned his pants, and a wave of pure terror washed over her. She knew what was coming, and it scared her to her core. He unzipped his pants, but before his fingers left the zipper, he looked her in the eyes. Danielle knew he could see the fear, plain as day, on her face.

"We can stop if you want, Dani," he said, his voice surprisingly gentle.

As terrified as she was, she wanted him. A confusing, terrifying mix of desire and fear warred inside her. "No… I want this."

He smiled, a slow, knowing curve of his lips, and zipped his pants back up. "We can wait. I don't want to rush anything. I like you too much for that."

Disappointment and relief warred within her, leaving her breathless and confused.

"Let's go," Nick said, his tone decisive. "We're going to go get coffee at the diner, and then I'll take you home. We're going to go on real dates, just you and I. We can take it slow." He kissed her one last time, a soft, lingering promise, before jumping out of the truck and waiting for her at the end of the bed, a silent, patient guardian in the dark.

Chapter 24 Danielle

Danielle stepped into the church the next morning, her stomach flipping as memories of the night before rushed back, how close she had come to taking things too far with someone she barely knew. She was excited that Nick liked her enough to want more, to move things forward, but deep down she knew it was happening too fast. A voice in her gut whispered warnings, he was too much, she wasn't enough, something wasn't right. Still, she couldn't pull away. There was something about Nick, something magnetic that kept drawing her in no matter how loudly her instincts protested.

As she made her way toward her pew, she heard Mrs. Johnson's bright laughter carry across the room. The older woman leaned into George, the mayor, her hand resting lightly on his shoulder as she beamed up at him. Danielle had always thought Mrs. Johnson was a little too friendly, too welcoming, but she reminded herself not to judge. Some people just lived louder than others, and Mrs. Johnson was the kind who filled every space she entered. Danielle was nothing like that.

Sliding into her seat, Danielle glanced around. Emily had already texted to say she would be late, so Danielle placed her purse beside her to save the spot, ignoring the disapproving looks from a few older members. If that was the worst thing she did in church, she doubted it would land her on God's bad side.

The microphone crackled softly, drawing her attention to the front where Father Hale stood on the stage, his warm smile already in place.

"Good morning, everyone," he said, his voice echoing gently through the sanctuary. "If you could find your seats, we'll begin shortly. Let us take this time to quiet our hearts and open them to His word."

Danielle watched as people shuffled into place, some moving faster than others, and she let out a quiet chuckle. Every Sunday, without fail, people seemed surprised that the service started exactly when it always did.

"My dear congregation," Father Hale continued, folding his hands in front of him, "today we turn to Genesis, chapters eighteen and nineteen, a story of warning, of mercy, and of judgment."

Danielle listened as he spoke about Sodom and Gomorrah, about how God looked down and saw the corruption that had taken hold. Father Hale compared it to the modern world, places like Las Vegas, where temptation thrived, and spoke about the importance of living a life aligned with God's expectations.

"God saw what the people of Sodom and Gomorrah had become," he said solemnly. "Abraham pleaded for their lives, asking that the city be spared if even ten righteous people could be found. But there were none. Not ten. Not enough. And so the city fell. We must ask ourselves, are we living in a way that would spare us? Or are we walking a path that leads to ruin?"

Danielle sank slightly in her seat, guilt tightening in her chest. She had almost slept with someone she barely knew. The thought made her stomach twist. She didn't want to be that girl, the one whispered about, judged, and labeled.

A gentle hand slipped over hers, and she turned to see Emily beside her, offering a small, knowing smile. The simple touch steadied her, easing the knot in her stomach and helping her sit a little straighter.

"In closing," Father Hale said, his tone softening, "we are called to reflect, to examine our lives, and to strive each day to walk in His light. None of us are perfect, but we must try. We must choose better when we can."

The congregation murmured in agreement as soft organ music began to play, filling the space with a calm, reverent hum.

People bowed their heads as Father Hale led the final prayer, his voice steady and reassuring.

"Amen," echoed through the church as the prayer ended, followed by a gentle swell of music. People began to rise, greeting one another, giving way to soft conversation.

Danielle turned and wrapped Emily in a tight hug, smiling. "I'm glad you made it. That was an amazing sermon, right?"

Emily shrugged, a playful grin tugging at her lips. "I mostly come for you, girl. I sin every day." She laughed under her breath.

Danielle rolled her eyes, though she couldn't help the small smirk that followed. Emily didn't believe the way she did, not really. For Danielle, God was everything, a constant presence guiding her choices. She just hoped that if things moved forward with Nick, he might one day find that same faith.

She glanced toward the front and saw Father Hale making his way through the crowd. Politely excusing herself, Danielle stepped out of the pew and approached him.

"Excuse me, Father," she said. "That sermon was beautiful. Thank you for always giving us something to think about and keeping us grounded."

Father Hale smiled warmly. "Thank you, Danielle. That means a great deal. It's my duty to care for my flock." He gave her shoulder a gentle pat before moving on to greet others.

Stepping outside, Danielle was met with the warmth of the day wrapping around her. She closed her eyes for a moment, breathing it in, silently thanking God for the sunlight and the fresh start.

"Hey!" Emily called, jogging toward her. "You want to hang out at your place?"

"Absolutely," Danielle said, smiling. "I'll make lunch."

"Perfect. See you soon, love."

Danielle climbed into her car and headed home, her thoughts shifting lighter now, focusing on the good parts of Nick, not the ones that had unsettled her the night before.

Chapter 25 Nick

Nick sat slouched on his worn leather couch, the cabin dimly lit by the single lamp in the corner. A half-empty beer bottle rested in his right hand, beads of condensation running down its neck and pooling onto his fingers. He wasn't drinking it so much as holding it, its weight and chill grounding him while his mind wandered. Outside, the wind whispered through the pines, the distant creak of branches echoing through the dark. Somewhere out there, an owl called out into the night.

And all he could do was think of her.

She was naïve, sweet, and shy in a way that didn't feel manufactured. She had this way of looking at him, eyes soft and trusting, like she couldn't even fathom the thought of him hurting her. Nick thought about her nervousness and an excitement went through his body. The looks she would give him as he defiled her and ended her. Yet he was pissed. He hated that she would only go so far with him and then she would shy away. He knew she was a good Christian girl, he was going to have to work really hard to reach his end goal. He hated that he had to keep acting as if he cared that she was nervous to have sex with him. He could not wait to make that a reality. It was not a want but a need to feel her blood on his fingers, her pleading eyes on him as she clawed at his hand. The wait would be worth it.

A noise snapped him out of it.

Three sharp knocks on the cabin's front door. Nick's eyes flicked to the clock on the wall. Eleven o'clock. No one should be here at this time.

He set the beer on the coffee table with a quiet clink and reached for the side drawer of the end table. His fingers closed around the grip of his handgun. He didn't point it, just kept it ready in his hand as he moved toward the door. The sound of his own breathing seemed louder than usual in the quiet cabin.

At the door, he hooked a finger around the edge of the curtain and pulled it just far enough to see outside.

Chuck.

The man stood on the porch, shoulders squared, hands hooked casually into the belt loops of his jeans. His silhouette was solid against the wash of moonlight, his posture calm. No immediate danger.

Nick set the gun on the table by the door, then unlocked it and pulled it open.

"Hey," Chuck said, his voice low, almost sheepish. "Sorry to drop in this late. Mind if I come in for a minute?"

Nick stepped aside. "Sure."

Chuck walked in, pausing just inside the door. "I wanted to apologize again. About Nicole's mom. And… well, the whole mess earlier. I know that kind of thing can stir up a lot of… stuff." He glanced toward the couch, toward the half-finished beer. "Didn't mean to interrupt your night."

"It's fine," Nick said, his voice even. "You want a beer?"

"Yeah, sure. Thanks."

Nick grabbed another from the fridge, the hiss of the cap twisting off breaking the momentary silence. He handed it to

Chuck, then sat back down on the couch. Chuck lowered himself into the recliner.

For a while, they talked about Nicole and the night they had found her. The pale, lifeless body in the woods. The shock of it. The sickening stillness of her chest, and the bruise marks on her neck. It had been hard on everyone, Chuck said. Nick nodded, letting his voice soften as he spoke about how much it had hurt, how long it had taken before he could even think about being with someone else.

"Honestly," Nick said, leaning back, "I never thought I'd give my heart to anyone again. But… I'm falling in love."

Chuck's face lit up. "No kidding? That's great, man."

Nick smirked faintly, knowing the truth was a much darker shade than Chuck could ever guess. Still, some small, buried part of him meant it. Some part of him, tiny but persistent, really did have strong feelings for Danielle, maybe not love yet but somewhere in the back of his mind, he felt maybe one day he could, and that scared the hell out of him.

They moved on to talk about the recent murders in the area, the unease that had settled over the community like fog. "This shit's gotta end soon," Chuck said, his tone grim. "People are scared. We've got the holidays coming up, and I want kids to be able to go trick-or-treating without parents worrying."

Nick nodded, feigning concern. "Yeah. Hopefully it all dies down soon." Inwardly, he knew exactly what he had to do. For now, he would stick to out-of-towners. People who wouldn't be missed here. People whose disappearances wouldn't lead back to his park. If the locals felt safe again, the heat would be off him.

As Chuck spoke, Nick's thoughts began to drift to that night with Nicole. The heat of her skin, the sudden fight in her eyes when she realized she wasn't walking away. The way her breath had hitched and then stopped. The power of it. The godlike rush.

A voice broke the moment. "Nick?"

He blinked, refocusing. Chuck was leaning forward, elbows on his knees. "Sorry. I guess I'm keeping you up. Didn't mean to go on so long."

Nick shook his head. "It's fine. Really."

Chuck stood, finishing the last sip of his beer. "Thanks for the drink. And the talk. I'm glad to see you doing better, man."

Nick followed him to the door. "Yeah. Take care, Chuck."

He watched him walk down the porch steps, his boots crunching against the gravel drive until he disappeared into the dark.

Closing the door, Nick leaned back against it for a moment, and the cabin went silent again. Then he went back to the couch, sinking into the worn leather; the beer bottle cold in his hand once more.

His thoughts returned to Danielle. He imagined her in his kitchen, barefoot, her hair down, smiling up at him as if he were the safest place in the world. Could he be like some of those other men, serial killers who had wives, kids, and normal lives? Men who loved their partners deeply, kept them safe, even as they slaughtered others in secret.

Could he love her forever? Marry her? Keep her close and untouched by the darkness that lived in him, while still feeding the hunger on others?

Part of him wanted that desperately. He didn't know why. He always killed. Always. It was who he was. Yet something about her made him hesitate. Made him think twice.

But another part, just as loud, still wanted to feel her life drain beneath his hands. Still wanted the shudder of that final moment.

The two urges wrestled in his mind, each one clawing for dominance. One painting her in white lace, standing beside him in the soft glow of a future he didn't deserve. The other painting her face pale and slack, lips parted, eyes glassy as she crumpled at his feet.

It was a war that he didn't know how to win.

The beer grew warm in his hand, but he didn't drink it. He just sat there in the dim light, listening to the faint ticking of the clock on the wall, waiting for the sound of his own mind to quiet.

Chapter 26 Chuck

Chuck sat at his desk, staring at the manila folders stacked like headstones. The last five murders. Everything was so clean, so perfectly staged, it was a mockery. He couldn't understand how someone could kill some of the best people in this town. The first two victims were married women, murdered two weeks apart in identical fashion. They looked as if they'd had intercourse, but with no signs of struggle, so there was no way to prove rape. Their necks were strangled, yet the rest of their bodies were strangely devoid of bruises. Again, no evidence, as if everything had been wiped clean, as if they were meant to be found that way. The first two bodies were discovered deep in Broad Mountain State Park, yet there were no footprints, no tire tracks. No one saw anything, and every potential suspect in town had an airtight alibi. There was no proof. Then, for a while, things had gone quiet. They never found the rapist or the murderer.

It had been right after Nicole died.

Chuck's eyes dropped to her folder, to the photo of her neck. The strangulation marks seemed to leap off the paper, so dark against her pale skin. The bruises covering her body, her swollen lips. Even her nails had been clipped clean, as if someone had meticulously scrubbed away any trace of their DNA after she died. There was no proof anyone had touched her, other than the marks left behind.

Nick had been cleared almost immediately. He had been a wreck, wrapped in grief, barely holding it together. He started drinking more, having trouble just functioning. Chuck remembered the dozens of calls, Nick's voice cracking as he cried about how much he missed Nicole, how he couldn't understand how someone could do this. Chuck had scoured that park with him, looking for any sprinkle of evidence, hours and hours of combing every leaf, every tree, examining every piece of evidence again and again. There had never been a time that Chuck would have suspected him.

Not until the day of the fair, when Nicole's mom had started screaming that Nick was the one, telling Danielle to stay away. The thought had never entered his mind before, but as he sat there now, staring at every folder, every murder, every staged piece of evidence, the pattern was undeniable. All the girls, wiped clean as if they were meant to be displayed that way. Every murder was the same: strangled or their throat slit, all of them nude, their necks covered in bruises. Except for Carly and Tina, who had been burned so badly in a fire you could barely tell they were human. The only thing that linked them was Chuck's memory of telling them to go to that spot, their phones pinging from that location.

"Every other murder," Chuck muttered to himself. "Was exactly the same."

He had gone to Nick's house that morning, needing to confront him, to see his face when he talked about Nicole. He needed to know if that same sad, grieving mask was still present. He remembered Nick at the fair, hearing her name, the fear and sadness that had ripped across his face. But was it all staged? Was the grief only real because he saw Nicole's mom? He had gone over there to look Nick straight in the eye, to see if he could sense anything out of the ordinary, anything that might prove he had murdered her. Because he was starting to realize Nick might be behind all of this.

He was in the Coast Guard, but they were trained to shoot. Chuck remembered Nick going for extra shooting certifications when he joined the police division to become a forest ranger. As a kid, he had taken martial arts and other self-defense classes, always saying he needed to make sure no one could ever hurt him again. He had become a black belt quickly. After Carly and Tina's death, when the suspicion first started to creep in, Chuck had called some of Nick's old instructors. They told him how obsessively he had trained, day in and day out, sometimes getting thrown off the mat for being too forceful, for getting this look in his eyes. They knew he was dangerous. Chuck had seen that look in his eyes many times lately.

But this morning, looking at Nick, all he saw was the sad, grief-stricken face of a man who had lost someone he loved, tears still welling in his eyes. Chuck didn't know what to do, what to think. Either Nick was an amazing actor, or he was innocent, and Chuck was wasting his time chasing a ghost while the real killer was still out there.

He didn't know what to do as he searched the folders repeatedly. Nothing came up because there was no evidence. The only thing Nick shared with these girls was that he knew them, that he had "protected" them in the park. He knew them from around town. Chuck had seen Nick's eyes shift before, but was it shifty because he was upset, just like everyone else, or was it because there was more that Chuck just couldn't seem to catch?

Then he thought about Dr. McGrath. They still hadn't found her or her dog, Henry. There was no proof she was even dead, but in his gut, he knew she was. He remembered the day she came into the station, terrified that she was being stalked. Chuck had gone to her house every night and never saw anyone.

He didn't know if his patrol car presence was scaring the stalker away, or if there was no stalker at all and Dr. McGrath had psyched herself into a panic because of the other murders and her stalker. Yet he knew she was gone. Had she fled the town because she was terrified? Did she not want anyone to know because she was afraid the murderer was after her? Maybe she had something on him, maybe she'd seen him and was now a witness, running for her life.

So many questions, and he was no closer to an answer. Every time he thought he had a handle on it, Nick would pull that poker face, and Chuck would feel himself being led in the wrong direction.

He slammed all the folders shut and pushed them away, disgusted. They were no closer. He knew there would be more victims, and he couldn't keep anyone safe. He would patrol late at night and see girls walking, and he would scream at them to get home. The next day, he would ask them why, and it was always the same thing: "It'll never happen to us." Or, "Those girls were just dumb. They didn't know how to fight back." The worst one: "We wanted to see if we could outsmart the Ravensburg murderer."

Chuck was getting more disgusted, more nervous about the town he loved, about all the women in it who were so loved and yet so in danger, and he couldn't save them.

He opened his desk drawer and pulled out his whiskey and a glass. Normally, he would only pour a little, just enough to take the edge off. This time, he poured half a glass and chugged it, needing the numbness to set in as fast as it could. He was starting to lose it. He was feeling hopeless. What kind of chief detective was he if he couldn't find a single shred of evidence in five murders and one disappearance?

Were there more he didn't even know about?

His stomach turned, and he threw up in the trashcan. Tears slid down his cheeks as defeat rolled in, hard and suffocating.

Chapter 27 Danielle

Danielle put the car in park, her heart skipping as the thought of Nick settled in. She still could not quite believe this was happening, an actual date at a nice restaurant with Nick Chambers. In a town like this, that alone would be enough to get people talking.

She still didn't understand why he had chosen her, why she was the one he was taking out, the one he didn't seem interested in hiding. The thought made her stomach flip all over again.

She smoothed her hands down the front of her dress and stepped out of the car.

As she walked toward The Toasted Tomato, nerves buzzed through her, sharper than she had expected. She swallowed hard. She had never felt this nervous before, not even close.

She opened the door, and the familiar scent of garlic and onions wrapped around her instantly. Italian food. Her favorite. She had been here plenty of times before, the food was always incredible but tonight felt different.

The bar sat to her left. As she scanned the area her eyes landed on him and she felt her palms get sweaty.

She froze for a second without realizing it, just taking him in. Nick sat at the bar in black dress pants and a deep burgundy button-down, the sleeves pulled snug against his arms. His biceps strained against the fabric, and Danielle's stomach flipped at the thought of them wrapped around her.

As she moved closer, she caught his scent, pine and something warm beneath it. It was a familiar and comforting scent.

Nick shifted in his seat, clearly searching for her. The moment his eyes found her, that smile appeared, the one that could undo any woman in seconds. Dimples deep, ice-blue eyes bright, and his sharp features softened just enough.

Danielle felt rooted in the floor.

He stood and walked toward her, his movements confident and assured, like the space around him naturally parted to let him through. Not arrogant, just certain of himself.

"Hey, darlin'," he said, leaning in to kiss her cheek.

Danielle swallowed before answering. "Hey, Nick."

"You look absolutely stunning, Danielle."

You're looking quite dashing yourself."

Nick chuckled. "Dashing? I'll take it."

Danielle felt stupid. *Why had she said dashing?* She was a smart girl; she knew way better words than that.

She looked up at Nick, and his eyes were focused solely on her. She was mesmerized by him, everything about him made her stomach flip violently, making her more nervous and excited, and curious all at once.

Their stare was broken by the hostess clearing her throat. "I can take you to your table now."

Danielle blinked twice, her mind coming back to reality. Nick placed a hand on the small of her back and walked with her as they followed the waitress to the table. She loved how much of a gentleman Nick was as he pulled out her chair.

Everything about him was perfect. He was a gentleman all the time, he was handsome, and he could be funny. Nick asked for a bottle of red wine, and Danielle watched as the waitress stared at him for a little too long before making her exit to grab the bottle.

"How was your day, Danielle?"

"Good. Worked at the community center for a while and then went back to Emily's house to help decorate her yard for Halloween."

"Oh, nice. Halloween's my favorite holiday. Nothing like putting on a costume and being able to act like someone else for the night."

"Absolutely," Danielle beamed, loving that someone else enjoyed Halloween. "It's the best holiday. Love being scared and seeing all the creepy decorations and the darker vibe that comes with the holiday."

Before any more conversation could be had, the waitress came over with the bottle and poured the wine. She purposely bent over the table in front of Nick, her chest quite close to his face as she poured his glass instead of grabbing his glass and placing it closer to her. Danielle rolled her eyes. As much as she was happy that Nick chose her, she hated how all the other women acted around him, no respect for themselves or for her.

Danielle cleared her throat, and the waitress's head cocked up, her eyes narrowing at Danielle as if Danielle were ruining *their* moment. The waitress grabbed Danielle's glass, pulled it close to her, and quickly filled it before going back to Nick's side of the table and asking if he was ready to order.

Nick looked at Danielle and smirked. "Do you know what you want darlin'?"

Danielle smiled and told the waitress she wanted the eggplant Parmesan. Nick looked at the waitress, who clearly did not want to be talking to Danielle as she rushed through the questions and seemed to huff every time Danielle took a minute to think about what dressing she wanted on her salad and what type of pasta she wanted.

The waitress then turned to Nick and pushed her arms together to make her breasts seem fuller as she bent her torso closer to him. "And what about you, sweetie?"

Nick smirked and stared right into Danielle's eyes for a second too long. The waitress cleared her throat.

"God, sorry. My girlfriend looks stunning and made me completely forget what I wanted."

The waitress stood back, her shoulders going tight. She chuckled, clearly annoyed, then softened her face before speaking. "I could recommend you something to eat if you'd like?"

"Sure. What do you recommend?"

She smiled slyly. "The clams are amazing. One taste and you're hooked."

Nick chuckled and then winked at Danielle, and Danielle's face flushed pink.

"I'll just have the lasagna."

The waitress rolled her eyes, then asked him the same question about salad dressing preference and walked away.

The rest of the dinner went smoothly. Danielle loved her meal and may have let out a small, involuntary sound at the first bite. She caught Nick's eyes flick to hers, the look in them darkening just slightly, and she had to fight a grin. She enjoyed that far more than she probably should have.

They talked easily after that, discussing their days, Halloween plans, and Thanksgiving coming up. By the time the plates were cleared, Danielle's cheeks hurt from smiling so much. She had loved every minute of the date, every second she had spent with Nick.

Nick paid the bill and then walked around the table, holding his hand out to her. Danielle's stomach flipped as she placed her hand in his. His was twice the size of hers, his fingers closing around hers until her own seemed to disappear. She loved how large everything about him felt, his presence, his confidence, his body. Her thoughts drifted somewhere dangerous, and she swallowed hard, forcing them back before her palms betrayed her nerves. The last thing she needed was sweaty hands.

Outside, the town glowed in shades of orange and red. Halloween decorations filled every storefront; cobwebs stretched across windows, jack-o'-lanterns lined doorways, and skeletons posed playfully beneath streetlights. Witches' brooms leaned against shop entrances, and cauldrons sat waiting to be filled with candy. Danielle slowly turned in a circle, taking it all in. When she stopped, she realized Nick was watching her, a soft smile on his face.

"You look beautiful, darlin'," he said.

Her head dipped instinctively, heat rushing to her cheeks. She hated how easily her face betrayed her nerves. Nick's finger slipped beneath her chin, lifting her head before she could hide. His touch was gentle but deliberate, forcing her to meet his gaze.

"Don't do that," he murmured. "Watching you blush like that… it makes me crazy."

Her breath caught. His hand settled against her cheek, his thumb brushing slowly across her skin as if he couldn't help himself. Danielle found herself staring into his eyes, those impossible blues, her stomach flipping hard as the meaning behind his words settled deep. Her breathing quickened as he leaned closer, and she knew exactly what was coming. She closed her eyes just as his lips brushed hers, soft and warm.

When he pulled back, she opened her eyes to find him still staring at her, his gaze darker now, his thumb still moving gently against her cheek. Then he leaned in again.

This kiss was different. His mouth pressed against hers with more intent, more need. His hand slid to the back of her head, holding her closer as his lips parted. She tasted the sweetness of the wine as his tongue met hers. The kiss was slow and hungry. Danielle stepped closer, her hands gripping his shirt, pulling him in as if she didn't want even a breath of space between them.

A low sound rumbled in his chest as his hold tightened, the kiss growing deeper, faster. Her heart raced, and her knees went weak.

And then, without warning, he broke away.

The cool night air brushed her lips, and she wanted him back instantly. Her eyes fluttered open, her body still leaning toward him, chasing what was suddenly gone.

Reality hit just as fast. She knew where this could go. She felt it in the way he held her, the intensity of his touch. Her stomach dropped, dizziness washing over her. She wasn't ready.

Before he could say anything, she spoke quickly, cutting through the charged silence. "I'm sorry, Nick. It's late. I should head home."

She watched his brows draw together, regret flooding her instantly. Her gaze dropped, embarrassment burning through her as she wondered if she had just ruined everything. When she looked up again, his hands were clenched at his sides. His jaw was tight, but then he smiled, yet it didn't quite reach his eyes.

"Alright, darlin'," he said quietly. "Get home safe."

He kissed her cheek once, brief and restrained, then turned and walked away.

Danielle stood there, feeling foolish and hollow. She knew she had messed up. He would find someone easier, someone who didn't hesitate, someone who didn't overthink every moment. She wasn't ready. They had only been on a couple of dates. She was still learning who Nick really was.

And yet… something twisted in her chest as she watched him leave. A small, insistent voice whispered that she'd made the wrong choice, and no matter how hard she tried, she couldn't quite silence it.

Chapter 28 Nick

Nick clenched his fists, his jaw so tight his teeth hurt. He couldn't understand why she would go this far, pulling him in, showing she wants him. And at the last-minute back out.

This pure anger started taking over his mind. He could have any girl he wanted, and she must know that. Why was she acting like this, knowing she was fucking up, leaving him in this state of mind. This is her fault. She fucked up. This made him want to kill her even more, really watch her suffer.

He got into his truck and ripped out of the parking lot. He threw on the radio, the band Skillet blasted from the speakers. He did not care that he was speeding. He flew down the roads to his cabin, punching the steering wheel as the lyrics to "Monster," blared, while randomly screaming, "Fuck her!" at the top of his lungs.

His tires barreled onto the dirt path of the park. A yellow glow caught his eye. He slowed the truck and turned down the radio, watching the glow coming closer in his head lights.

As the glow came closer, he realized it was a sweatshirt. And the person inside the sweatshirt was a girl. She was jogging down the trail, her long brown curly hair bobbing in a ponytail. She was a shorter girl, and the sweatshirt hid her body for the most part.

His pulse quickened; this could be the key to fixing his anger for the night.

He hopped out of the truck and saw her body stiffen. She jogged closer to the other side of the trail, almost into the woods. He watched her as she watched him, never taking their eyes off each other.

"Hey, miss." Nick said, walking onto the trail towards her, flashlight shining on her.

She seemed to straighten her body more and move quicker. As she did, she tripped on a rock and flew forward, skidding her knees on the ground.

Nick ran over, acting like a concerned citizen.

She stumbled as she tried to get back up, her legs wobbly like a baby deer learning to walk.

"Miss, are you ok?"

She paused and looked up at him and a calmness came over her when she realized who he was.

"Nick. What the fuck. It's not nice to scare people at night."

Nick realized by the voice that it was Sienna. She was a local in town. Her dad ran the small bait shop and she helped out there often. Everyone in town adored her, she was a sweet girl but she had no problem putting people in their place. Nick had always loved that fire in her, it made him laugh when the grouchy old men would be throwing a fit because the computer was down and they couldn't get their fishing license on time.

"Sorry, Sienna. I was patrolling the ground. Are you ok?"

Nick held out his hand and helped her up. Sienna seemed to get her footing and then brushed herself off and brushed her hair back. Then she brushed herself off again, making sure to only brush her chest area.

Nick smirked, he loved that women fawned over him. It made what he did so much easier because they were always so willing.

"Sorry I startled ya, darlin'." He said as he brushed a pine needle off her shoulder. "But you really shouldn't be out here at night alone."

"I know." Sienna said, now looking around quickly, her hand fidgeting. "But I love to run, and I didn't have time this morning."

"Well, it shows. You look amazing."

Nick watched as her cheeks flushed a shade of tomato. He looked her up and down, knowing she would make a perfect distraction.

"Why don't we go back to my place so you can warm up, and I can clean up your cuts."

Sienna nodded and he held open the door of his truck for her and lightly touched her ass as he helped her in.

They sat on the couch, the air thick with the scent of antiseptic and whiskey. Nick tended to the scrapes on her knees, his touch surprisingly gentle as he placed a cartoon bandage over the worst of them. "All better, darlin'," he murmured, his hand lingering, his thumb stroking the skin just above the adhesive before slowly, deliberately, tracing a path up her thigh.

He watched her, a predator studying its prey, as she licked her lips and took another sip of her whiskey, her eyes never leaving his. Nick smirked, a slow, dangerous curve of his lips, and slid his hand higher, eliciting a low, breathy moan. He watched, fascinated, as her legs fell open a little wider, a silent, unmistakable invitation. He took the glass from her trembling hand and set it on the table, the clink of glass on wood the only sound in the room. When he turned back to her, his touch was no longer gentle. His fingers slid along her jaw, tilting her head up before he claimed her mouth with his.

She kissed him back with a force that made something inside him snap. There was no hesitance, no shyness, just raw, unbridled want. He smirked against her lips. Good. He wanted this to be easy. Her hand slid along his thigh, trembling just enough to betray the depth of her need, and he hardened instantly in response. A low growl rumbled in his chest. He kissed her harder, deeper, his fingers threading into her hair and giving it a sharp, possessive tug. Her moan vibrated against his tongue, a sensation that drove him dangerously close to the edge. Her soft grip tightened on him as he pulled her into his lap, settling her exactly where he wanted her. She ground against him without thinking, her body acting on pure, primal instinct. He loved it. Loved how she yielded to him, how easily he could draw the need out of her.

Nick's arm wrapped around her waist, while his other hand slid up the delicate curve of her throat. His thumb brushed the frantic line of her pulse before his fingers tightened, just enough to make her breath catch. "You like that, baby?" His voice was a low, smoky rasp, edged with command. Her hands fumbled at his belt, shaking with a desperate urgency. He let her try for a moment, enjoying her struggle… and then his grip tightened around her throat, halting her completely. "Not yet."

Her eyes widened, a flicker of fear finally piercing the haze of her lust.

"I need you to tell me," He murmured, his voice dropping into a dangerous whisper. "Tell me how much you want this before you lay another finger on me."

She struggled for words, her breath shuddering beneath his hold. He tightened his grip a fraction more, feeling her pulse hammer against his palm like a trapped bird.

"Say it, Sienna." His tone darkened and became a threat. "I want to hear how badly you want me."

Her throat bobbed under his grip. Her lips parted, and a soft, desperate sound escaped from her. "I… want you, Nick."

His smile was slow and predatory. "Good girl." He loosened his grip just enough for her to drag in a ragged breath, then crushed his mouth against hers again, claiming, and devouring her need and feeding his own. Her hands returned to his belt, steadier now, driven by want and the undeniable command in his voice. He felt the tremor in her fingers, felt her urgency, felt her complete surrender. He slid her thong to the side, his fingers finding her clit and rubbing in tight, merciless circles. She gripped his cock, her thumb rubbing over the tip, smearing the bead of pre-cum that gathered there. The dual sensations sent a jolt through him. He tightened his hand around her throat, his grip a vise, the restriction making his own excitement mount to a fever pitch. She rubbed him harder, while her pussy was grinding into his hand, a desperate, frantic rhythm.

His hand tightened, a spasm of pure, unadulterated power. He could feel himself getting close, so close. Her eyes popped open, her lips freezing in mid-moan. He could see it then, the dawning terror, the realization that she was having trouble breathing, and the horrifying knowledge that he didn't care. He gripped even tighter and heard her try to cough, but only a wet, pathetic wheeze escaped. She squirmed, her hands pushing against his chest, trying to break free, but his hand got even tighter. She fought, her claws digging into his arms, his chest, but it was like trying to push a mountain. Her eyes bulged, her face turning a deep purple as she realized she was taking her final breath. Then she went slack.

Nick smirked. He knew he had probably only made her unconscious, but the thrill of it, the knowledge that in the next couple of minutes she would be completely dead, and he would finally have his release, was intoxicating. He slowly lifted his hands to take in her limp body, to enjoy this quiet, perfect moment.

His breath hitched when he saw her eyes snap open, and she smiled. She slammed the palm of her hand into his nose. Blood poured from it immediately, a hot, coppery flood. Nick screamed, a raw, animalistic sound of pain and shock, and threw her off.

"You fucking bitch! What the fuck did you just do?"

He watched as Sienna scrambled to her feet, but as she did, he lunged, grabbing her by the ankle. Blood dripped from his nose, splattering onto her, ruining her clothes. She tried to kick him with her free leg, but he blocked every attempt, laughing as she tried to roll away, an "alligator roll" he had seen a hundred times. He was stronger, faster, and he had control. He yanked her leg, pulling her body fast towards him, her skin scraping and tearing on the rough wooden floor. Splinters lodging in her flesh as she let out blood-curdling screams.

"You know I like it when they scream," he said, his voice a calm, terrifying contrast to her hysteria. "It makes my release even better. Keep screaming, princess. No one can hear you." He grabbed her by the throat and lifted her into the air, her feet kicking uselessly. He squeezed, tighter and tighter, as she clawed at his hand, his arms, a single tear tracing a path through the blood on her cheek. Then he squeezed one last time, so hard he felt something in her neck pop.

His body reacted instantly, his stomach clenching as his climax built. Her body went completely limp, and he heard the last, wet wheeze leave her throat. The moment he heard that final, pathetic breath, he felt his own release tear through him, warmth spreading across his thigh as his body trembled in a sick, shuddering wave of pleasure. He reveled in it, in the knowledge that she was gone, that he was the reason she had taken her last breath.

He laid her limp body back on the floor and shook his head, clicking his tongue. "You shouldn't have done that," he sighed. "Now I've got all these cuts, and I have to figure out what I'm gonna do with the clothes you ruined. You're gonna get cold in the ground, you know." He undressed her, his movements now gentle, almost tender, making sure not to bruise her beautiful skin any further. "Wouldn't want to mess you up, now would we?"

He decided he would cut her up and use the meat to catch coyotes. If anyone asked, it was just bait. He dragged her body to the basement and started cutting, his movements precise and practiced, as if he were skinning a deer, the muscle memory taking over. He threw her remains into a big metal bin and figured with the bones, he would use the woodchipper tomorrow, burning them just like he had the others, along with her ruined clothes.

After finally cleaning up his mess and tending to his own wounds, he went and took a long, hot shower, rinsing off the lovely release Sienna had given him. Now he could deal with Danielle again with a clear head. He wasn't so angry anymore that she hadn't come over. He couldn't wait for their next date. Maybe this time she would finally come back to his place. And for once, he didn't want to kill her. He just wanted her, all night. He wanted to touch her body, feel her, taste her, feel every breath, every shudder, every moment. And then in the morning, he would watch her leave, knowing she had been in the same spot Sienna had been in not that long ago.

Chapter 29 Danielle

Danielle woke the next morning to a soft ding from her phone. She rolled over, a sleepy smile already blooming on her face when she saw Nick's name flash across the screen. She opened the message, and her heart fluttered a little. "I really hope I get to see you on your walk today."

Her fingers flew across the screen. "Well, of course. I can't miss a day of seeing you, Nick Chambers."

She placed the phone back on her nightstand and flopped onto her back, her smile widening as she replayed last night in her mind. The kiss... his hands holding her face with such surprising gentleness, the sweet, lingering taste of him still a phantom on her tongue. A wave of relief washed over her; he wasn't mad that she had gone home. She just needed to be sure she was ready. She wasn't the type to fall into bed with someone, and they had only had two dates. She knew God viewed sex as a serious decision. Not something you do with just anyone. But the next time they hung out, she was positive. She was ready for all of him, not just a piece.

Then her phone dinged again. She grabbed it eagerly, but her smile faltered when she saw her friend Emily's name. She wasn't annoyed, but a part of her had wanted to spend the entire day lost in a text conversation with Nick.

"Hey, chick. Let's go for coffee and then hit the bookstore."

Danielle's stomach sank. Going out with Emily meant she would miss her walk, miss seeing Nick. Guilt pricked at her. She quickly switched back to Nick's chat. "Going out with Emily. How about we get together at your place tonight?"

Then she jumped back to Emily's text. "Absolutely. See you in an hour."

She threw on a pair of comfortable jeans, and a soft grey knitted sweater, then sat at her vanity to apply a quick coat of mascara. Danielle looked at her reflection. She knew she was pretty, in an average sort of way, but she never felt like the kind of girl who could hold the attention of someone like Nick Chambers. And yet, he wanted her. The thought gave her a small, potent boost of confidence. She smiled, swiping on her favorite, pink-tinted lip gloss and pulling her hair into a messy bun before grabbing her purse.

Her phone dinged again as she reached the door. Her stomach did a full-on flip when Nick's name appeared. She opened it, and her cheeks flushed hot. "Can't wait to kiss you tonight, Darlin'."

She let out a little screech of pure excitement, dancing in a small circle in the middle of her room with her hands thrown in the air. She took a deep breath, smoothed down her sweater as if it had somehow become wrinkled in her moment of glee, and walked out the door.

Her face lit up when she saw Emily at their usual table at The Roasted Bean Cafe, a table for two already occupied by two drinks and a huge, glistening cinnamon roll. The rolls here were legendary. The perfect balance of cinnamon and sugar, all drizzled with an obscene amount of cream cheese frosting, and they were humongous. Danielle waved back and slid into the seat across from her.

"Hey, chick, how ya doin'?" Emily grinned.

"Not bad. I'm excited to see you!"

Emily leaned forward. "So, how was the date with Nick?"

"Wow, no warm up at all, huh?"

"Hey, I'm living vicariously through you. I want every detail."

Danielle chuckled, tearing off a piece of the cinnamon roll and popping it into her mouth. Her eyes rolled back as a blissful moan escaped her lips. She swallowed, doing a little happy dance in her seat as she savored another bite.

"Ma'am." Emily laughed, tossing a balled-up napkin at her chest, "Stop procrastinating and tell me."

Danielle swallowed and laughed. "Okay, okay. It was amazing. He was a complete gentleman the whole night. Even when the hostess tried to dig her fangs into him. And then at the end of the night… he kissed me."

"Like a quick peck, or like…" Emily's voice dropped to a deep, husky purr. "Hey, baby, come back to my place and I'll dig my fangs in." She wiggled her eyebrows dramatically and laughed.

"The second one." Danielle said, laughing.

Emily slammed her hands on the table. "Shut up! And what did you do?"

Danielle shrugged, a wave of shame washing over her. "I was an idiot. I panicked, told him it was late, and ran."

Emily dragged her hands down her face in theatrical annoyance. "Whyyyyy?"

"You know why! I got nervous. I don't know him all that well. And I don't want God mad at me for making a decision with the wrong part of my body."

"I get it," Emily sighed. "But damn. I don't care. You should've just gone for it, thrown away all your damn reasons."

"I know!" Danielle said, hiding her face in her hands. "His lips were so intoxicating and I ran!"

Emily moaned in frustration. "Dani!"

"Well, I'm gonna see him tonight," Danielle offered. "Hopefully I'll have better details for you."

Emily's head shot up. "Oh my god! Forget the bookstore. We need to get you some lingerie!"

"What's wrong with what I have?"

Emily shook her head. "Okay, my cute little Christian girl. White is for grannies. Not fucking. We're going."

Danielle slouched back in her chair and stuffed another piece of cinnamon roll in her mouth, her fate sealed.

The next thing she knew, they were standing in a lingerie store. The air was thick with the scent of flowers and vanilla, and soft pop music played from hidden speakers. Bras of every color and style hung from mannequins; cute undies were perfectly arranged on tables, and sheer robes and bodysuits hung on hangers. Danielle felt completely out of her element. She had no idea what men actually found sexy, and none of it looked remotely comfortable. She picked up a red, lacy bra with a small gold heart hanging from the middle. She turned it over and saw what looked like padding for days. Confused, she looked at

Emily and pointed to the padded cups. "Where does your boob go?"

"Exactly," was all Emily said.

Danielle watched as Emily grabbed five different bra sets and ushered her into a fitting room. The first bra Danielle tried on seemed to offer a 50/50 chance of a wardrobe malfunction. "I don't know about this, Emily. There's nowhere to fit my actual boob."

Emily barged into the room, closing the door behind her. "That's how it's supposed to look. It makes them look bigger. You could use that, ya know."

"Ha, ha. Very funny," Danielle said sarcastically.

Emily picked up a blue lacy bra with black accents. "Try this one." Danielle grabbed it and turned around, fidgeting with the clasps. "Okay, this one isn't too bad." She turned to show Emily. The bra accentuated her curves perfectly without making her feel like she was about to spill out.

After trying a couple more, Danielle felt she had enough. "Alright, Emily. Bookstore now? Please?" Just then, her phone dinged. She looked down to see a message from Nick.

"You. Me. A boat ride tonight?"

A slow smile spread across her face. "That sounds lovely."

"Great. See you tonight, beautiful."

Chapter 30 Nick

Under the warm spray of the shower, Nick let his mind drift to Danielle. He pictured her on the trail, the subtle bounce of her chest with each step, the way her leggings hugged the curve of her ass as she walked ahead of him. Tonight, all of that would be his, riding him, taking him.

His body reacted instantly, heat pooling low in his gut. He clenched his jaw, forcing his hands to remain planted on the tile. He wouldn't touch himself. He wanted to wait. He wanted her.

When he pulled up to her house at six, his heartbeat quickened. He watched her emerge from the front door, and a predatory smile touched his lips. She was wearing a plaid brown mini skirt, a cute plaid shirt, and tall brown boots that made her legs look endless. She looked so adorable, so innocent. He couldn't wait to see that outfit crumpled on his floor.

"Hey," she said shyly, sliding into the truck.

"Hey, darlin'."

"So, how long have you driven boats for?"

"For as long as I can remember. My dad used to take me out on the river all the time. He would let me drive. I thought I was the coolest kid ever."

"I'm sure you were," she said, smiling before dipping her head, a nervous habit he couldn't wait to punish out of her. He smiled, knowing those sheepish looks would soon turn into something far more devilish. He couldn't wait to strip away that shyness.

At the river, he was out of the truck in a flash, opening her door and holding out a hand. She took it lightly, and he helped her into the boat before pushing off and hopping in himself. He grabbed the blanket he had stowed away and draped it over her lap.

"What a gentleman."

"For you, always."

"This park is so pretty at night," Danielle said, her voice full of wonder.

"Wait until we go around the bend and you see the mountain."

They drifted through the river, the soft sounds of the forest their soundtrack as they talked about their day. Then Nick spotted a moose in the distance and pointed it out.

He watched as her eyes lit up, her smile wide and genuine. "I have lived here my whole life, and I have seen these creatures quite a few times now, yet every time I see one, I am still as amazed and entranced with them."

"That's me every time I see you, darlin'."

Nick's eyes locked onto hers, and she smiled, bending her head forward in that familiar show of shyness. They came around the bend, and her head flew up, her eyes widening.

"Oh my god, Nick. This is such a different view from a boat."

"I know, right?" He killed the engine and moved to her side, grabbing a basket from near her feet. He pulled out a bottle of wine and two glasses. "Figured this would keep us warm."

She smiled and took a glass as he poured. Her eyes closed as she took the first sip, a soft hum of appreciation escaping her lips, and Nick watched with enjoyment. He could not wait to hear that sound again.

"I want you to know," Nick said, his voice dropping to a smoky whisper. "I have never brought anyone out here."

She looked up, an eyebrow raised in playful disbelief. "You expect me to believe that, Mr. Chambers?"

"Cross my heart," he said, making the gesture over his chest. "This is my quiet place. I come here when I'm stressed or want to be alone. It's too special to me."

"And I'm…?" She asked softly.

"You're extremely special, Danielle. I've never felt this way about anyone before. You are so different from anyone I've ever met." He could see the small kernel of doubt in her eyes, so he played his final card. "Even Nicole never came out here with me."

He watched as a blush crept up her cheeks, and she took another sip of her wine, a shy smile playing on her lips. He took her glass and set it down, placing his next to it. Then he cupped her face, his thumbs stroking her soft skin. "I mean it, Danielle. You're not just another girl."

Then he kissed her. It wasn't gentle; it was passionate, and possessive. And she kissed him back with the same fire. Her lips were soft and inviting. His hand moved to the back of her head, his fingers tangling in her hair, tightening just enough to make her moan. He smiled against her mouth, easing his tongue past her lips. She tasted sweet and tart, like the wine, and it made him want to devour her. He kissed her harder, his grip on her hair tightening. She grabbed his shirt, pulling him impossibly closer. He knew he had her right where he wanted her.

He broke the kiss, watching as her eyes fluttered open, her breathing heavy. “Let’s go back to my place and finish this bottle… and that kiss.”

Danielle just nodded quickly, adjusting the blanket on her lap. He turned the boat around, and the ride back was silent and thick with anticipation.

***

The wine was never reopened.

They sat on his brown leather couch, lost in each other. He grabbed the back of her head, pulling her in, her soft lips and the sweet taste of her making him go crazy. He fisted a handful of her hair and kissed her harder, bruising her lips as he listened to her moan into his mouth. His other hand palmed her breast through her shirt, his jeans becoming painfully tight.

A sharp knock at the door shattered the moment.

“Sorry, darlin’. I’ll be right back.” He lifted her off his lap and grabbed his shirt, striding to the door. He pulled it open to find Chuck standing there, his expression grim.

“What’s up, Chuck?”

“Sienna has gone missing. Her mom is freaking out. We gotta go search the park.”

“Oh, shit. Okay. I’ll be right out.”

“You got someone in there, Nick?” Chuck asked, raising a knowing eyebrow.

"Yeah. A pretty special girl."

"Well, damn, Nick. Is that Danielle in there?"

"You caught me," Nick said with a short laugh. "Let me just say goodbye and I'll be right there."

He walked back into the living room. Danielle was sitting there, her lips swollen from his kisses, her hair delightfully disheveled. She looked so fucking hot. At that moment, a dark part of him wanted to say screw Chuck, fuck the search, he needed her, but he knew that wouldn't look good.

"Hey, darlin'. Something's come up. Chuck needs me."

"Everything okay? Not another murder?"

"No. But I can't say anything more than that. You can either stay here and wait, or I can bring you home."

She looked around the room, considering it. "I wouldn't mind staying here. You guys won't be too long, will you?"

Nick smiled, loving the thought of coming back to his cabin and finding her here.

"Not at all, darlin'. My bed is just down the hall if you get tired." He bent down and kissed those pink, plump lips one more time before walking out the door to join Chuck.

They walked the trails in silence at first, the beam of their flashlights cutting through the darkness. Then Chuck broke it. "Her mom is pretty worried. Thinks she might have been the next victim."

"I think her mom needs to calm down. It's too early to think that way. She needs to stay positive."

Chuck looked at him, his eyebrows scrunched. "You know, we found some new evidence that might link us to the killer."

Nick paused for a fraction of a second. "Oh yeah? That's good. What did you guys find?" he asked, his voice a carefully constructed mask of indifference.

"Tire tracks. We had them analyzed and figured out the type of vehicle. We also found DNA evidence on the flip flop from the fire murder. We think it's someone close to the park. Someone who has the ability to be stealthy and not recognized as a threat."

"What do you mean by that? You think it might be a camper?"

"That… or maybe someone with more experience and knowledge of how a crime scene works and knows the park well." Chuck looked at Nick, a fierce, calculating glint in his eyes.

"The way you're wording that, it seems you're insinuating it's someone who works at the park." Nick's voice rose, a controlled fury. "Who do you think it is, Chuck?"

Chuck just smiled. "The evidence is stacking up. That's all I can say right now."

Nick tripped on a branch and grunted, pissed off. He picked it up in frustration, ready to hurl it into the woods. Then he thought about how easy it would be to swing it, to knock Chuck out and drag him back to the cabin. That would end the suspicion. He dropped the branch. Killing Chuck now would be stupid. If they did have evidence, killing a cop would put him at the top of their list.

They combed the woods for hours until Chuck finally called it off, muttering about daylight and fresh leads. Nick nodded but said nothing as he watched Chuck leave. He walked slowly towards the cabin, his mind racing. How could he have left evidence on the flip flop? He had been so careful. He retraced every step, every movement. Nothing came up.

He needed to get the evidence, or what he thought was evidence, into the woods soon. Dispose of it. Every minute it sat where it was, he could feel the walls closing in.

As he moved closer to the cabin, the beam of his flashlight cut through the now darkening forest. The woods had gone eerily quiet around him, and then he heard a twig snap somewhere off to his left. Nick spun instantly, his flashlight jerking toward the sound as his pulse slammed against his ribs. Between the trees stood a shaggy golden shape, half hidden by the shadows. For a split second his mind raced somewhere darker, until the animal shifted forward and he realized who it was.

Henry.

The dog stood trembling between the pines, his tail tucked tightly between his legs as a low whimper escaped him. His fur was dirty and matted in places, and his wild eyes darted nervously through the woods like he expected something terrible to emerge from the darkness behind him.

Nick's chest loosened with relief. He slowly lowered himself into a crouch, careful not to make any sudden movements. "Hey Henry," he called softly, his voice low and steady. "It's alright. Come here."

Henry hesitated. The dog took one cautious step forward, then froze again, ears twitching toward the surrounding woods. Every few feet he stopped to look around, his body tense and uncertain before inching closer once more. Nick stayed perfectly still, one hand stretched out patiently in front of him. He could feel his own heartbeat pounding as he waited.

Finally, Henry reached him. Nick kept his breathing even as the dog cautiously sniffed his hand. For a couple long seconds neither of them moved. Then Henry's tail gave a small wag.

Relief hit Nick so hard he nearly sagged forward with it. He let out a breath he hadn't even realized he had been holding and gently ran his hand over Henry's head before quickly scooping him into his arms. The dog clung against his chest as Nick stood and headed back toward the truck, his flashlight bouncing across the trees with every hurried step.

He drove straight to the vet, exhaustion and adrenaline batting inside him the entire way. After checking Henry over, the vet assured Nick that aside from being frightened and dehydrated, he was alright. She explained that Henry would be placed with Jenny's family and thanked him for bringing the dog in safely.

By the time he climbed back into his truck, the adrenaline that had carried him through the woods was finally beginning to fade, and thoughts slowly drifted back to Chuck and what he might already know.

Then, like a switch flipping in his mind, it clicked.

Chuck lied.

There was no evidence. If there was, they wouldn't be playing mind games in the dark; they would have hauled him in for questioning. This was a bluff. A carefully orchestrated attempt to scare him, to make him panic, to make him fuck up and lead them right to what they were looking for. They wanted him to slip up. He knew better. He wouldn't let that happen. He walked into the cabin, no longer worried. His body ached from the past couple of days.

He stepped into the shower, letting the hot water beat against his back, rinsing away the day's dirt and the sharp edge of his panic. The steam filled the small bathroom, but his mind drifted somewhere far warmer, far more dangerous. His thoughts settled on Danielle, on the couch. He remembered the feel of her lips, the soft weight of her breast through her shirt. He could almost hear her moan as her fingers tangled in his hair, gripping, pulling herself closer, needing more of him.

And then it dawned on him, a thought so potent it made his breath catch. She was in his bed right now.

He shut off the water, his movements hurried, distracted as he dried his skin. His thoughts were no longer on Chuck, or evidence, or the woods. Only her.

He was completely nude as he walked into the bedroom. The moonlight through the window cast a pale, ethereal ribbon across the bed, and there she was, curled beneath his covers, her soft, even breathing the only sound in the room. For a moment, he just stood in the doorway, staring. Something dark and possessive unfurled in his chest, a cold, creeping satisfaction that eclipsed everything else.

Sorry, Danielle, he thought as he stepped closer, the shadows sliding over his skin like a second skin. It's time to get up.

Chapter 31 Nick

Nick stood at the edge of the bed; a statue carved from shadow and restraint. Every muscle in his body was coiled, a taut wire humming with a violent energy as he watched her sleep. Her breathing was slow, steady, utterly oblivious to the storm standing less than a foot away. He eased the covers back, a predator unveiling its prey; his movements calculated and silent. The moment her body came into view, his breath caught in his throat. Soft pink fabric. Bare skin. The rhythmic rise and fall of her chest pulled at something feral inside him, a primal tide.

His gaze dragged over her slowly, mapping the slope of her waist, the curve of her hips, the faint, delicate pulse in her throat. There was something almost obscene about her innocence, how utterly exposed she was, completely unaware of the man looming above her. A dark ache twisted low in his gut. He wasn't just looking; he was memorizing, possessing her with his eyes because he wasn't allowed to touch. Not yet. His jaw clenched as his gaze dipped lower, to the thin pink lace of her underwear hiding what he wanted most. The barrier infuriated him, tempted him, and dared him. He swallowed hard, his pulse a frantic drum against his throat. She had no idea what she did to him just by existing in his bed. No idea how close he was to losing control, how deeply he wanted to mark her with something she would never forget.

Heat throbbed through him, sharp and relentless, as his thoughts spiraled into darker places. Places where she woke beneath him with his name on her lips, where she reached for him because she belonged to him and nowhere else. His fingers curled into tight fists at his sides. God, he wanted her. Wanted her in a way that was dangerous, in a way that felt like hunger and possession and something he didn't dare name out loud. He stood there, breathing hard, staring at the woman who had no idea how close she was to being devoured.

He brushed a stray piece of hair from her face, his knuckles barely grazing her cheek. She stirred beneath his touch, her lashes fluttering. A soft, sleepy sound left her throat. Then her head rolled toward him, her eyes foggy with sleep. God, she was beautiful like this, unguarded, and completely his. Cute didn't even cover it. She was dangerously adorable; the kind of soft that made something savage in him want to protect and ruin her in the same breath. When Danielle smiled, slow and sleepy, Nick felt his cock throb. He imagined those lips wrapped around him, taking him deep, and his pulse jumped.

He leaned down and kissed her gently, a quick brush of lips before sliding into the bed beside her. Her warm skin pressed against him, and she instinctively began to roll onto her side. His hand clamped onto her shoulder, keeping her on her back.

"Stay just like that," he ordered, his voice a low rumble. "I want every inch of you right where I can see it."

She froze, her breath catching, and Nick smirked. She was perfect.

His lips found her shoulder, soft at first, then trailing heat up her neck. She moaned faintly when he grazed her skin with his teeth, and he smiled against her throat. His thumb stroked her cheek once before his lips found hers once more. He slid his tongue into her mouth, claiming her, swallowing her soft gasp. He would never get over her taste; he wanted it imprinted on him permanently. Her soft lips moved perfectly with his as he sucked her tongue, hearing her moan for him as her hand gripped his arm. His hand slid down her neck, resting there as he bit her lip before lifting his head, needing to see her face, needing to see how she looked with his fingers around her neck. Her eyes were staring at him with need. *Fuck.*

He pulled her bra aside without breaking eye contact and circled her nipple with his thumb. It tightened in response, and he could feel his cock throbbing, aching to be inside her. When she moaned, he crashed his mouth back onto hers, trapping the sound between them. He grazed her nipple one more time before letting his mouth wander down her throat. Across her collarbone. Lower. He stopped at her breast and kissed the tight peak lightly. Her moan was sharp and immediate, and the sound shot straight to his cock. He swirled his tongue around it, savoring her reaction, before closing his lips around it and sucking hard. Danielle arched into him, fingers diving into his hair, gripping fiercely. Nick growled and bit down lightly.

"Fuck," she gasped.

He smirked, sliding the other side of her bra away until both breasts were bare for him. He latched onto the other nipple, sucking hard while rolling the first between his fingers. He lifted his head, needing to see her. "You like that, darlin'?"

Her moan was the only answer at first. Her hips lifted off the bed, desperate, pleading. He bit her nipple a little harder, and she cried out.

"Use your words," his voice dropped into a command.

Her breath shuddered. "Yes…"

"Good girl." His hand left her nipple and moved down her stomach, stopping at the lace of her thong. Heat radiated off her. He groaned softly. He wanted her. Now. He wanted to fuck her hard, hear her scream. He pushed the thong aside and felt himself get harder with need as he looked at her pussy, pink, glistening, and perfect. Her scent made his mouth water. He needed her on his tongue.

His finger pressed to her clit, circling slowly. Her hips reacted instantly, a soft cry spilling out of her. "Fuck, Danielle," he muttered. "Tell me how badly you want my fingers."

Her voice trembled. "I need them."

"Beg."

A beat. Then soft, breathless. "Please… I need them."

Nick's smirk sharpened. "Good girl." He slid one finger into her. She was incredibly tight, and a dark curse left him before he could stop it. *She is going to feel so fucking good around my cock.* He eased his finger in and out, letting her body adjust, her hips rolling with every movement. He felt her hand grip the back of his neck as she let out a low whimper. He wanted her louder. He slid a second finger inside of her.

"Fuck, Nick…" she gasped.

His fingers moved faster, deeper, rhythmically as she cried out in pleasure. His thumb circled her clit, dragging more desperate sounds from her lips. Her body tightened, and he could feel her climax building, feel her losing control as her fingers tightened around his hair. He kissed her abdomen as he worked her, hearing her breath hitch, watching the tension coil tight in her stomach. He felt her body tighten and her breathing go quiet. Then her pussy clenched hard around his fingers. Danielle let out a loud cry, as her orgasm tore through her. She shook, her breath breaking, her thighs trembling. Nick watched her fall apart and felt something dark and possessive curl tight inside his chest.

When her breathing slowed, she lay still, smiling faintly at the ceiling, one hand pressed to her chest. Then she sat up on her elbows and looked at him. And that soft smile, warm, trusting, and undeniably his, hit him like a punch. *She is going to change everything.*

"I need you. Now," he commanded.

He moved onto his knees and spread her legs wide, admiring the view. Then he slid her panties down her thighs and tossed them to the floor. Danielle was still propped on her elbows, staring at him. Her gaze flicked down and froze. Her eyes widened at the sight of his cock, thick and hard and ready for her. Nick felt a slow, dangerous smile pull at his lips.

"Nick," she said nervously.

"Don't worry. I'll be gentle."

"Nick. That's not going to fit." Her legs tightened defensively.

"Danielle. Open your legs," he commanded. "You will be fine."

"Nick. I don't know. I've never done this, but science dictates that something that large will not fit into something my size."

He chuckled. "Dani…" Then he froze. Had she just said…? Nick sat back on his heels and stared at the scared girl before him, her eyes wide and her body trembling. "Are you a virgin?"

Danielle nodded and then bowed her head in that embarrassed stance he wanted to spank out of her. That motion made his cock twitch, and he wanted her even more now. Needed to thrust into her. Knowing he could claim her as only his, it made that animal instinct in him roar. He needed to claim her.

"I will be gentle. I promise." He laid on top of her, his forearms bracing his body. "Put your hands on my biceps. If it hurts, you squeeze and I'll slow down. You will dictate how fast I go."

Danielle stayed quiet, but her eyes stared worriedly back at him.

"Danielle, I need you to speak," he said, his voice a low command.

"Yes, Nick."

He kissed her again, his tongue sliding into her mouth as if he needed to show her how slow he could be. He felt the precise moment her fear eased, her body softening beneath him, her breath mingling with his. *God, she trusts me* he thought, a dark current running beneath the surface of his desire. *She has no idea how much danger lives in my bones.*

He shifted closer, slow, and deliberate, feeling the tremor that ran through her when his hips aligned with hers. Every instinct in him screamed to take, to claim, to bury himself in her until she forgot everything that wasn't him. But she was trembling… and she was innocent… and for the first time in his life, he cared what someone felt beneath him.

He kissed down her neck, each slow drag of his mouth meant to coax her deeper into him, to pull her mind away from fear and into want. Her soft little moan vibrated against his lips, and her fingers curled around his biceps like she needed him to anchor her. That small sound nearly broke his restraint.

He moved slowly, inching into her. The moment he felt her sliding around his cock, he almost lost it. She was so tight, so warm. He carefully adjusted his weight. Her breath hitched, her hips jolting as nerves and desire warred in her body. Her nails pressed into his skin, not out of pain, but to steady herself. He felt his cock sliding deeper and then he heard her whimper.

"That's it…" he whispered against her throat. "Good girl."

He felt her tense suddenly, a soft cry catching in her throat, and Nick froze. Her eyes squeezed shut, her breath trembling, and the weight of her innocence hit him like a blow to the chest. In that moment, something dark and primal surged up inside him. She was his now. The certainty of it settled deep, absolute, and it terrified him how fiercely he felt it. He didn't just want her. He claimed her. She mattered in a way no one ever had. She was his and only his.

He slid into her the rest of the way slowly, deliberately, forcing himself to stay controlled even as every instinct screamed to take her harder, to mark her, to hear her say his name. His body wanted to consume her, to drive her breathless. His mind told him this moment mattered, that she mattered. He moved with restraint, feeling how tight she was around him, her slickness barely easing the stretch, and it nearly undid him.

When he felt her relax, and felt her body finally accept him, his control loosened. He began to move faster, deeper, savoring every second, loving how perfectly she held him.

Danielle gripped his biceps, and he looked up to see her biting her lip.

"Okay. Got it. Slowing down." Her grip loosened by degrees, her shoulders dropping, her throat arching back as her body slowly adjusted beneath him. Nick lowered his lips to that exposed curve of her neck, kissing her there, slow, and claiming, designed to pull her out of fear and into him entirely. As her breath steadied, he let his movements follow her cues. Each slow shift met with a soft sound, each gentle coaxing of his mouth earning a little more trust.

When she relaxed fully beneath him, her hands sliding away from tension and into something closer to surrender, a darkness in him unfurled. He kissed her again along the line of her throat, deeper this time, letting his pace grow just enough to feel her respond. Her quiet moan vibrated against his lips. He sucked gently on her neck as he slid in and out of her. He could feel her anticipation, her nerves, her heat, everything in her trembling for what came next. Her fingers tightened on his biceps as she moaned.

"There you go," he whispered against her throat. "Good girl."

The realization that he had just claimed her darkened something inside him, but he forced himself to breathe slowly because one wrong move, one moment of giving in to the instinct to take, could frighten her. He leaned up, looking into her face. "You're safe," he said quietly. It wasn't soft, it was a command, a truth he intended to enforce with his life. "And I'm right here."

She relaxed beneath him, tension unwinding little by little, her trust settling into his hands. He kissed her again deeply, his tongue swirling with hers, and then he lowered his mouth to her neck once more, savoring the sound that slipped from her throat. Her touch grew bolder, her breath shorter, her body arching toward him without thought.

"Nick…" she whispered. That single word almost broke his control. He held her tighter, his breath growing harsher, the dark animal part of him clawing at the edges of restraint as her legs wrapped around him and her nails scraped down his back.

"Tell me what you need," he growled.

"Faster," she whispered, trembling.

He froze, not from doubt, but from the sheer force of wanting to obey, to give her everything she asked for and more. But he held himself steady, forcing the heat into something measured and controlled. He breathed, kissing her jaw, her cheek, and then her lips. "Then hold on to me."

He slid in and out of her harder, making sure to still hold back, knowing she could not handle him fully yet. He felt his own release building as he moved within her. She was incredibly tight and wet as he slammed into her, as if she was made for him. She clung to him as he fucked her, every thrust he gave met with a loud moan.

Her eyes drifted shut as he felt her body begin to clench around him, a familiar signal that she was right on the edge. "Open your eyes," he commanded, his voice low and firm. "I want to see you when you come."

Her lids flew open, and the sudden intensity in her gaze was matched by the way her body tightened, a desperate grip on him. He noticed her breath catch and still, the tell-tale sign he knew so well, the way she held her breath on the cusp of release. His hand circled her throat, and a slow, wicked smirk spread across her lips. The sight of her utter enjoyment sent a jolt straight through him. He tightened his grip, cutting off her air completely. There was no struggle, no panic. Instead, her eyes darkened with a feral hunger, and her inner muscles squeezed him even tighter.

A tremor started deep within her, a violent, beautiful wave that he felt ripple through her entire body as her walls pulsed around him. He released his hold, and she sucked in a ragged gasp. A raw moan of pure ecstasy tearing from her throat as her back arched off the bed. Nick watched, captivated, as she came for him, her eyes locked on his the entire time. As the tremors subsided and her body softened around him, something primal took over. He began to move again, driving into her with a hard, demanding rhythm. He stared into her eyes, watching the pleasure and the slight wince of pain as he slammed into her, a combination that only spurred him on. Her nails dug into his arms, sharp points of pain that bloomed into exquisite pleasure, pushing him closer to his own breaking point. He fucked her harder, chasing his release, needing to claim every part of her. Her loud cries were his undoing. With a final, powerful thrust, the pressure snapped, and he poured himself into her. The release was absolute, a blinding wave of pleasure that left his body shuddering and his arms weak, his ragged breath mingling with hers as he stared down into the eyes of the woman he had just completely consumed.

"Fuck, Dani," he murmured, his voice rough.

Sliding out of her felt wrong immediately, like tearing himself away from something that belonged to him. He already needed to feel her again.

Her hand drifted across his abdomen, tentative and warm, before she curled instinctively into his chest. The moment she did, something in him locked into place. He didn't hesitate. He didn't question it. His arms wrapped around her, firm and unyielding, pulling her tight against him. He had never been a man who cuddled or cared. He never wanted to be, but with her, letting go wasn't an option.

She's going to ruin me. He thought. *One way or another.*

Chapter 32 Danielle

Danielle turned over, her hand landing on the cold, empty space beside her. Her eyes fluttered open to find Nick's side of the bed vacant. She rolled onto her back, letting them drift shut again as flashes of the night before ignited behind her lids. Her breathing quickened, a phantom echo of his hands on her skin, the memory of his lips tracing every curve. Her body stirred, a deep, visceral response to the thought of his fingers slipping into her, of his grip on her throat as she came around his cock.

The sharp clank of a pan from the kitchen interrupted the memory. She slipped out of bed, grabbing his button-up shirt from a nearby chair and pulling it on. After quickly putting on her thong, she followed the rich scent of coffee and bacon down the hall. She was smiling sleepily when she reached the kitchen and then she stopped dead.

Nick was at the stove. Shirtless. His tattoos, an intricate tapestry of ink, wound over his arms and back. Gray sweatpants hung low on his hips, exposing the deep V of muscle that she had absolutely no business staring at first thing in the morning, but she could not look away. It was not just the body that rooted her to the spot. It was the way he moved. Soft metal music drifted from a speaker on the counter, and Nick, dangerous, brooding, guarded Nick, was quietly drumming along to the beat with a pair of tongs. Not for show. Not for an audience. Just… relaxed. Completely unaware of her. He tapped the counter with his knuckles, his shoulders swaying slightly, the tattoos along his arms shifting with the rhythm. For a moment, he looked like a man without weight, without ghosts, just someone who genuinely liked the song.

Danielle felt her heart pull tight in her chest. He was… cute. Stupidly, dangerously cute. A side of him she knew no one else ever saw. And then the dark ache hit her. Her eyes traced the ink across his arms, remembering how each muscle had flexed beneath her hands last night, remembering the red scratch marks she had left on his skin, still visible, still claiming him. Her breath hitched. The mix of sweetness and raw want nearly knocked the air out of her.

He flipped the bacon, drummed lightly on the pan, and when he reached for his coffee mug, his dimples appeared, softening every sharp line of him. She almost melted on the spot.

"Morning, darlin'," he said, finally noticing her. His voice was warm, a little raspy.

"Morning," Danielle whispered, her chest fluttering. She stretched, the hem of his shirt lifting to reveal the pink thong beneath. Nick's eyes dropped instantly. The playful softness vanished, replaced by something darker, hungrier. Her heart skipped.

He cleared his throat, looked away, and poured her coffee exactly how she liked it, cream, and one spoon of sugar, without a word. He set the mug in front of her with a quiet, "Here."

She took a sip, her eyes fluttering shut. "How do you know how I like my coffee?"

His lips twitched. "Our first date."

Her stomach flipped. He remembered. Of course he did.

"Thank you, Nick."

"Anything for you." The words seemed to slip out so easily.

She stared at him, at the tattoos, the dimples, the unconscious rhythm he still kept tapping with his fingers and she felt utterly undone.

A sharp knock at the door broke the moment. Nick's entire body shifted, muscles coiling, posture hardening. The drummer disappeared; the predator returned. He killed the stove, rolled his shoulders back, and walked to the door with that quiet threat in every step. Danielle watched him go, heart pounding. He was beautiful and all hers.

Nick opened the door, and she saw Chuck on the other side. She could hear Chuck murmuring something and then watched Nick turn and grab his coat. He smiled at Danielle. "Sorry, darlin'. I'll be right back."

She assumed they were talking about the recent trouble in the park, but curiosity gnawed at her. Still, she knew better than to spy; Nick didn't seem like the type to tolerate his privacy being violated.

She wandered into the living room, her attention drawn to the pictures on the mantle. Her hand slid over the cool rock as she took them in. A young Nick, proudly holding a fish with a man who must be his father. Another, a few years older, in a river tube with a beer hoisted high, surrounded by friends. She smiled at a photo of him and his Coast Guard crew, everyone grinning. Then her fingers brushed against a metal tin, the embossed Coast Guard emblem cool to the touch. Tucked behind it was a picture of him in his forest ranger uniform, shaking hands at his graduation. He looked so happy and young, yet he filled out the uniform just as powerfully as he did now. Her head snapped toward the front door as it opened. Chuck walked in first, followed by Nick.

"Whoa. Sorry, Danielle," Chuck said, turning his back quickly.

Heat flooded Danielle's face as she looked down, suddenly remembering what she was wearing… or more what she wasn't. Her cheeks burned as she fled to the bedroom and threw on her clothes. When she walked back out, her face still felt sunburned.

"Sorry, Chuck. I, uh, completely forgot what I was wearing."

"No worries, sweetie. How are you doing?"

"Good. Everything okay?"

Nick walked back to the counter, grabbing a to-go cup. "Yeah, just normal park business."

Danielle nodded and took another sip of coffee. Nick placed the cup on the table and walked over to them. "Alright, I'm just going to get dressed. I'll be right out, Chuck."

Chuck nodded, and they both watched Nick disappear into his room. Then he walked over to Danielle and lowered his voice. "You really need to be careful, Dani."

Danielle's eyebrows scrunched. "Because of the murders?"

"That, and… watch yourself with him, Danielle."

She was even more confused. Chuck and Nick had known each other forever. "Nick?"

"Yes. You're a good kid, and I just need you to keep your head on straight and be safe."

"Chuck, Nick is the safest person I know. I trust him with my life."

Chuck shook his head, his expression grave. "Please don't be naïve. Not with him. Please."

The door opened, and Chuck took a step back. Nick walked out in his uniform and watching him move with that easy authority made Danielle's mouth go dry. He strode toward her, his musky pine scent filling the air. His arm wrapped around her waist, pulling her close as he claimed her lips with a kiss that was both a promise and a brand.

"Have a good day. Hope to see you later." He smacked her butt lightly, smirked, and grabbed his cup, heading for the door.

She glanced at Chuck as she passed him. The look he gave her wasn't judgment, it was worry, heavy and unguarded. Before she could ask, he turned and followed Nick out, leaving her alone in the quiet cabin. Danielle sank onto the couch, letting out a breath she didn't realize she had been holding. Her head spun in a strange mix of adrenaline and something softer. She didn't know if it was the intensity of Nick's kiss lingering on her lips… or the echo of Chuck's warning whispering through her mind. And then something clicked. A slow smile curved her lips, warmth swelling in her chest. Of course Chuck was worried. He had known her since she was a baby. He had watched her grow up, stumble through heartbreak, and avoid dating altogether after one attempt that crashed and burned. He wasn't doubting Nick. He was watching over her. Like he always had. That realization soothed something deep inside her and Danielle's smile widened. She loved that so many people cared enough to worry. Loved that Chuck cared enough to pull her aside, even if it was awkward. It felt safe. Like having a family she didn't have to ask for. And she loved that gruff, quiet Chuck was still one of the people watching out for her.

Chapter 33 Nick

Nick followed Chuck to his cruiser. "I need your help today," Chuck said, his voice clipped, all business. "Some of the boys from my hunting class want to learn how to set traps. I need you to meet them at the camping area and run the drill. I got called in on something else." He opened his door and slid in without another word.

A knot of ice formed in Nick's gut. He and Chuck had been friends for years, but this… this was different. No jokes, no banter. Just cold delegation. He watched the cruiser pull away, Chuck not even glancing back. Nick's hands clenched into fists at his sides. Either Chuck had found actual evidence, or he was acting on a gut-deep instinct. Either option made his skin crawl with a nervous energy he despised. Nervousness led to mistakes. It led to losing control, and that was a luxury he could no longer afford.

He forced a few deep, steady breaths and headed for the shed beside his cabin. He grabbed a heavy metal bin of "coyote" bait and heaved it into the truck bed. The meat inside was already rotting, the stench thick enough to make the boys gag when he opened it. Good. The stronger the smell, the faster it would draw in an animal, and the sooner this task would be off his plate. He went back for the traps. He preferred these models; they were designed to restrain, not maim. A clever system of springs left a small gap when fired, preventing the leg from being crushed while ensuring a secure hold until the animal could be relocated. He tossed the traps into the back and headed for the campground.

Heavy metal blasted from the truck speakers as he bounced down the trail, but he didn't hear a note of it. His mind was a loop of last night, of Danielle. The feel of her body under his, the sound of her moans, the way she moved with him. The certainty that he had claimed her. His thoughts zeroed in on the moment his hand circled her throat, how her hips had risen to meet him, how his tightening grip had only drawn a louder cry from her lips. He had savored the sound of it so completely that the thought of hurting her never even entered his mind.

He wracked his brain, trying to pinpoint what made her different. Why didn't he feel that familiar, dark urge to kill her? He replayed the moment she found her release, the way it had sent him hurtling toward his own. His whole body had vibrated with the sound and feel of her, his head growing dizzy with a primal need to hear more, to feel her pulse around him until every nerve was alight. He had lost himself inside her, letting go completely.

He had never finished inside a woman before. He had never wanted to. It was too intimate, an act of trust he had never felt, and he would be damned if he left his DNA as evidence. But Danielle… Danielle was different in every way that mattered, and he couldn't grasp why.

The first time he had met her, all he could think about was murdering her, about feeling her last breath. Now, he couldn't imagine a world without her in it. She was rewiring him, changing the very way he saw things, and he hated it. He hated the feeling of his own mind turning against him. He was a man of logic, of methodical planning, not of messy, uncontrollable emotion. He knew if he wasn't careful, she could make him slip. And with Chuck already acting strangely, he couldn't afford a single mistake.

He had to get his head straight. He needed to start thinking of Danielle as just another potential victim. Nothing more.

As he drove into the camping area, he saw the boys standing near a tent waiting for him. Larry stood near them, making them laugh at something, and as he heard Nick's truck pull in, his head snapped up and he started waving enthusiastically.

Nick was not a huge fan of Larry. The man drank like a fish and had definitely lost a lot of brain cells from it. He could not stand people who drank like that, making an imbecile out of themselves and not being in control. He had punched out a lot of men when he was in the Coast Guard for being drunk. He could remember being young and dumb, walking into bars with his shipmates. People around them would start talking shit about how they were just glorified fishermen. Then they would say other shit just to get under their skin, talking about how while they are gone, men are back home fucking their girls and mommas like whores.

Nick had pounded men's faces into the floors of bars more times than he could count. He quickly shook the thought away. He needed to be the professional forest ranger in front of the kids.

He put the truck in park and jumped out. "Hey boys, you waitin' on Chuck?"

Larry spoke up for the boys, his words already slurring this early in the morning.

"Yup… boys're pretty 'xcited t' learn how to set traps."

Nick nodded and gave a tight smile.

"Alright boys, well, Chuck got pulled away on important police business, so you're stuck with me today."

The boys smiled wide. He had known many of these kids when they were little and had seen them grow up at this campsite and in the park for Boy Scouts.

Larry beamed as he looked at the kids. "You guys're g'nna have a blast with Nick... Have fun. And don't... don't none of you come back missin' fingers. Yer moms'll kill me."

Nick tapped the bed of his truck a couple of times. "Alright boys, hop on into the bed of the truck. I'll drive you down to the area where we're going to set the traps."

The boys waved to Larry and jumped in, one after the other, excitedly.

Nick chuckled and shouted, "Be careful of the traps, guys."

Nick hopped in and drove towards the deeper part of the woods, making sure to be far enough away from where people would be walking. As he drove, he looked in the rear-view mirror. The boys shouted as he went over bumps, hopping off the floor of the bed a little and then laughing hysterically, high fiving each other.

Nick chuckled. He remembered being a kid and his dad would let him ride in the back. His dad would purposefully hit ruts in the road or go over a hill a little too fast to see Nick fly through the air laughing.

He slowed down and came to a stop when they had gone far enough in. Nick grabbed the bag sitting next to him and stepped out and the boys hopped quickly out of the bed. "Alright boys, each of you grab a trap. I'll grab the meat bin."

Nick crouched in the dirt clearing, the morning light barely breaking through the trees. The six boys formed a half-circle around him, all wide-eyed and trying a little too hard to look tough.

"Alright, gentlemen," Nick said, tugging on his gloves. "Today you're learning how to set an offset jaw spring-coiled trap." He grabbed gloves from inside the bag and handed them to the boys. "Put these gloves on, and before any of you ask… yes, this can take your fingers clean off if you're stupid."

The boys exchanged looks.

"Cool," one of them whispered.

"No, Caleb. Not cool," Nick corrected sharply. "Cool is walking out of here with all ten fingers."

He tapped the metal trap on the ground. "Okay, step one, safety. This thing is strong, like, snap a tree branch in half strong. So rule number one, fingers stay OUT of the jaws. You hear me?"

All six heads bobbed quickly.

Nick pointed to the trap's parts. "Now, look at what you're working with. These are the jaws, the big metal teeth on the sides. Those springs. They're what make it slam shut." He tapped the center. "This flat plate in the middle is the pan. It's basically a button. The coyote steps on that, and boom."

One of the boys jumped at the word "boom." Nick smirked. "Relax. It's not loaded yet. And this little bar here is the dog. No, not the barking kind. It's what holds the trap open. Think of the whole thing like a giant mousetrap for something way bigger and way meaner."

The boys leaned in closer.

"To open it," Nick continued, "you gotta press your heels down on the springs. This is the hardest part. You push both heels down at the same time and lean your weight on them. They're tough, so don't whine."

He pressed his feet onto the spring arms and shifted his weight. The metal creaked as the jaws slowly opened.

"Once the springs are down," he said, grunting a little, "you use your heels on the outside edges of the jaws, and never inside, to open it all the way."

"That looks like it hurts," Mason muttered.

"It does if you do it wrong," Nick said cheerfully. "So don't."

He grabbed the dog bar and hooked it onto the tiny notch on the pan. "This part's delicate. You place the dog right onto this notch. That keeps the trap open. Kinda like propping a door open with a stick."

He stepped off the trap, watching to make sure the trap held. "Now we make sure it's steady. I tap the frame, again, frame, not the pan. If it stays open, we're good."

He gave it a light tap. The trap held strong.

Nick nodded. "Perfect. Now you put it where you want it. Ground needs to be level, so the trap doesn't wobble." He shifted the trap into position near a tree root, nudging the dirt flat with his boot.

"Now we hide it. Just a thin layer of dirt or leaves. Don't bury it like a pirate chest, or it won't snap fast enough."

The boys watched him scatter leaves lightly over the trap.

"Last step, the bait goes *behind* the trap. Not on it." He stood up and dusted off his hands. "Coyote steps forward to get it, steps on the pan, and the trap does the rest."

Nick walked over to a metal bin that had been sitting in the shade. The boys stiffened as soon as he popped the lid.

A wave of stench rolled out, thick, sour, and rotten.

"Oh, my God!" Liam gagged, covering his mouth.

"What *is* that?" Mason choked out.

"Coyote meat," Nick said casually, reaching in with one gloved hand. The meat was warm and thick.

All six boys recoiled, some turning away entirely.

"Dude, that's disgusting!" Caleb said, eyes watering.

"That's the point," Nick replied, lifting a dripping chunk that looked like it had been dead for far too long. "The smell travels. Coyotes can pick it up from a long way off. The worse it smells, the better."

One boy dry-heaved. Nick grinned. "Welcome to real wildlife management, boys."

He tossed the bait a few feet behind the trap. "And now? We walk away. Carefully. Like ninjas. Don't step on the trap, don't trip, and don't act like idiots." He eyed them one by one. Most of them nodded, pale. Nick watched as each boy set a trap. "We only need a couple in one area. Most of yours won't stay set but I need to see that you can do it."

The boys seemed to have more fun unsetting the traps as they stuck long sticks onto the pad of the trap. Nick chuckled as the boys jumped and screamed each time the clamps bit the stick.

"Alright boys, time to bring you back to the campsite. Grab the unset traps and get in the bed."

Nick looked at the three traps set a bit apart. The meat was strong, and he knew by tonight it would be devoured. Especially when he came back after to unset the three traps. He needed to show the boys how to set them, but he did not want the coyotes or any other wildlife to get trapped and be too scared to eat. He needed to make sure this meat was eaten pretty quickly. Nick turned towards the truck and saw the boys talking excitedly amongst each other. "Good job today, boys."

"Thanks Nick." They all seemed to say it in unison.

Nick smiled, he had really enjoyed today.

Chapter 34 Chuck

Chuck pushed through the precinct doors and gave Darla a tight nod. She was a sweet girl, pretty and determined, but she was drowning. This was her second attempt at the police exam, and the defeat in her eyes was palpable. He had tried to help her study; she knew the material like the back of her hand, but she claimed the moment she walked into the test hall, she felt like someone had taken an eraser to her brain.

He moved past the reception area to a door in the back hallway, swiping his badge. The light flashed green, followed by the familiar buzz and clunk of the lock disengaging. Muffled voices drifted from the detectives' bullpen as he stepped inside.

"Hey, Officer Braider," one of his men, Parker, called out, hand already half-raised.

"Hey Parker. Anything? Any leads? Anyone see anything?"

Parker just shook his head. "Sorry, sir. No calls. Nothin'."

Henry chimed in from his desk. "Calvin and I re-gridded the land around the last two sites. There's nothing. This guy is a ghost."

Chuck sank into his chair, rubbing his face with his hands, trying to physically smother the anger building in his chest. This was insane. He just knew Nick was involved, and the inability to prove it was eating him alive. He lifted his head to find his detectives staring back at him, waiting for a directive. They looked like deer in the headlights, lost and directionless.

"This is bullshit," Chuck snapped, pushing himself to his feet. "Every serial killer leaves something behind. A calling card or clue. So, where the hell is his?" He strode to the evidence board, a chaotic collage of smiling victim photos, a park map dotted with red pins, and pictures of the few, pathetic clues they had found. "What are we missing?" He demanded, his voice laced with frustration. "Four of us, and we can't figure out the next move?"

He scanned their faces, pleading for a spark of an idea, but they all found something fascinating to look at on the floor. He hadn't told them about his suspicions about Nick. Everyone in town, including himself not so long ago, loved the guy. They would think he had lost his mind.

He tried to steer them back on course. "We know it's someone who knows these woods. It's not an out-of-towner. No new vehicles, no unfamiliar faces at the diner or campgrounds. That leaves our own residents."

Parker finally spoke up. "Maybe we should ask Nick to help with some night patrols? Set up some game cameras."

The mention of Nick's name as a helper made Chuck's stomach flip. He was trying to rattle Nick, to make him slip, but it wasn't working. The man seemed immune. Chuck wished they had found DNA on that damn flip flop, or anywhere. He had been sure when Nick found Jenny's dog that it would lead to something, maybe blood. But another dead end. They interviewed nearly everyone in town. No one saw anything. It was like the killer was a phantom.

Henry's voice cut through his thoughts. "What if we set up a decoy? Have one of our people jog the trails at night. We can watch them and keep them safe. It's been a while since his last kill. He's got to be getting antsy."

Chuck considered it. It wasn't a terrible idea. But Nick was smart. They would have to be invisible. He wouldn't be surprised if the man had the nose of a bloodhound. "Alright," Chuck conceded. "But it must be someone Nick doesn't know. Otherwise, he'll immediately—"

Parker interrupted, his brow furrowed. "Nick?"

Chuck froze. He had slipped up. The other detectives were now looking at him like he had grown a third head.

"Uh," Chuck stammered. "I didn't mean to say Nick. We were just talking about him, so his name is stuck in my head."

The officers just stared, their trained eyes dissecting his every word. Calvin took a step closer, his expression hardening. "I don't know why you'd even think it's Nick. He's done nothing but help us for years. He was a groomsman at my wedding, Chuck. Look somewhere else."

Parker and Henry nodded in agreement. "I thought we were a team here?" Parker added, his voice tight.

Chuck's jaw set. "We are."

"No, we're not," Calvin said, closing the distance between them, his voice low and dangerous. "If we were, you would've told us why you were looking at Nick. And then we would have told you to look somewhere else."

Chuck stood his ground, his own voice dropping to an icy authority. "Last time I checked, you three work for me. I will tell you what you need to know, and you do not question my orders. Now, go find us our next victim."

Calvin turned and, with a sharp sweep of his arm, sent a cup of pens flying off his desk. Chuck's heart hammered against his ribs as he watched them walk away, their backs rigid with betrayal. Sweat dripped into his eye, making it sting. The last thing he needed was to make enemies within his own department.

And then a thought, far more terrifying than insubordination, surfaced in his mind.

What if he was wrong?

Chapter 35 Nick

Nick took one last pass around the trails, a final sweep to ensure everything was in order. He hated how the darkness crept in early; seven o'clock and the forest was already buried in a midnight gloom. He drove slowly toward the back of the woods, listening for any signs of bears or coyotes drawn to the bait. Thankfully, the woods were still. He parked a short distance from the traps and grabbed the long stick the boys had used earlier. He made quick work of disarming all three, the heavy jaws snapping shut with a satisfying thud. The meat was still where they had left it. He had made it easy for them, taking it off the bone, skinning it, and preparing the meal. All they had to do was eat. He took one last look around, his gaze sweeping the shadows for any movement, before tossing the branch into the truck's bed.

As he shifted into reverse, a familiar, low growl rumbled from the dense undergrowth. A slow smile spread across his face, he knew the meat would be gone by morning. He backed out quietly, not wanting to spook his dinner guest.

Nick turned the truck around and eased down the narrow trail toward his cabin. The woods swallowed the headlights, branches clawing at the air, until a strange flicker of pink drifted across the beam like a lost wisp of cotton candy. He frowned. As he drew closer, the shape sharpened: a woman jogging alone, her bright puffy jacket a neon beacon against the oppressive dark. She looked like a piece of candy dropped in the dirt.

When she noticed the truck, her eyes widened, and she moved to the side of the trail, her breath pluming in the cold. Nick slowed and rolled down his window.

"Miss, you really shouldn't be out here."

She tugged out her earbuds, still catching her breath. "What?"

"This park isn't safe at night."

She froze mid-step. "What do you mean by that?"

Nick slid the truck into park. "You're not from around here, are you?"

"No. I'm here for the week. I live out west."

He let out a short, humorless laugh. "This is a terrible place to vacation in late fall."

"I'm on a retreat," she said, a little too bright. "Thinking of moving back up here. I love this weather."

Nick nodded slowly. "Well, hop in. I'll give you a ride back to your car. I don't want anything happening to you."

He saw the exact moment her internal alarm blared. Her eyes flicked from him to the truck, then back again. *Smart girl.*

"You're safe with me," he said, letting his tone soften just enough. "I'm the forest ranger. Here to protect and serve."

But she didn't relax. If anything, her jaw tightened. "I think I'll just jog back," she said.

"Ma'am," he replied, his voice dropping, losing all its warmth. "It's cold, it's dark, and you've got miles to go. Don't be stubborn."

She stepped closer, cautiously, her eyes scanning every inch of the truck from the tires to the bumper, and then to the cab, like she was committing it all to memory. A prickle of awareness traced its way down Nick's spine. Why was she cataloguing his vehicle?

"You got heat going in there?" She asked, rubbing her hands over her jacket arms.

"Full blast."

He watched as she quickly ran in front of the truck to the passenger side and climbed in. Five feet of bubbly blonde energy, pin-straight hair, and dimples, smelling like sugar cookies and frost. She looked up at him with wide, assessing eyes. They weren't admiring; they were studying.

"Thank you for letting me warm up," she said softly.

"No problem," he muttered. "Seatbelt."

She clicked it on, then scooted a little closer, as if testing a boundary. "Such a gentleman. Worried about my safety and all."

Nick turned to her, his brows raised. Three minutes ago, she had been ready to freeze to death rather than step inside. Now she was flirting? He didn't trust her for a second.

"So… Ranger…" she said, touching his shoulder lightly. "I'm sorry, I didn't get your last name."

"Chambers." His tone was clipped and cold.

Her dimples deepened. "Well, Ranger Chambers… you always pick up damsels in distress?"

"What damsel?" Nick asked, completely unimpressed. "You looked pretty ready to jog the whole way back."

She shivered dramatically. "You saved me from the cold. Though I wouldn't mind finding another way to warm up…"

Her hand slid onto his thigh.

Nick's reaction was instantaneous. He grabbed her wrist, his grip firm but not bruising, and placed her hand back in her own lap.

"I'm trying to keep you safe," he said, his voice dangerously low. "And my girlfriend wouldn't appreciate you touching me."

The color drained from her face. She curled inward, turning toward the window, suddenly very small and very quiet. Nick said nothing else. By the time they reached the main parking lot, she already had her hand on the door handle. The moment the truck stopped, she jumped out and sprinted to her car without a backward glance.

Nick huffed a laugh to himself. "Wow. Not even a thank you." He pitched his voice high and mocking: "'Oh, thank you, Nick, for keeping me safe… even though I clearly just wanted your cock.'" He rolled his eyes and gave a dismissive wave out the window as he drove off, heading back toward the one person he actually wanted to see. His stomach fluttered at the thought of her, his heart skipping a beat. He was thankful for Danielle in that moment; that entire interaction had reeked of a poorly executed setup.

"Good job, Chuck," Nick thought, shaking his head with a low chuckle. "But not good enough."

Chapter 36 Danielle

Danielle sat in her room, putting the final touches on her "Get Ready With Me" video. She loved the quiet ritual of editing, the connection she felt with her subscribers and fellow creators. With a final click, she hit 'Publish' and leaned back in her chair, stretching her arms over her head. Now, it was time to get ready for tonight. Her stomach did a familiar little flip at the thought of seeing Nick, her mind instantly drifting to the memory of his hands on her body, his fingers gliding over her skin, his lips claiming hers…

Her bedroom door swung open, shattering the moment. "Hey, chick," Emily announced, flopping dramatically onto Danielle's bed. "You're not dressed yet?"

"No," Danielle laughed. "We've got a couple of hours."

Emily rolled her eyes. "Yeah, and?" She bounced off the bed and made a beeline for Danielle's closet, disappearing into the depths. She emerged a few minutes later with an armful of tops. "Okay. Start trying stuff on."

Danielle smirked, grabbing the clothes and giving Emily the middle finger. Emily just giggled. "Oh, stop. You love me."

Danielle tried on a few outfits, but none of them felt right. They all screamed 'good girl' and tonight she wanted to look stunning for Nick. "These suck, Emily. I look like an Amish girl on Rumspringa."

Emily burst out laughing. "Oh my god, Danielle." Then she dove back into her overnight bag. "I figured you might say that, now that you've…" She wiggled her eyebrows suggestively. "…you know."

Danielle pressed a finger to her lips. "My parents are home."

Emily mouthed a silent 'sorry.' "Try it on. I brought it from home."

Danielle shed her clothes and slipped into the dress. It was innocent in shape but sinful in color. A bright, attention-stealing red. The short, fluttering skirt showed just enough leg to make her own heartbeat trip. She had chosen it for one reason, to see Nick's eyes darken the way they did last night.

"Perfect," Emily breathed, bouncing on the balls of her feet. "Nick is going to lose his mind!"

Danielle looked at her reflection, tugging nervously at the hem. She still felt a flicker of self-consciousness in clothes this bold.

"Stop it, Danielle," Emily commanded. "You look drop-dead gorgeous. Do not second-guess this."

Danielle looked at her friend and stuck out her tongue. "Alright, brat. What are you wearing?"

Emily rummaged in her bag again and pulled out a tiny scrap of black fabric. "Is that a lingerie nighty?" Emily rolled her eyes. "No! Just wait." She shimmied out of her clothes and slipped into the dress. Danielle's eyebrows shot up. It was a very short, strappy number that didn't leave much to the imagination. If Emily bent over, the whole bar would get an eyeful.

Danielle whistled. "Damn, girl."

"Thank you. I can't wait for Luke to see it."

"Luke? Who's this new mystery man?"

Emily sat on the bed, a dreamy look washing over her face. "Oh, you know. Only the most attractive new lumberjack at Pete's lumberyard."

Danielle's jaw dropped. "Ooh, do tell."

"Not much to tell, really. We met at the bar last night, he brought me back to his place… I'll let your imagination do the rest."

Danielle sat stunned for a solid second before grabbing the pillow from her lap and hurling it at her. "Oh my god, Emily!"

"What?" Emily laughed, dodging the pillow. "Alright, chick. Let's get going. Make sure you wear your long trench coat. We don't need Mommy and Daddy freaking out."

Danielle rolled her eyes but grabbed the coat. Her stomach fluttered again as she imagined Nick's face when she took it off. She quickly went back to her computer, double-checking that the video had finished publishing. Satisfied, she shut it down. She had thought about telling Nick about her YouTube channel a dozen times but had always chickened out. What if he thought it was stupid or childish? She knew she shouldn't care, but she did. Nick was unlike anyone she had ever met, and the thought of losing him was terrifying.

"Danielle, hurry up!" Emily called from the hallway.

Chapter 37 Nick

Nick sat at the bar, nursing a Samuel Adams while he waited for Danielle and Emily.

"You want another?" Gary asked, already reaching for a fresh bottle.

"Sure. Thanks, Gary." He watched as Gary popped the top with practiced ease, the motion pure muscle memory. He slid the beer down the bar, and Nick stopped it with a steady hand, raising it in thanks before taking the first sip. He loved that first hit of cold, rich malt rolling over his tongue, followed by the clean, sharp snap of bitterness.

His gaze drifted over the bar's usual cast. The newly twenty-one crowd, already too loud and drunk, cackled at their tables. On the dance floor, girls moved with a calculated dirtiness, hoping to snare a guy for the night. Near the pool tables, an older crowd laughed and boasted, their cheers erupting when one of them sank the eight ball. Nick chuckled, watching two friends celebrate their victory.

He took another swig, the bitter taste barely registering, because the moment the front door opened, something hot and sharp cut through him.

Danielle stepped inside. Her wavy blonde hair bounced over her shoulders as she shivered out of the cold, her long black coat clinging to her frame. The delicate flats on her feet made her look smaller, easier to gather up, easier to hold against him. Every inch of her pulled at him like gravity. Her eyes swept the room, and when they landed on his, her whole face lit up. Nick's breath caught. His heart kicked hard against his ribs, harder than it ever had on a hunt, harder than any kill. She did this to him. Something no one else had ever managed.

Her warm rose scent hit him first as she approached, something soft and intoxicating that made his jaw tighten. It filled his lungs, a vivid reminder of how she had smelled tangled beneath him, how her skin had felt under his hands…

"Hey, Nick," she breathed, her cheeks flushed from the cold… or from him.

"Hey, darlin'."

She set her purse on the counter and began unbuttoning her coat. Nick forced himself to stay still, but tension coiled through his muscles. Then the coat slipped from her shoulders, and he forgot how to swallow. Her dress was sinful, making heat pulse through him in one dark, possessive wave. He wasn't thinking about the dress anymore. He was thinking about how easily it could be removed. How easily she came apart in his hands. His gaze climbed back up her body, slow and claiming, until it locked with her eyes.

"You look," he said, his voice low and rough, "absolutely delicious."

Danielle's face flushed deeper, and she dropped her gaze in a shy smile. Nick didn't allow it. He reached out, hooked a finger under her chin, and lifted until her eyes met his again.

"Do not ever look down when I compliment you," he murmured, his voice dark velvet. "You own it."

Her breath caught. He was so confused. He wanted to only see her as his next victim, but she was doing something to his mind and body. He saw her as his possession, his girl. No one was to touch her. He felt this new feeling come over him, a fierce need to protect her, to make her feel cherished. *What the fuck!* He screamed in his head. He was obsessed with her.

"You are beautiful," he continued, his eyes never leaving hers. "Don't you dare lower your head like you're doubting me."

Her lips parted, her eyes softening, and Nick felt something fierce settle inside him.

Danielle smiled and nodded.

Just then, Emily walked up with a tall man in tow. "Hey, Nick."

"Emily." Nick nodded. "And who's this?"

"This is Luke. He's new in town."

Nick whistled. "And already sunk your teeth in."

Danielle giggled and Emily shot her a look. Danielle immediately put her hands up in a don't-shoot motion. "Hey, I just laughed. I didn't say it."

Emily rolled her eyes. "Have fun, kids. We're gonna go dance." Nick watched as Emily dragged Luke to the dance floor, immediately putting her back to his chest and sliding down his body before rolling back up, her ass grinding against his jeans perfectly.

Nick looked at Danielle, who was watching them intently, her eyes following Emily's every move. "Do you want to dance?" He asked.

He watched as her focus broke, and she looked at him, her eyes wide as she shook her head. "Oh god, no. I'll need a couple of drinks before I do that."

Nick chuckled. "What do you want to drink?"

Danielle's head cocked to one side, and she pursed her lips. The face she made when thinking was adorable. "Twisted Tea, please."

Nick smiled, a low sound in his chest. "Can't wait 'til you're saying *please* later for a different reason." He watched as Danielle blushed and started to dip her head before snapping it back into place. "Good girl," he whispered in her ear. He called Gary over and shouted his order above the music. Gary slid the bottle down the bar, and Nick gripped it. "My lady," he said, handing it to Danielle.

She lifted the bottle in thanks and took a sip. He watched as her lips wrap around the glass, her head tilting back. His gaze was fixed on her mouth, a sudden, desperate need to have them on him overwhelming him.

"Nick?" His head shot up to meet her eyes. "You good?" Danielle said, laughing.

"Yeah," he said, his voice thick. "Just mesmerized by you."

She rolled her eyes and took another sip.

Emily appeared out of nowhere, breathless. "Hey guys… want to get some air? It's suffocating in here."

Nick barely had time to respond before Danielle hopped off her stool and headed for the door, her blonde hair bouncing with each step. "Come on, Nick," she called over her shoulder.

He followed, watching the way she moved, the way she always seemed to pull him with her without even realizing it. The cold air slammed into them the moment they stepped outside, sharp and icy. Danielle stood next to Emily, arms wrapped around herself, shivering. Nick crossed the distance in two strides and wrapped his arms around her from behind, pulling her into his chest.

"Let me grab your jacket," he murmured.

Danielle's hands shot up and held his arms in place. "No. Stay."

Something inside him tightened, a mix of fondness, hunger, and pure possession. His palms slid slowly along her arms, warming her. Then his hands settled on her hips. He gripped her firmly and tugged her back against him. Her body pressed into his instantly, like she needed his heat, his closeness. Him. His hands drifted lower, rubbing her thighs, while her skin pebbled under his touch, goosebumps rising along her flesh. Her legs trembled, and he wasn't sure if it was from the cold, from him, or maybe both.

"Danielle," he said softly but firmly, "I'm either grabbing your coat… or you're coming inside."

She turned, meeting his eyes, and he watched her cheeks redden. "Fine. Back inside. It's too cold anyway."

Good girl, he thought, smirking.

Nick took her hand and led her back into the bar. The blast of heat hit them like stepping from a freezer onto a tropical beach, and he pointed to her stool. "Sit." She did, immediately. He liked that. His hands slid along her sleeves, warming her, and Danielle leaned into him. The moment her back touched his chest, something dark and possessive curled in his gut. His hand slid to her throat, a gentle hold, a promise, a reminder. He leaned down, his lips grazing her ear.

"I need your mouth on something else later," he whispered, his voice thick with intention. "I'll be right back, bathroom. Do not leave this spot." She nodded obediently. He disappeared into the bathroom, a rare grin pulling at his mouth. He couldn't wait to get her back to his place. Last night had not been nearly enough.

He zipped up, washed his hands, and stepped back into the bar… and froze. Her stool was empty. His pulse jolted as his eyes swept the room once, then twice, faster each time. A sharp, unwelcome panic crawled up his spine… until he heard squealing laughter. His head snapped toward the noise. His body relaxed a little as he saw Danielle and Emily were dancing on the crowded floor, laughing and singing. Danielle threw her head back and twirled, hands in the air, joy radiating off her like light.

Nick crossed his arms and leaned against the wall, watching them. His eyes never left her as she dropped low, her hips swinging, her dress riding up her legs. He felt his pants get tight as he watched her. The way her body moved and swayed. He thought about what it would look like with her on top of him, her head falling back as she rolled her hips on him. His attention was snagged away as he saw a guy watching her, pointing to his friend. The guy started making his way closer to the dance floor, his eyes locked on Danielle like she was prey.

Nick's fists curled instantly. The guy moved with purpose. Intent and Nick's vision narrowed. *Don't you fucking touch her.*

The guy reached her first, slipping behind her, hands finding her hips and sliding lower. Danielle startled, turning quickly. Her reaction said everything. She realized it was not Nick, and as she stepped back, Nick saw her hands go up as if she was going to push him away.

Nick's blood detonated. He stormed onto the dance floor. The guy tried to step closer again, but Nick didn't give him the chance. His fist connected with the man's face so hard the impact shuddered up his arm. The guy stumbled, shock written across his face.

"What the fuck, dude?"

"Stay away from my girl."

"She's free game," the man spat, laughing. "Everyone knows Nick Chambers doesn't claim anyone, just fucks and ducks."

Something inside Nick snapped. His fury surged, white-hot, obliterating rational thought. He struck again, harder, feeling bone shift beneath his knuckles. Danielle shouted his name, but he didn't care. He punched again, watching the man's eyes roll back as he crumpled to the floor. Nick lunged for him, ready to crush his face into the ground, but hands seized him from behind, he turned to see Gary and the bouncer.

"Nick, stop! It's not worth it!"

Nick didn't care. He wanted the man's blood on the floor. He wanted to make sure no one ever thought they could touch her again. But then he saw Danielle. Frozen. Wide-eyed. Emily holding her back. Something twisted in his chest, rage, fear, and desire, all tangled into something he didn't want to look at too closely. He ripped himself free and stormed outside, the cold air a welcome shock.

He hated this. He hated the loss of control. Hated that she could get into his head like this.

A hand touched his shoulder and instinct took over. He spun, ready to break someone's jaw. Danielle stumbled back, eyes wide, and he exhaled sharply. "Sorry, baby. Thought you were that pathetic excuse of a man."

Her voice came out small, and fragile. "Thank you."

Nick blinked. "You're thanking me?"

She shrugged, looking almost shy. "You… might've gone a little far. But your intention was to protect me. I liked that."

Something dark flooded him, tightening like a vice around his ribs. She liked it. She liked him like this. He stepped closer, unable to hide the way her reaction ignited him. "Get in the car," he said, his voice rough, and commanding. His eyes locked on hers, no space left for misunderstanding. "Now."

Chapter 38 Danielle

Danielle walked into Nick's cabin and turned slowly, already feeling the air shift. Nick stood there, the faint rise and fall of his chest the only movement. She watched as his gaze dragged over her body, slow, deliberate, and claiming, like he was deciding exactly what he wanted to do to her the moment she crossed his threshold. When his eyes finally met hers, they had turned almost pitch black.

He still radiated violence. She could feel it rolling off him in waves as he stalked toward her. His knuckles were split, his chest heaving, his eyes still burning with the fury he had unleashed on the man who dared touch her.

Before she could speak, he spun her, shoving her back against the door with a force that stole her breath. Her heartbeat spiked, thundering in her ears, but her body leaned into him instinctively. His hand cupped her face, not gentle, but claiming, and then his mouth crashed against hers.

His lips were soft, but the kiss was anything but. It was fierce, hungry, and punishing… like he needed to erase the memory of anyone else even looking at her. His tongue pushed past her parted lips, tasting, taking, his mouth moving against hers with a desperate, perfect rhythm that made her knees weaken. He tasted like beer and adrenaline and something uniquely him, something she knew she would never get enough of.

His hand dragged from her cheek down her body, fingers gripping her thigh so hard she gasped into his mouth. Heat pulsed violently between her legs the moment he squeezed. And when he pressed his growing hardness against her hip, grinding into her as his tongue tangled with hers, she could barely breathe. He gripped her thigh tighter, pulling her closer, forcing her to feel exactly what she did to him.

Then his hand slid between her thighs.

Her mind blanked. Her knees buckled.

His fingertips grazed the damp silk of her thong, then shoved it aside like it was an insult to his progress. A sound rumbled out of him, low, and feral. "Fuck… you're already wet for me."

Her stomach twisted sharply, desire flaring so hot it burned. She didn't even try to hide how badly she needed him.

His fingers pushed into her slowly, stretching her, filling her. Danielle's eyes fluttered shut as pleasure tore up her spine, sudden and electric. He worked his fingers in and out of her at an agonizing pace, curved just right to hit that spot, his thumb brushing her clit with devastating precision. Her mind fogged. Her legs shook. Pressure coiled deep inside her, pulling tight.

His fingers sped up just as her control began to slip. His thumb circled her clit harder, faster, dragging a moan from her throat she was powerless to stop. Her whole body melted into him, trembling, surrendering. She moaned into his mouth as he kept kissing her like he owned every sound she made.

Then, just when she was seconds away from coming, his fingers slid out of her.

Her eyes snapped open in time to see him lift them to his mouth and taste her.

"Fucking perfect." He said, smirking.

She didn't even have time to catch her breath before his hands were on her again. He lifted her effortlessly, her legs wrapping around his waist because her body had no other instinct left. He didn't speak. He didn't need to. The look in his eyes, dark and blazing with possession, told her everything.

Nick carried her toward his room like he was taking what was his, and she wanted nothing more than to be claimed.

Chapter 39 Nick

Nick dropped her onto her feet. The red dress swayed at her thighs, a vibrant slash against her skin, and he needed it off of her.

"Turn around."

He watched Danielle obey without a flicker of hesitation, and a dark satisfaction curled through him. He unzipped her dress, then gripped the hem and lifted it over her head in one smooth motion. Her perfectly round ass was presented to him, a flawless offering. His hands ghosted over her hips and thighs, leaving a trail of goosebumps in their wake. He hooked his fingers into the delicate string of her thong and slid it down her legs, his own body lowering with the descent. As he rose, his hand slid up the inside of her thigh, and he heard her soft moan.

He quickly unhooked her bra, letting it fall to the floor.

"Get on the bed. I need to taste you."

He watched her crawl onto the mattress and turn onto her back, propping herself on her elbows. Her eyes, heavy-lidded and dark, followed his every move. Her body was a masterpiece, from her full, parted lips, down to the perky swell of her breasts, to the perfect, glistening folds of her pussy.

Nick walked to the bed and slid her legs apart. He growled at the sight of her, so wet, so ready to be licked. He knelt, grabbing her calves and sliding them up until her heels nearly touched her ass. He held her gaze as his hands roamed over her thighs, watching her eyes roll back as he touched her between her legs, feeling her slick heat.

He dragged his tongue against her slowly, savoring the choked sound that slipped from her throat. Her moan wasn't just pleasure; it was laced with surrender, and he smiled against her skin. He wanted her trembling. He wanted her breathless. He wanted her so undone she couldn't remember anyone's name but his.

He kept her trapped under his mouth, taking his time, forcing her pleasure to build in controlled, unrelenting waves. He wanted her begging before he ever let her fall apart. When he slipped his hand between her thighs, her reaction was immediate, her whole body jolted, a sharp gasp tearing from her lips. Her hips jerked toward him, desperate in a way she probably didn't even recognize.

Nick smirked, the darkness in him sharpening. He slid one finger in and out of her slowly, matching the pace of his tongue. He felt the first slick evidence of her surrender and pressed a second finger inside, a slow, careful stretch that earned him a sharp, shaky gasp. His fingers curled inside her, tilting to find that sensitive spot he now owned. His tongue began to circle her clit as he felt the tension coil deep within her. He sealed his mouth over her and sucked, a hard, pulling pressure that made her hands fly to his hair, her fingers digging in, anchoring herself. The sharp sting only made him groan, the sound a dark vibration against her flesh as he fucked her faster with his fingers, his tongue a relentless, swirling torment.

Her thighs tightened around him as her moans grew louder. "Don't stop," she whispered.

He kept his pace as she gripped his hair, her hips jerking. His tongue loved the taste of her as he slid it up and down, teasing.

"Fuck, Nick."

His fingers quickened as he felt her body pause, her thighs tightening around him, her breath catching. He smirked, and with one more swirl of his tongue, he heard her moan loudly as she pulsed around his fingers. His fingers kept their pace as she screamed his name again, grabbing the sheets now. He didn't stop until she was a panting, trembling mess, her grip loosening on the sheets.

Slowly, he withdrew his fingers and moved up her body, covering her with his weight. He looked down at her flushed face, her eyes wide and dazed with pleasure.

"Mine," he whispered, the word a final, possessive brand. "Only mine."

He crushed his mouth against hers, his tongue forcing past her lips, so she tasted exactly what she had left on him. The kiss was deep, demanding, and claiming. And while her mouth was still tangled with his, he felt her wetness coat the length of him. He slid into her in one slow, merciless push.

Her lips faltered, breath catching as her body stretched around him. For a moment she went still beneath him… then he felt her melt, her lips moving again, kissing him back with a low, hungry sound.

He broke the kiss, bracing himself on his palms above her. "Mmm, that's my good girl."

His hips snapped forward, faster, harder, he needed to fuck her. Needed to feel her take every brutal thrust. Her screams broke open beneath him, her nails dragging down his arms in desperate, stinging streaks. His hand found her throat, fingers curving around it with controlled pressure. She looked up at him and smirked before moaning louder, and something dark and hungry surged through him.

"Come for me, darlin'."

He slammed into her again, tightening his grip. Her body locked up beneath him, breath pausing as she clutched his arms, her nails sinking so deep he felt the burn of skin breaking. It only pushed him harder. Then she came around him, pulsing violently. He released her throat, as she cried out, gasping as air finally tore back into her lungs, her orgasm coating him, pulling a groan straight from his chest. Her body trembled, every aftershock rippling around him.

When her eyes fluttered open, he saw those wild, green eyes staring at him, and he felt something low and primal snap inside him.

"Fuck… you're gorgeous."

Danielle smiled, unguarded and bold. Nick smirked back, loving that she had no shyness left in her, only hunger.

"Get on your knees and bend over, darlin'."

She flipped onto her knees instantly, arching her back with perfect obedience. Her ass lifted for him, full and inviting, and he knew she wasn't ready for everything he wanted to do to her, but the thought of that future made heat coil viciously in his gut. He leaned over her, sliding his hand up the back of her head. His fingers tangled in her hair, and he yanked, forcing her head back as he drove into her with violent precision.

She screamed, the sound drenched in pleasure. Every thrust pulled her head back further, her cries rising, raw and desperate, her body clenching around him as if she couldn't get enough.

And he wasn't about to give her mercy. He needed to hear her scream, needed to know there was a small amount of pain mixed with her pleasure. He needed to hurt her just enough.

His fingers glided down her back like a warning before he slammed into her, hitting the farthest depths of her until pleasure and pain blurred. He brought his hand down hard on her ass, the crack echoing off the walls. Her sharp yelp melted into a desperate moan, and the sound only fueled him. He spanked her again, harder, and her response was a trembling, breathless whimper that told him the sting had only made her wetter.

Nick groaned low in his throat and seized her hips, fingers biting into her skin. "Fuck," he murmured, voice rough with want. He slammed into her in one brutal thrust. "I want you so sore you can't sit for days." His hand crashed against her again, heat blooming beneath his palm. "Your body will remember exactly who did this to you. I want you wet for me on command."

The warmth radiating from her skin was intoxicating; he knew he had put it there. He held her steady, using her body like something meant to be controlled, his thrusts so punishing he had to haul her back into position every time she slipped forward. She trembled beneath him, every moan louder than the last until suddenly, her body went taut and silent. He felt the shift, the tightening, the way she braced for the fall.

Nick fisted her hair and yanked her head back, forcing her arch against him as he growled into her ear. "Soak me, darlin'."

His fist tightened in her hair, just enough to drag another raw scream out of her, and he felt her clamp around him again, pulsing hard, her release tearing through her body in waves. The sound of her screaming, gasping, soaking him with every convulsion shredded whatever control he had left. His own climax ripped through him, brutal and consuming, as she trembled beneath him, her orgasm fading into broken breaths.

When he finally slid out of her, her body collapsed forward onto the sheets, limp and shaking. Her breath came in ragged shivers, her muscles quivering from overstimulation. He stayed where he was, kneeling behind her, just watching her fall apart and slowly piece herself back together.

A darker part of him, the part that once craved breaking things beyond repair, went silent. It always roared during moments like this, hungry and vicious, but not with her. Not anymore. The instinct to wreck, to ruin, to take it too far… it simply wasn't there when she was beneath him. She had become the exception. His exception. He couldn't imagine a version of his world where she wasn't here, panting, shaking, and marked by him.

Her breathing softened, slow and steady, drifting into sleep. He looked down at the deep red bloom across her ass, heat radiating from the skin he had claimed with his hand. A dark satisfaction curled through him at the sight, followed by something unfamiliar, unwelcome, and yet impossible to ignore. He was going to have to take care of her, and he actually wanted to. He brushed his thumb across the flushed skin, light where he had been brutal moments before. He loved hurting her, loved the way she met his darkness without flinching. But for the first time in his life, he also felt the pull to soothe what he had created… to tend to what was his.

"You are never going to leave me", he whispered into the quiet room.

Chapter 40 Chuck

Chuck walked into the precinct mail room and found Holly standing with her back to him, sorting letters onto a cart. She was a beautiful girl, and Chuck never minded the excuse to stop by. She was on the shorter side but had curves that made a man's thoughts wander. Her long blonde ponytail swayed with every movement, and the whole room smelled faintly of sugar cookies.

He cleared his throat as he entered, not wanting to startle her. She turned, and the moment she registered who it was, her face broke into a smile. Chuck loved that smile, but his favorite part was her dimples. She looked so wholesome, and when she smiled, her eyes did too. She lit up the room, making you feel like you were the most important person in it, regardless of who you were.

"Hey, Chuck."

"Hey, Holly. How's the morning going?"

"Not bad. The usual." She smiled, but it didn't quite reach her eyes.

"So, Holly," Chuck began, his tone shifting. "I'm sure you know why I'm here this morning."

Holly's smile faltered completely. "Yeah… I don't have anything for you. He was a gentleman."

Chuck's eyebrows furrowed. "Did he give you any indication he wanted to hang out longer? Maybe take you somewhere private?"

Holly shook her head. "No. He just wanted to make sure I was safe. I even tried to act shy and nervous, like I'd be an easy target. Then I switched gears and tried to act like I wanted extra privacy. Nothing. You said he was easy, but that was the farthest thing from the truth."

Chuck rubbed his forehead, his thumb and finger pressing into his temples. "He must have said something. Didn't he want to meet up later? Try to convince you to come back another time?"

Holly shrugged and sighed. "I don't know what you want me to say, Chuck. He really was a gentleman. If anything, he tried to push me away. Told me his girlfriend wouldn't like that I was so close to him. I tried acting hurt, none of it worked. I really think you've got the wrong guy."

Chuck's head shot up, a scowl etching itself onto his face. Girlfriend? In all the years he had known Nick, he had never once dated anyone. He had seen him flirt, seen him take girls home, but he had never seen him with anyone for more than a night. Except for Danielle. But Danielle was a good girl, she would never be able to give him what he wanted. What was he planning?

"Thank you again, Holly, for helping out. Glad you're safe."

Holly offered a small, tight smile and went back to sorting mail. As Chuck turned to leave, he glanced over his shoulder. Holly had dropped a piece of mail and was bent over to pick it up. He couldn't help but watch as her skirt slid up her thighs. Just as she grabbed the letter, it rode up a little higher, revealing the gentle curve of her ass. His jeans tightened as he watched, wanting nothing more than to be right behind her. He knew he shouldn't be looking, but he couldn't help himself. He had wanted Holly since the day she had started at the precinct, but he had always been too afraid to ask her out. She was a beautiful, vibrant woman, and he was an older, balding detective. He figured she would never go for him, so he had never taken the chance. But seeing her like that, he really wished he had.

He adjusted himself quickly and walked out of the room before she could catch him staring. He waved to Darla at the reception desk as he passed, then badged into the detectives' room. The smell of stale coffee and donuts hit him like a wall. Calvin sat behind his desk, flipping through a folder, his face pinched in concentration. Henry walked out of the break room, donut in hand, and gave Chuck a nod.

"Mornin', Detective Braider."

Chuck waved back and retreated into his office, closing the door behind him. He didn't feel like hearing Calvin tell him he was right, that Nick was a good guy. He still didn't believe it. Every instinct told him there was something off about Nick. He just needed to figure out how he was pulling off these murders so perfectly. Not one trace of evidence. No hair, no blood. It was as if these girls never fought back. Why? Why weren't they fighting back? Even if they were in the middle of… it, at some point they would have to realize something had changed and fight, right?

Chuck rubbed his temples; a headache was brewing, and no amount of Tylenol was going to fix this. He needed to figure out how Nick was doing this, and where he was hiding the bodies. He needed to change tactics. He would have to befriend Nick again, get him comfortable, and then make him slip up.

Chapter 41 Nick

Nick drove back up the dirt trail toward the clearing where he had set the coyote traps. Early morning light spilled through the trees in thin gold bars, but the forest felt too still. As he rolled the window down, he noticed it immediately. The heavy, putrid stench of rotting meat was gone. The air was crisp, clean, and deceptively innocent. A slow, satisfied smile crept across his face. The bears and whatever other scavengers lurked out here had done their job. They had finished off Sienna completely. Nature had taken care of his mess, just like he had counted on.

He killed the engine and climbed out, his boots crunching through the frost-kissed grass. He scanned the field with a trained eye, walking forward with deliberate steps. Even though he knew any remaining trace would be dismissed as animal remains, he was never sloppy. But lately, a thin thread of irritation pulled at him whenever he thought of Chuck. Chuck had changed. Something in the man's eyes was different, watchful, calculating, and suspicious. Nick didn't know exactly what Chuck had pieced together, but he knew one thing: Chuck was paying attention. And Nick hated being someone's project.

He reached the first trap and looked down. It was exactly as he had left it, unset. Not a scrap of meat remained. Not a smear of fat. Not even a stray hair. The grass was pressed flat, disturbed only by the frantic rush of animals fighting over the meal he had provided. Nick's smile widened. He checked the other two traps and found the same thing, nothing. Absolutely nothing. Sienna had been devoured down to the last molecule.

He smirked, the familiar rush of victory warming his chest. Another kill erased. Another loose end tied up. He had gotten away with it again. He tossed the traps into the truck bed with a hollow clang. A faint flicker of guilt nudged him as he remembered the boys helping him lay the bait, laughing and gagging, totally unaware of what they were participating in. But guilt, to him, was like a fly that occasionally buzzed near his ear. Annoying, but meaningless.

Before he could turn back toward the driver's side, he heard tires crunching over gravel and pine needles. Nick froze, adrenaline tightening his muscles. A police vehicle appeared between the trees, rolling slowly toward him. Perfect timing, he thought bitterly. He forced his body into a casual stance and raised a hand in greeting. The driver returned the gesture before parking. Chuck stepped out, slamming the door behind him, his expression unreadable.

"Hey, Chuck," Nick called, forcing friendly ease into his voice despite the pounding in his chest. "What brings you way out here?"

"Thought I'd come see how the boys' work went." Chuck seemed to look past Nick, his eyes searching the grass. His eyebrows furrowed. "No bears?"

"Those bastards are getting smart," Nick said, crossing his arms. "They ate all the meat without setting off the traps. Have no clue how they did that."

Chuck whistled. "They are getting smarter. Scares me. We do not need them getting close to the campers and hikers."

Nick nodded. "I'm going to set up the traps differently. Make them harder to smell the metal. I think that's giving it away."

"Ahh, that makes sense. That's why we pay you the big bucks."

Nick watched Chuck, wondering why he was suddenly acting friendly. Everything in him screamed suspicion, yet he decided to play along. If Chuck had something up his sleeve, he would figure it out.

"Hey," Nick said, pulling his knife from its sheath. "Look at this beauty." He held the blade, offering the handle to Chuck.

Chuck took it, his eyes appreciating the woodwork on the handle before he slid a finger across the flat of the blade. "Wow, Nick, she is a beauty. Where'd you get her?"

"My uncle gave her to me when I graduated from the Ranger Academy."

Chuck whistled, still staring at the knife. "He has a good eye for knives." He handed it back. Nick grabbed the blade and quickly slid it into the sheath.

"Yeah, he really does."

Chuck tapped the bed of the truck. "Well… I better be going. Police business never stops."

Nick nodded and smiled. "I hear that. Have a good day, Chuck."

He watched as Chuck got back into his vehicle and made his way down the trail. He knew Chuck was definitely up to something. If he was a betting man, he would wager Chuck was hoping he would slip up. He was very wrong if he thought that, and Chuck would find out very quickly that you do not play games with Nick Chambers.

Back at the cabin, Nick grabbed the coyote traps and headed into the shed. He took his bleach spray off the bench and started cleaning them one by one, slowly swirling the paper towels over the metal, watching it glisten. The clean, sharp smell of the bleach filled his nose. He thought about his last kill, remembering how Sienna had looked right before she took her last breath. The fear in her eyes as she realized his grip was getting tighter, and not for her pleasure. The scent of fear that came off her as she gasped for air, her hands scraping his skin, begging him to let go.

Yet as he cleaned the traps and thought of Sienna, the urge to kill again, the urge that usually thrummed through him was gone. That urge to hear them gasp one last time, to feel their body go limp in his hands, to feel their pulse stop. All of that want was gone. Ever since Danielle.

He didn't know if that was a good thing or a bad one. He loved killing; that feeling he got from it, the power, the thrill of seeing their blood coat his hands as he came hard. It was an erotic experience he never thought he would get bored of. He enjoyed every second of it, down to cleaning up the mess the girls had made, and the mess he had made. He couldn't understand why Danielle had changed that.

Even when he was being rough with her, choking her until she struggled for breath, he never wanted to end her. He never wanted fear to enter her eyes, didn't want her digging her nails into him unless it was for pleasure. When he had his hand around her throat and her breath hitched, he never wanted to see fear. He wanted her begging for more. And she did.

He remembered the first time he had fingered her, watching as she made herself stop breathing right before she came. Maybe that was why the urges had stopped. She gave him all the same feelings, but instead of fear, she egged him on, begged him to tighten his grip, moaned louder as he hurt her, screamed in pleasure through the pain. She loved the sadistic side of sex, and for some reason, it fixed a small part of him. He was able to have those urges with her and enjoy them in a completely different way.

He loved watching her squirm in pleasure as he hurt her, but then he wanted nothing more than to mend the areas he had hurt. He loved that when he commanded her, she never questioned him, she did as she was told without hesitation. She gave him everything he needed, without the annoying inconvenience of disposal. She took the darkness in him and didn't flinch; instead, she fed it, tamed it, shaped it into something he could use and enjoy. She was obedient, eager, and responsive. She was the perfect victim because she did not need to die for him to feel powerful.

She was not just an urge he would get over. He needed her. She was going to be his willing victim, forever.

He finished up with the coyote traps and grabbed the paper towels. He made his way to the cabin and down the stairs to the wood stove. With a flick of his wrist, he lit the kindling, the smell of burning wood filling the area. He loved that smell; it reminded him of camping with his dad back home in Georgia, the scent of wood mixing with the warm air as they sat beneath the stars, his dad telling him stories of his time with Grandpa Jack. He missed his dad every day, hated that he was gone. Hated that he would never hear his dad's voice on the other end of the phone again.

He wiped his eye with the back of his hand and shook his head free of the memories. He needed to focus. He threw the paper towels into the stove and watched as they immediately scorched to ash. Whatever blood may have been on them dissolved into the fire. He swept the area, making sure there were no bone chips lingering on the floor. He threw the small scraps in, added a couple of logs, and shut the door. Fire could fix most issues, and today it was cleaning up his mess, a mess he didn't think he would ever have to clean up again.

He made his way up the stairs to finish tying any other loose ends. Chuck might think of himself as a clever guy, nosing around for clues, but all he would find, if he dared to dig, was a community that adored Nick Chambers. And without evidence? Not even suspicion could touch him. Because around here, Nick wasn't a monster. He was a hero. And he planned to stay that way.

Chapter 42 Danielle

Danielle walked into the community center with a smile she couldn't seem to shake, one of those soft, lingering grins that crept onto her face at random moments and refused to leave. For days now, every time she blinked, memories of Nick's bedroom replayed in her mind. The warmth of his hands, the rough scrape of his stubble against her skin, the way he said her name in that low, coaxing voice. Each memory sent her stomach twisting and her heart tripping over itself. At this point, she was convinced she had developed a permanent heart murmur from the way her body reacted to simply breathing the same air as him.

Before she could gather her thoughts, Mrs. Jenkins bustled toward her, waving frantically as if Danielle were returning from war rather than walking through the door.

"Hello, Dani," she sang, smiling with all the pride of a grandmother watching her grandchild make good life choices.

Danielle mustered a polite smile. "Hello Mrs. Jenkins. How are you today?"

"Oh, I'm just fine, dear," she said, swatting a hand in the air as if health and aging were too boring to discuss. Her eyes lit up, sharp and nosy. "But I heard you and Nick have become quite close. And by close, I mean closer than two people need to be unless they're planning babies or a wedding."

Heat exploded across Danielle's cheeks. She opened her mouth to respond, then promptly shut it again, mainly because she had no earthly idea what to say to that.

Mrs. Jenkins chuckled, delighted. "Oh, you don't need to say a thing, dear. Your face said it all. I think it's lovely. That boy needed a sweet girl like you to ground him."

Danielle forced a polite smile. "Thank you, Mrs. Jenkins."

"But may I add," Mrs. Jenkins continued, raising her eyebrows with wicked delight, "you didn't do too badly yourself. He is quite the handsome man. If I were thirty years younger, I'd let that man handle me… maybe even teach him a few tricks."

Danielle choked on her own breath. "Oh… okay, Mrs. Jenkins." She laughed nervously. "You have a wonderful day. I'm going to… um… go see where I'm needed." She hurried away before Mrs. Jenkins could share any more nightmare-inducing fantasies. Danielle pressed a hand to her warm cheek and shook her head, trying to scrub the mental image from her brain. She adored the community here, but sometimes their lack of boundaries was enough to make her sprint.

As she crossed toward the front desk, she noticed eyes following her. A few people whispered behind their hands. Others openly stared with amused smiles. The back of Danielle's neck prickled. Great. She and Nick were officially the town topic of the week.

"Well hello, Dani! How are you today?" Sally's cheerful voice cut through the tension, grounding her. Danielle instantly relaxed. "Hi, Sally. I'm doing pretty well. How about you?"

"Oh, can't complain. Things are good," Sally said, though Danielle doubted she had ever heard Sally complain in her life. The woman radiated sunshine even on stormy days.

"That's good to hear. Where would you like me today?"

"If you could work on sorting the clothes," Sally said, tapping her clipboard. "Yesterday was fill-a-bag Friday and people tore through those tables like wolves. They're a complete mess."

Danielle smiled. "On it."

She made her way to the four long tables against the back wall. Clothing was piled everywhere, tangled, wrinkled, overflowing like a textile tornado had blown through. She loved seeing how excited people got on Fridays, how much they appreciated the program. But lord, the chaos made Black Friday look organized. She decided to start with the children's clothes. At least adorable dinosaur shirts and unicorn onesies were a distraction from the stares. She folded carefully, sorting by size, letting herself drift into a peaceful rhythm. Her mind wandered back to Nick's hands, his mouth, and the way he—

A warm hand suddenly settled on her hip. Danielle gasped and spun around, straight into Nick's chest. His uniform fit too well, outlining every muscle. His scent of pine, clean soap, and something entirely him wrapped around her as he grinned down at her like she was his favorite sight in the world. God, that smile was enough to melt every woman in the room.

"Hello, darlin'," he drawled, leaning in to kiss her cheek.

Her breath caught. "Nick! You scared me."

He didn't look remotely sorry. If anything, he looked proud. And when someone across the room openly stared at them, Nick's arm slid around her waist in a deliberate, claiming gesture. Her face heated instantly.

"What brings you here?"

He held up a to-go cup and a small white paper bag in his other hand. "Stopped for coffee. Figured my girl might want something too."

My girl. Her stomach flipped, and her insides turned to syrup. "That was really sweet of you. Thank you."

Nick stepped closer, his voice dropping as he leaned near her ear. "Honestly? I just wanted to see you. And those cute cheeks that flush every time I'm around."

"Nick!" Danielle swatted his arm, scandalized and thrilled.

He raised both hands in surrender, grinning until a woman nearby chimed in loudly. "I saw her hit you! I can be a witness for that brutal attack," the woman teased, clearly flustered by Nick's attention.

Nick chuckled. "That's all right." He lowered his voice conspiratorially. "I liked it."

The woman giggled, and Danielle covered her face. "Oh my god, Nick."

"What?" He said innocently. "If they're gonna stare, we might as well give 'em something worth staring at."

Danielle shook her head and grabbed the cup and bag from him. "You are very popular around here, you know."

"Oh?" Nick raised an eyebrow. "Do tell."

"Mrs. Jenkins told me what she would do to you if she were younger."

Nick burst into full, hearty laughter. "She's always been a spicy one. Zero filter."

Danielle hummed as she sipped the coffee. Perfect, exactly how she liked it. He remembered. Of course he did.

Nick lowered his voice, leaning in again. "You know they're lookin' at you too, right?"

She blinked. "Me?"

His eyes dropped to her lips before returning to hers with heated purpose. "Yeah. Can't blame 'em. Look at you." His hand brushed her hip again. "But they need to understand somethin'."

"What's that?" She whispered.

"That you're mine." His voice was quiet, intimate, meant only for her. "And I don't share."

Her breath stuttered, and she went mute, her mind completely blanking.

"Well, darlin', I gotta get back to work," Nick said, brushing a thumb across her cheek. "I'll see you later at my place?"

Her breath hitched. "Absolutely."

Nick's smile deepened, dimples appearing. He cupped her face and kissed her slowly, and a little too heated for public, which only made her heart race harder. When he pulled back, mischief glittered in his eyes.

"And now they've got something new to gossip about."

Danielle groaned, cheeks blazing. "Oh my goodness. Go, before Mrs. Jenkins jumps you."

Nick laughed, gave her one last quick kiss, and headed out. Danielle watched him walk away, nearly every female eye in the building following him like he was a parade float made of sin.

She rolled her eyes. These women, honestly. Half of them were married, and yet if Nick showed even a hint of wanting them, they would sprint.

Turning back to the table, she started folding again. Except now, her mind wasn't quiet or drifting. It was loud with memories of Nick's hands, his mouth on her skin, the way he made her feel like she belonged to him. Warmth pooled low in her stomach. She couldn't wait until tonight. Until he touched her again. Until every part of her woke up under him all over again.

Chapter 43 Danielle

Danielle sat at her vanity, slowly applying her blush, her brain somewhere else completely. Two weeks had passed since the first time she and Nick had done anything. Yet she had lost count of how many times since then they had done things. She smirked, thinking about all the things they had done, the positions alone he had taught her, the accessories that had come with those positions, and every scream and moan.

She knew she needed to film this "Get Ready With Me" video, but she was having so much trouble focusing. Her ASMR videos were already faltering. Every time she walked through the park, she was no longer met by beautiful forest views and the sounds of animals. She was met by Nick, standing in his uniform, his stance making him the only thing on the trail. He would smirk at her, and immediately her body would react. The next thing she knew, he was on her, pulling her into the woods or his truck or even a duck blind, making her moan into his mouth while he pleasured her into oblivion. She was obsessed with him and wanted nothing more than his hands on her body forever. She didn't even sleep at home anymore; every night was spent in the sheets with Nick, yet she didn't get much sleep, and she didn't care.

Her fingers brushed the highlighter, but her gaze snagged on the inside of her wrist. A bracelet of purplish-blue bruises stained her skin, a stark and violent mural against the pale canvas. They weren't just bruises; they were claims. Her mind didn't wander; it was dragged back to the source, to the cold, definitive click of steel locking around her flesh. To the short, unforgiving chain he had clipped to the cuffs, the other end bolted to the bed frame, a tether ensuring she could never escape.

A flush crept up her neck, a phantom heat from the memory of being on her back. His hands had been vices on the backs of her thighs, forcing her knees toward her chest, opening her, owning her. He had slammed into her, each thrust a brutal, punishing act of possession. The metal had bitten into her wrists as she had pulled, a desperate, primal need to touch him, to dig her nails into his back and mark him as he was marking her. He had felt her struggle, her silent plea, and answered by fucking her harder. Her scream was torn from her throat, a raw sound of agonized pleasure. He drove so deep he bottomed out, a sharp, blinding nerve of pain that shot through her and melted into a guttural moan. He had growled low in his chest, a predatory sound of approval, and the words he whispered were a brand. "Good girl." The praise was a weapon, making her toes curl and her pussy clamp down around him like a vise. One hand abandoned its post on her thigh, his thumb finding her clit and rubbing in a merciless, demanding circle. Just as the crest of her climax began to break, he leaned over, his breath hot against her skin, and sank his teeth into her nipple. The sharp, exquisite pain was the final key, unlocking a release so powerful it felt like destruction. Her body convulsed, a trembling mess of pleasure and pain, a beautiful, agonizing symphony he had composed and conducted.

Her brush clattered onto the vanity, snapping her out of the moment. Her hands rubbed the bruises as she smirked. She couldn't wait to see what he had in store tonight. She quickly finished up the video, applying a cute light pink lip gloss and hitting the stop button on the camera. She figured she would just finish editing later; right now, she needed to get to the community center. Emily was going to be there today helping, and she couldn't wait to see her.

She jumped up, grabbed her purse, and ran out the door.

***

She opened the door to the center and immediately felt everyone's eyes on her. It's fine, she thought. *You opened the door and people are nosy. It has nothing to do with you in particular.* That thought was erased quickly as she walked over to Sally. Every step she took, she saw eyes watching her. She wanted so badly to look at them and snap, "Never seen a girl before? Eyes on your own business, people!" But she didn't. Her head dropped toward the floor as she walked toward Sally.

Then Nick's voice came into her mind. "Eyes up. If they're looking, it's because they want you… or they're jealous they will never be you."

She picked up her head and walked toward the desk, a smile on her face as she remembered the last time she was in here, Nick making every woman in the room jealous as he kissed her possessively.

Her train of thought was broken by Emily screaming her name. "Dani! Hey girl!"

Danielle turned to Emily, embracing her. She adored this girl and felt so guilty that they hadn't spent much time together lately. "Hey Emily! What's…"

"Oh no. We don't care about me. I want to hear about you!"

Danielle's eyebrows furrowed. "And what exactly do you want to hear?"

Emily rolled her eyes and placed a hand on her hip. "Don't play dumb. I heard from your mom that you haven't been home. Are you guys that serious?"

Danielle felt her cheeks redden as she shrugged. "Honestly, I have no idea. I'm just enjoying the ride."

Emily laughed. "Oh, I bet you are," then wiggled her eyebrows.

"Oh, shut up, Emily," Danielle said, swatting her arm.

"Come on," Emily said, pulling Danielle's hand. "I got us a spot at the toy area. Figured it's a quiet space for us to talk. I want all the details."

Emily dragged Danielle over to the toy area where a kid of about four was playing with a fire truck, making siren noises and lightly screaming for backup. She loved how imaginative kids could be but also wondered what shows he watched that he knew to scream for backup. She chuckled and walked to the table where boxes of toys were stacked, waiting to get out on display.

"Spill, chick. What is going on? You don't even do your ASMR videos anymore. What have you been up to?"

Danielle grabbed a box and looked at the contents inside. She grabbed a small blue teddy bear with a black bow around its neck and pulled it out. She fiddled with it as she thought of how much to divulge to Emily. "Honestly, I'm not sure. I try to make the videos but…" Danielle really did not know what to say. She didn't want to tell Emily about their sex life and the things he did. Her mom had always taught her that you do not talk about things others may covet. She loved Emily to pieces, but some things were private, and she didn't want anyone else to hold the memories of what she and Nick did together.

"I'm just not feeling them anymore. It's basically the same thing every day. I still go on my walks, and I still wear the camera just in case I see something amazing, but I stopped posting them.."

Emily studied her for a second before shrugging. "I get that. So, what are you going to switch up to? Or are you just going to stick to your 'Get Ready With Me's'?"

"I don't know. I need to figure something out so I can keep volunteering here."

A lady came up and started looking at some of the toys. Emily and Danielle looked at each other and knew by the look that they would come back to the Nick conversation. The lady grabbed the teddy bear, inspected it, then put it down and walked away. Danielle loved helping out here; everything was dirt cheap so that they could help people out. With Christmas coming up soon, she knew this place would start getting packed.

"So have you moved in with him, or just a temporary roommate?"

Danielle rolled her eyes; she knew Emily would never give up on these questions. She had to give her something. "He actually asked me to move in with him last night."

Emily's jaw dropped and she froze, eyes wide. "What!"

Danielle put her finger to her lips. "Can you not scream? People are looking."

Emily slapped her arm. "How have you waited this long to say anything to me?"

Danielle laughed and put her hands up. "I'm sorry. I haven't made a decision yet. I told him I would think about it."

"What's there to think about? He is Nick fucking Chambers!"

"I know, Emily. I know… but…" Danielle didn't know how to convey that she was nervous that if she moved in with him, he might get bored and then everything would end. What if she wasn't enough for him?

"No buts, chick! You are an amazing girl, and he is lucky to have you. He will not get bored of you or leave you. He is the winner in this by getting you."

Danielle stared at Emily, dumbfounded. *Had she said the words out loud instead of just in her head?*

"I know you, Dani. Way better than anyone knows you. I know you're scared, but you deserve happiness, and I have never seen you this happy. You think you hide it well, but there is a smile and a twinkle in your eye that you can't hide."

Danielle felt her heart get even more full, and the love she had for her best friend made her throat choke up. "Love you, Emily."

"Love you too, chick. Now spill. I need to live through you. Give me something."

Danielle laughed and went to speak when someone cleared their throat on the other end of the table. Danielle and Emily both looked over, annoyed that their moment was being interrupted.

Chuck stood before them, his hands on his belt, a stern look on his face. "Danielle, can I see you in the back? I need to ask you some things in private real quick."

"Umm… sure." Danielle looked at Emily, and Emily looked at her and then at Chuck.

"You do realize how small this town is?" Emily said in a sarcastic tone. "Like there's anything private around here?"

Chuck looked at Emily, and his lip curled. Danielle's heartbeat skipped; she had never seen Chuck like this. He was the guy who always had a smile on his face and a joke ready in his back pocket to make you laugh.

"Stay out of this, Emily."

Emily lifted her hands and whistled. "Okay, Officer Sunshine." Then she turned around and grabbed a box.

Danielle followed Chuck to the back of the building, where they kept all the things they didn't have room for and things that still needed to be sorted.

"What is this about, Officer Braider?"

Chuck raised his eyebrows and crossed his arms. "Dani, you do not need to be so formal."

"Am I in trouble?"

"No. I just have a couple questions I need to ask you, and I don't need anyone to know what's going on yet."

"Okay," Danielle said, a worried tone in her voice.

"Your videos in the park. We need them."

Danielle looked at him, puzzled. "My videos? Why?"

"We're hoping your camera caught someone in them that would show who has been committing these murders."

Danielle's eyes grew. She had never thought of that before. Then her mind went to her and Nick. She never turned off the camera when they were doing things. Granted, it didn't show much because it usually got thrown off, but there were definitely noises, and she didn't always have her clothes on. She knew she needed to at least erase those ones before they got them.

"Okay. I can drop it off today."

"Thank you, Dani. I also wanted to ask you a couple questions about Nick."

"Like?" Danielle did not like that. She again thought about the fact of how private of a person she was. And not only that, but Danielle knew she did not know anything about Nick's work life or what he actually did. How much help could she be?

"How long have you been seeing Nick?"

"Umm… I don't know… around two months. Why?"

"Have you noticed him acting different?"

Danielle wasn't sure how to answer that because, before this, she didn't really know Nick. She just knew he was a forest ranger. Other than the night that he had become very possessive and beat that guy up in the bar, he seemed the same to her.

"No. I mean… I don't know him that well, but he has been the same with me. Why are you asking?"

"I can't divulge that. I need to know how often you've been around him. Are there times he's by himself at night?"

Danielle felt anger filling her body. This was none of his business. "I am not comfortable with these questions. Is there a reason you need to know about my private life?"

"Dani!" Chuck shouted. Then she watched him close his eyes and breathe. When he opened them, he seemed calmer. "I need to know. I have my reasons that I can't talk about. Police business."

Danielle's eyebrows scrunched together. She didn't believe him for a second. Then the time that he had caught her pantsless at Nick's cabin came into her mind. Him telling her to be careful.

Danielle spoke quickly and with annoyance in her voice. "Look, Chuck. I don't know what this is about, and I don't care. I spend every night there, and you have nothing to worry about. He has been nothing but a gentleman."

Chuck's mouth tightened as he looked at her. She looked at him, and something in the back of her brain told her this was not his concern, as if it had nothing to do with her well-being and everything to do with Nick.

Before Chuck could respond, the back door slammed open.

Nick filled the doorway like he owned the building and every breath inside it. His eyes locked on Danielle first… then slid to Chuck with a coldness that made the room shrink. He stalked forward, every step slow and controlled.

"Mind telling me," Nick said quietly but with force, "why you've got my girl cornered in the back of a building?"

Chuck exhaled sharply. "Jesus, Nick. It's part of an investigation."

Nick tilted his head, eyes narrowing. "Investigations usually happen at the precinct. With witnesses. Cameras. Supervisors."

"That's not how this works…"

"Then let me make it easy for you," Nick cut in, his voice now edged with something lethal. "You don't pull Danielle away from a crowd. You don't isolate her. And you don't ask her a single personal question unless I know why."

"Whatever." Chuck said and waved his hand. "Thank you, Dani, for the answers. This will help the investigation more than you know." Then Danielle watched as Chuck walked away, shaking his head annoyed and slamming the door closed.

Nick was now standing in front of her, taking up her entire view. "What did he want? He didn't bother you, did he?"

Danielle shook her head. "I'm not actually sure. He was asking about you. Where you've been. If we've been together every night." Danielle watched as Nick's eyes grew dark, but not out of need, with anger.

"What the fuck could he possibly need to know that for?"

Danielle shook her head. "I have no idea."

"And what did you say?"

"At first, I told him it was none of his business, but then he kept pushing. He said he needed my camera for evidence, and then…"

"Your camera? What camera?"

Her stomach twisted into knots. She had never meant to tell him this way.

"I… I make videos," she whispered.

"What kind of videos, Danielle?" His voice sharpened. His posture didn't move, but she felt him close in on her, choking the air. Her pulse hammered in her ears.

"ASMR videos. For YouTube. They're calming videos."

Nick's tension loosened. His shoulders dropped slightly. "Okay. And why would he need them?"

"I record in the park. He thinks the killer might've been caught on the footage."

Nick tilted his head. "How often do you wear the camera?"

Her gaze slipped downward only for a second. Nick's hand was instantly at her chin, gripping, angling her face up to his.

"What did I tell you about looking away from me?"

Her breath hitched, and heat rushed under her skin. "Only at the park," she whispered.

Nick's mouth curved dark and pleased. "So, you've basically been filming our porn sessions."

"Kind of," she muttered, cheeks flaming. "I was going to delete them before giving him the camera."

Nick smirked, eyes dark with hunger. "No. Save those. On a private card." He leaned close, lips brushing her ear. "I want to watch what you look like when you think I'm not paying attention."

Her knees nearly buckled.

"Fuck, Dani," he growled. "You blush for me, and it makes me want to make your ass the same color."

Danielle's eyes went wide, and her face reddened further.

"Fuck. Bend over. I need to fix you for looking at the floor."

Danielle felt butterflies swarming in her stomach. She turned around and braced her hands on the table in front of her as she felt Nick's hands slide down her leggings. A shiver ran through her body at the touch. Then she felt the sharp slap to her ass. She gasped, the sound catching in her throat before melting into a soft moan as warmth instantly bloomed across her skin. The sting lingered in the best way, sending heat rushing through her as her pulse quickened, and to her surprise, she liked it far more than she wanted to admit.

"You will not look away from me again," he said, low and commanding. His hand came down again, harder. "And remember," he breathed, leaning over her, possessive and absolute, "you belong to me." Then she felt his hand make contact again, harder this time. "And that's for not telling me about the camera."

Danielle felt Nick slowly slide her leggings back into place before his hand moved gently over the spot he had just punished, the soft touch sending a completely different kind of shiver through her. A second later, he spun her toward him and captured her lips in a deep kiss, leaving Danielle breathless as she melted against him. Then Nick straightened, turning toward the door. He paused with his hand on the frame, glancing back at her with a slow, wicked smirk. "Oh… your coffee and danish are waiting at your table," he added, as if he hadn't just unraveled her.

Danielle stood frozen, pulse roaring in her ears, stunned as he walked out without another word.

Chapter 44 Nick

Nick pushed through the precinct doors like a storm rolling in, his boots echoing off the tile. Darla sat up straighter at her desk, her cheeks turning pink the second she saw him. "Well hello, Ranger Chambers," she practically sang, twirling a pen between her fingers. "Nice to see you."

"Likewise, Darla," Nick said with a polite grin, tipping his hat just enough to charm without offering anything real. His voice dropped, darker, all business. "I need to see Officer Braider. It's important."

Her smile faltered at his tone. "Oh… of course. I'll buzz you in right now."

The heavy door buzzed, then clicked, and Nick pushed through the hallway with long, purposeful strides. The fluorescent lights hummed above him, but nothing could drown out the pounding anger in his chest. He reached for Chuck's office, already picturing his face, when Calvin stepped out from a side room.

"Hey Nick! What brings you in?" Calvin asked, easygoing as always.

Nick forced a small smile. Calvin didn't deserve the edge simmering under his skin. "Hey, man. Need to talk to Chuck."

"Gotcha. Been a while. We should grab a beer after work."

"Love to. Six?"

"Perfect." Calvin brought his fist out. Nick bumped it, both men laughing for a moment until Chuck's office door opened. The laughter died instantly.

Nick turned. Chuck walked out with that self-important swagger, the kind of walk that only pissed Nick off more. Acting like he was in control. Acting like he hadn't backed Danielle into a corner with questions that weren't his damn business.

"What's up, Nick?" Chuck asked casually, like they were still friends. Like he hadn't just crossed a line.

Nick didn't bother with the fake pleasantries. He slammed Danielle's memory card onto the nearest table so hard it rattled a coffee mug. The entire bullpen went silent.

"Heard you wanted my girl's memory card," Nick said, his voice low, and controlled. "The videos of her in the park."

Chuck's face flushed instantly. Three detectives sitting nearby paused and turned, confused by his words. Nick stepped closer, crowding into Chuck's space. "Poor Danielle was shaking when she told me you cornered her. Asking her private questions you had no right to ask. Pressing her for videos of her doing very private things."

Calvin spun toward Chuck. "What the fuck, Chuck?"

Chuck raised both hands, defensive. "It's not what it sounds like. She records herself walking in the park. I thought maybe it caught something about the killer."

Nick grabbed the memory card, held it up between two fingers like it was evidence… then threw it against Chuck's chest. "Yeah? And mixed in with those peaceful little walks were videos of us. Of me and my girlfriend. Half-dressed. Half out of the frame. She was crying when she handed that to me, knowing people would see her doing things."

Gasps. Whispering. One detective muttered "Jesus Christ" under his breath.

Chuck's jaw tightened as he straightened. "Nick, that's not what I asked for. I needed the park videos. Not anything else."

Nick stepped in so close Chuck had to tilt his head back. "Fun fact, Chuck… I fucking live in the park."

"That's not what I meant," Chuck stammered. "You're twisting my words."

"Bullshit." Nick's voice dropped to a growl. "Stay the hell away from my girlfriend… you sick fuck."

As he walked out of the room, he could hear the detectives yelling at Chuck, saying worse things than he had. Nick smirked. Everything was working out exactly as he wanted it to.

"Nick!" He turned to see Calvin jogging up to him. "Here's the card. Tell Dani I'm really sorry. None of us will be watching that, especially Chuck."

"Thanks, dude." He grabbed the card and clapped Calvin on the shoulder. "Anytime, bud. See you tonight. And again, let Dani know we're sorry. We're not all like that."

"Will do. See you at six."

Nick walked out of the precinct and got into his truck, placing the card of them being intimate in his glove box.

***

Nick walked into the bar like he owned the place. The neon lights washed over him, shadows clinging to his shoulders like old friends. Gary looked up from behind the counter and grinned. "Well hello there, Ranger Chambers." He slid a Samuel Adams across the bar with a chuckle. "No bar fights tonight, man."

Nick smirked, taking the bottle. "No fights tonight. Scout's honor." He took his seat, claiming the space with casual dominance.

Calvin dropped onto the stool beside him. "Hey, Nick."

"What's up, man?" Nick lifted a finger at Gary. "Another one."

Gary nodded, popped the top off a second bottle, and slid it expertly down the counter. Nick caught it and handed it to Calvin.

"Thanks, dude."

Silence settled, comfortable, broken only by the game on TV and the clinking of glasses. After a few minutes, Calvin sighed. "Man… I can't believe what Chuck is doing. He's been acting off lately."

Nick nodded. "How so?"

"I don't know, man," Calvin said, his hand playing with a coaster. "He keeps looking in the wrong places, asking questions that don't seem right, and he's been snapping lately."

"Sounds like Chuck is bothered by something. Maybe his private life?"

Calvin shook his head and shrugged. "Not really sure, man. I don't like it, though. He's going to mess up and miss something, and we'll never catch the dude with the way he's acting."

"Maybe he needs to step back from this one. He was pretty close to the girls that went missing or died."

Calvin took a sip of his beer, then seemed to stare at his bottle a little too long. "He said something weird the other day about Jenny. Said he'd been watching her. Said he was shocked she went missing."

"And you think…?"

"I don't know, dude. He started acting weird not too long after that."

Nick took a long sip of his beer, trying to figure out how to reply. "I know he had a thing for her. She never reciprocated."

Calvin looked at Nick, his eyebrow raising. "What are you getting at?"

Nick shrugged. "Just sayin'. Maybe he's mad that she never wanted him. Maybe he feels guilty for pushing his feelings on her. I heard he pushed pretty hard."

"From who?"

"Oh, God. You know all the old biddies in this town love to talk."

Calvin chuckled. "Yeah, that's for sure. God… you think he may have gotten mad? Reacted?"

Nick lifted his hands. "No clue, man. I'm just telling you what I heard. If he was acting weird after that, maybe it's guilt, or something else."

"Shit. I hope not."

Gary came over with two more bottles. "How's Dani? She okay?" Gary asked.

"Yeah. She's good. Thanks for asking, Gary."

Gary nodded and grabbed the empty bottles. "She's a really sweet girl. Comes from a good family."

"Yeah." Nick's jaw tightened. "I'm lucky." He meant it, but hearing another man say it made something dark coil in his gut. Even harmless comments felt intrusive. Danielle wasn't for men to discuss.

"Man… you and Dani," Calvin said, laughing. "How the hell did you end up with sweet, holy Dani?"

"By being her angel," Nick said with a smirk.

Both of them laughed and clicked bottles. "For real though, really happy you have her. You seem happier."

"Thanks, dude." And then he quickly changed the subject. "How's being a detective? Everything you hoped for?" Nick did not want to talk about Danielle to anyone. This was his girl, his. No one else should be able to get an insight into what she was like around him and what she did to him to put a smile on his face.

"It's good. More paperwork than I thought," he said, laughing. "Really thought I'd see more action."

"In Ravensburg?" Nick laughed.

"Yeah… I know. It was pretty quiet until these murders."

"Any leads?"

Calvin shook his head. "No. This guy is good. He makes sure to cross every T and dot every I."

"Damn."

Calvin nodded and took another sip of his beer. He tapped his hand on the bar. "Alright, man, I'm tired. Gonna go knock out."

"Alright. Night, man. Nice seein' ya."

Calvin raised a hand to Gary and then tapped Nick on the shoulder. Nick turned to watch Calvin walk out and smirked. Everything was falling perfectly into place.

Then he heard the door open and turned to see Larry walking in.

"Heeey, guys. Th' party's… here."

Nick took that as his moment to leave. He threw money on the bar, raised a hand to Gary, and walked out the door.

As his hand gripped the door handle of his truck, he heard someone say his name.

"Hey, Nick."

He turned to see Mrs. Johnson standing there, a tiny dress that left nothing to the imagination, walking toward him. He rolled his eyes. *Here we fucking go again.*

"What's up, Mrs. Johnson?"

"You're leaving pretty early. You don't want to come back in and hang out. We can play pool, and I can show you how I handle a stick."

Nick's hands gripped into fists. He hated when women acted like this. She was married and had made invitations to him multiple times, completely disrespecting her husband. Her husband really needed to get her in line.

"I'm sure your husband would love that invitation."

She moved in closer and pushed her chest out, her breasts almost falling out of the dress. "He's not here tonight. Come show a girl a good time."

Nick laughed and moved in closer. "Oh, I'm about to show a girl a great time. Make her scream my name 'til she loses her voice."

"Oh yeah?" Mrs. Johnson said breathless, biting her lip.

"Yeah." Nick stepped closer and dropped his voice. He was so close he could hear her heavy breathing. "I fucking love when Dani screams for me."

He stepped back and watched as her face dropped. She quickly adjusted her dress and stood straighter. "Well… good for her," she snapped.

"Every night," Nick said with a slow, mocking tilt of his hat before walking away.

He climbed into his truck and started the engine. Skillet poured from the speakers, and he tapped the steering wheel, a predatory smile on his lips. He was shocked at his reaction to Mrs. Johnson. Every time someone made an advance toward him, he either wanted them punished or wanted to be the one to punish them until they could not speak. He did not have any of those feelings now. All he thought about was punishing Danielle, and not for pure pain, but to pleasure her.

He backed up the truck with the thought of her bent over the table at the community center. He pulled onto the road and headed toward his cabin, and her. The only woman he wanted to break… and the only woman he would die to protect.

Chapter 45 Danielle

Danielle stood in Nick's cabin, waiting for him to get home. He had texted saying he was grabbing a quick drink and would be back soon. She checked her phone again, then let her gaze wander, the walls suddenly feeling too close, too silent. She drifted toward his bedroom door, her steps slow, and cautious. Curiosity tugged at her harder than she liked to admit. She wasn't a snooper, but Nick kept so much of himself locked away. He gave her pieces, never the whole picture.

Her fingers brushed the door. She hesitated, then nudged it open. "Oops," she murmured to no one, a small shrug lifting her shoulders. "Might as well."

She walked in and flipped the light switch. The room was immaculate. The bed was made with military precision, the sheets smooth and tight, the pillows aligned perfectly. No clothes on the floor. No clutter. Nothing out of place. It didn't surprise her. He was the type of guy who needed control, clearly in every aspect of his life.

She walked closer to the bed, her mind replaying the moments they had shared here, late at night. The biting, the spanking, the screaming, no-holes-barred sex. Goosebumps prickled her arms as she thought about the things they had done, and she felt her cheeks warm. The way he controlled her here, the strength he showed as he fucked her hard, in positions she never thought her body could achieve. Hearing him praise her and talk dirty to her as he did vile things to her, things that made her body react, feeling herself getting wet, her pussy yearning for his cock.

She walked to his dresser. The top was bare except for a six-slot mahogany watch holder. The watches inside were stunning, heavy, and expensive, gleaming beneath the light, yet one of the slots lay empty. Her fingers slid over the top of the dresser, and she was shocked not to feel a speck of dust.

She walked to his closet and opened the door. A walk-in closet of perfectly color-coded clothes stood before her. Suits, dress shirts, and uniforms to the left; casual shirts and jeans to the right. She stepped inside and saw the back wall, where sneakers and boots sat perfectly arranged, looking like she had walked into a Famous Footwear. Hats hung perfectly on the wall above them. In the corner of the closet sat a hamper with a lid. He didn't even want to see his dirty clothes, hiding them from view. A spot of red on a white shirt caught her eye.

She pulled the white undershirt from the hamper and saw red smears on the fabric. It looked as if he had been wrestling with something. Her mind went to hunting, remembering him talking about getting a pretty big buck not too long ago. He really needs to soak that. She put the shirt back in the hamper and walked out of the closet, making sure to close the door perfectly. He seemed like the type of guy who knew exactly how he had left things. She was shocked that throughout the entire cabin, there were no personal effects. The only things were the pictures on the mantel, and that was it. She turned the light off and closed his bedroom door.

Making her way back to the living room, she went back to the pictures. She loved the one of him as a young boy, a fishing pole in his hand, a huge smile on his face, a small trout hanging from the end. She assumed it was his dad behind him, smiling wide, proud of his boy. Her finger slid across the metal tin again. Her mind burned with what he might hold inside. Her gut told her not to look, yet she couldn't help herself. She popped the top of the tin and was shocked. Inside, nestled in faded velvet, was a single, delicate silver necklace. She picked it up carefully, studying it. A small, heart-shaped charm hung from the fine chain, simple and worn smooth with age. She set it back gently, her mind already spinning. She realized she saw no pictures of Nick's mom and wondered if this was hers. Maybe it was the only thing he had of her. She was curious about the piece but figured if he ever felt comfortable enough, he would tell her.

She placed the tin back on the mantel and went to the fridge, grabbed a beer, and plopped onto the couch. She wondered how many other girls had sat on this couch, waiting for him to come home, or doing much more than that. She quickly swatted the thought from her mind. She did not want to think of that. Nick was with her now, and the way he acted, she knew he was quite obsessed with her, the way she was with him. She did not feel she had anything to worry about.

She heard tires crunching through the gravel as headlights came closer. Nick was close to being in here, touching her, making her go just as crazy as she had last night. Her body shivered as she thought about him and how much she needed to feel his touch. The door creaked opened. Before she even turned her head, she could already smell his musky pine and soap scent, and her body reacted immediately, her pussy pulsing, her body aching for his cock.

Chapter 46 Nick

Nick saw the lights on in the cabin and smiled, his thoughts instantly going to Danielle. He felt his stomach flutter and his cock instantly harden. His body had never reacted this way for anyone. He was still shocked that Danielle was having this effect on him.

He put the truck in park and sat there for a moment, thinking of her. Him standing in the bedroom, his arms around her ass as she wrapped her legs around him, holding her in the air as he fucked her hard, lifting her off him only to slam her back down onto his cock, her tightness enveloping him and making him go crazy. Hearing her moans as she gripped his neck hard, her nails digging into him, making him go even more wild with need. Feeling her tighten even more around him, feeling her breathing stop, knowing she was seconds from soaking him. He had wanted his hand around her throat so badly in that moment; it always made her cum harder, gasping for breath after, every pulse on his cock making him harder, his need to release stronger.

His jeans tightened as he hardened even more, the fabric screaming to be unzipped. He adjusted himself and headed for the cabin door. He was going to have a lot of fun with her tonight.

The door opened and there she was, curled on the couch, beer in hand, wearing nothing but his shirt. The sight punched the air from his lungs. His mouth went dry. Possession surged through him, hot and immediate.

Danielle smiled when she saw him. Nick didn't smile back. He didn't want conversation. He didn't care what she had done all day, what she wanted to eat, or what plans she thought she had. None of that mattered. The only thing that mattered was the way her body responded to him and how easily she gave it over.

He crossed the room in long, decisive strides.

"Hey N—" was all she got out.

"Don't talk unless I tell you to." Nick bent down, his hands on either side of her, and kissed her hard. His mouth consumed hers, needing her badly. His tongue slipped past her lips, and she tasted of beer and her own sweetness. His tongue swirled with hers, sucking her tongue, wanting every bit of her. He pulled back and bit her lip, making her moan.

"Fuck, Dani," Nick said breathlessly.

He dropped to his knees in front of her, deliberately slow, forcing her to watch him. He looked up at her through his lashes, studying her face, the way her breath had changed, the way she waited. Nick smirked. "Open your legs."

His chest filled with pride as he watched her smirk and open her legs without question. Her dress bunching up her thighs, and he smirked at the sight of her not wearing panties. He could smell her want before he had even moved, and his mouth watered. Her pussy was beautiful and slick, ready for him.

Nick knelt forward and slid her ass to the edge of the couch. He slid his tongue up her slit as she moaned and grabbed the edge of the couch. Nick growled low in his throat at the taste of her. He could eat her all night long. He slid his tongue against her semi-swollen clit, making her hips buck. His tongue swirled the area as Danielle grabbed his hair.

"Fuck, Nick."

He smirked as he listened to her moan his name and grip his hair harder, the sting sending pleasure waves through his body. Nick slid a finger inside of her, feeling how slick she was. His cock hardened further.

"You want more, darlin'?"

"Please," she said breathlessly.

He growled. "I love when you beg."

Nick slid another finger inside of her, her hips jerking again as he swirled his tongue around her clit. He knew she was close by the way her screams got louder. He fingered her faster as she rode his hand. His other hand gripped her thigh hard as he said low, "Come for me, darlin'." He slapped her hip, feeling the sting in his own fingertips. "Now."

Nick bit her clit hard enough to make her scream from pain and pleasure. As he did, he felt her body tighten, her breathing stop. His fingers slid in and out of her faster as he sucked on her clit. He bit her clit again, a little more forceful, and felt her body react, her pussy pulsing around his fingers. She gasped and screamed as her body released, as he felt her wetness dripping on his hand, her body trembling.

"Good girl," he growled.

His fingers slid out of her, and his tongue took their place as her hands gripped hard on his hair.

"Please. Stop."

Nick smirked and slid his tongue along the outside of her folds. While still on his knees, he growled authoritatively, "Turn over. Knees on the couch."

She moved without a word, her ass pushed out to him as her arms lay on the back of the couch. Nick's hand made contact on her ass hard.

"You do not tell me to stop." His hand cracked against her ass again, harder this time. "Ever."

She yelped, but beneath the sharp sound was unmistakable pleasure, the kind that only pushed him further. He spanked her a couple more times, each smack echoing through the room until her skin burned crimson beneath his hand, the outline of his fingers stamped across her like a warning. Nick stared at the marks with dark satisfaction. He loved seeing evidence of himself on her body. Loved knowing she would feel him long after this moment. He stood up before bending behind her, his arm braced beside hers as he leaned near her ear.

"Understand?"

He watched as she nodded. His mouth twitched before his hand came down once more, sharp enough to make her cry out and jolt forward in surprise.

"Use your words, Danielle."

"Yes, Nick. I understand."

Nick moaned in satisfaction as he slid two fingers into her. She was still drenched, and her hips moved to deepen his finger placement. "Ride my fingers, Danielle."

He watched as her hips slowly ground against his hand. He slid his fingers out and rubbed her now-swollen clit, his lips nipping at her neck. Nick smirked as she ground into his hand harder, his fingers sliding over her, his thumb sliding up and down her lips and rubbing the entrance of her pussy.

“Fuck,” was all she could get out, her breaths ragged.

“Come for me, darlin’.”

Nick felt her grinding slow down, her movements methodical. Her body tightened, and his stomach flipped. She was going to come for him, on command, again. Just like she always did. He loved how receptive she was to his control, the way it made her wetter, hotter, more ready for him. He slid his hand to her neck and gripped her tightly. His fingers felt her pulse as he gripped tighter. She ground onto his hand slowly, his fingertips curved as she moved into them, her body shaking. Then he felt her body tremble and her head bend forward. He released her neck as she gasped for air. The scream that came from her was animalistic and raw as she came all over his hand again.

Nick sank to his knees behind her, drawn by the primal urge to claim every trace of his dominance. His tongue traced a deliberate path up her inner calf, the taste of her flooding his senses, awakening a hunger that made his cock throb with brutal need. His tongue traveled higher, exploring the sensitive flesh of her inner thigh. He felt her muscles tense and quiver beneath his touch, and a smirk twisted his lips.

When his tongue finally reached the swollen folds of her pussy, he didn’t hesitate. He started licking with a possessiveness that left no doubt to who owned her. Her sharp intake of breath and the soft, desperate sounds escaping her lips were music to his ears.

“Fuck, you taste so good.” he growled against her flesh, his voice rough. The vibrations made her legs tremble further.

His tongue ventured upwards, needing to taste an area he had not ventured to yet. He felt her attempt to pull away, a futile gesture of defiance that only fueled his need. His fingers dug into her hips, holding her in place as his other hand came down hard on her ass, which was followed by a yelp. He pressed his tongue between her cheeks, circling her entrance. As he breached the tight muscle with the tip of his tongue, he felt her try to push away and then freeze.

"Don't you dare, Danielle. You know what will happen."

He felt her body tighten as he slid his tongue against her, tasting her, enjoying her. After a few seconds, he replaced his tongue with a finger, sliding it inside of her. The moan that came from her was muffled. He looked around to see her face buried in the couch. Nick slapped her ass. "I want to hear you. Move your face."

With a smirk, he slid two fingers into her ass, sliding in and out of her, her body moving with his fingers. She moaned loudly.

"Stay there. Do not move at all."

Nick walked into his room and grabbed the vibrator he had bought for her. He was going to need a little help tonight; he wanted to hear her scream louder than she ever had. He walked back over to where she knelt on the couch and smirked.

"Good girl."

His hand rubbed her very red ass cheek before sliding two fingers back into her ass slowly, easing himself in. He could feel her pussy getting soaked as he fucked her ass hard with his fingers, listening to her moan loudly.

"What I do to you next, you are not allowed to move away."

He felt her body go rigid. He dropped his pants, his cock pounding, needing to feel her. He placed his cock at her entrance and felt her body tighten.

"Loosen up. I promise I will go slow… at first."

He felt her arms loosen a tiny bit and took it as a win that she was at least trying. He slid into her slowly, the tightness of her making him crazy. He fucked her faster, her tightness pulling him in and not wanting to let go. After a few seconds, Nick's pace picked up. He heard her moaning lightly, her hands gripping the back of the couch. As he moved faster, he could feel her body moving with his, her moaning getting louder.

That's when he placed the vibrator on her clit.

Her body jerked, and she moaned louder. "Fuck, Nick."

"Hold this. I need you to play with your clit while I fuck you hard."

Nick felt her fingers slide over his, her hand staying in place, the vibrator's buzzing sound coming through her moans. Nick gripped her hips harder and slammed into her, her one arm barely able to hold herself up with how hard he fucked her. He felt her body tighten and knew she was about to unravel for him again. He slammed into her harder, his body hitting hers with such a force that he knew her ass cheeks would be very red and sore tomorrow, and not from the spankings she had received.

The scream that left her throat was raw and loud as she came again, her body shaking underneath his hands. He could feel her body wanting to give in and collapse. He slammed into her one more time before he felt his own release, his head going fuzzy as he came hard inside of her, his hands gripping her so hard he knew she would have deep purple bruises on her body.

As his mind cleared and his body finished, he slowly slid out of her. He watched her body tremble against the couch, her head falling forward as she tried to catch her breath. Her eyes stayed closed, chest rising and falling in uneven breaths, completely spent beneath him.

Nick brushed a hand along her side before slipping his arms beneath her and lifting her effortlessly against his chest. She barely stirred as he carried her down the hall to the bedroom, exhausted to the point of collapse, and something dark inside him eased knowing he had been the one to unravel her like that. He had needed the release more than he wanted to admit.

When he reached the bed, he lowered her gently onto the mattress and pulled a blanket over her. For a moment he simply stood there watching her before leaning down and pressing a soft kiss to her forehead.

"Rest," he said quietly. "You'll need it."

Because he wasn't finished with her yet. Nick just needed to make a phone call, and then he would be back to ravage her again.

Chapter 47 Calvin

Calvin dropped the receiver and picked up his jacket. He had received the weirdest call from Larry. He knew he needed to check it out, but he wasn't excited about it. People like Larry never called for real emergencies. Yet, Larry had seemed very off, nervous, upset, slurring his words the entire time, but it didn't feel like a typical drunken call.

"Hey, Henry. We need to go check something out really quick. Grab your coat."

Henry looked at him, confused, but shrugged and grabbed his jacket. When they got in the car, Calvin started toward the park.

"So," Calvin began, feeling like an idiot for going off drunken Larry's words, "Larry called. Said there's something we have to see."

"Larry?" Henry said, confused. "Drunk Larry?"

"Yeah. I know how it sounds. But he seemed real upset. Not himself."

"Larry hasn't been himself since the day he was nineteen and picked up his first can of beer."

"I know," Calvin said, holding a hand up. "But we still have to take it seriously."

Henry shook his head but didn't say anything else about Larry.

"Hey, Calvin?"

"Yeah?"

"What's up with you and Chuck? You guys used to be close."

Calvin looked at Henry, his eyebrows scrunched together. "You heard him. He's been after Nick for a bit. And putting Danielle in the mix now… Something's off with him."

"That part's messed up, I'll admit," Henry said. "But he's just covering every angle. Nick lives in the park… he has to check that."

Anger crawled up Calvin's spine, his jaw tightening. "Are you kidding me? He didn't check Nick, he accused him. Big difference."

"True."

"And not only that," Calvin snapped, "girls keep going missing, and Chuck always seems to be right there. Watching. Pointing them in the right direction. You don't think that's strange?"

"Coincidence, at most," Henry said. "Chuck loves this town."

"Maybe. But he's way too close. He needs to be pulled off the Ravensburg murders."

"That," Henry said, nodding, "I can get behind."

They fell silent the rest of the drive. Gravel crunched under the tires as they pulled into the campground. Larry stood outside his RV near a small fire, a beer can clutched in his hand. Calvin stepped out as Larry approached, his eyes wide, his head shaking slightly like he couldn't stop.

"Hey, Larry. What's going on?" Calvin asked.

"H-hey, guys… thank God you came. I found somethin'… somethin' that ain't right."

"You said it's in one of the cabins?"

"Yup… th-the run-down one. Y'know… basically in the woods."

"What did you see?" Henry asked, stepping closer.

"Coolers," Larry said. "Two of 'um."

Henry and Calvin exchanged a look. Henry shook his head. "We came all the way out here for coolers?"

Calvin raised his hands. "Let's just go look." He grabbed a flashlight, and the three of them headed toward the run-down cabin.

Calvin walked in first and saw a blue tarp covering a lengthy area. He pulled the tarp away, and a knife clattered to the floor.

"I didn't think we'd need evidence bags, but maybe you should go grab some," Calvin said to Henry.

Henry nodded and ran back to the car. He came back breathless with the bags.

"You didn't have to run," Calvin said, laughing.

Henry shrugged. "Didn't wanna miss anything."

Calvin grabbed the knife with his gloved hand and dropped it in the bag. "Why are there two coolers? I don't understand what you could possibly be keeping cold way out here," Calvin said to Henry.

Henry just shrugged. "Guess we should open one up."

Calvin flipped the latch. The lid popped slightly, and the smell hit them like a wall. All three men stumbled back, gagging.

"What the fuck is that smell?" Larry choked. "That… that ain't no deer."

Calvin grabbed a stick and pried the lid open. One look inside, and the stench punched him in the face. He turned just in time, emptying everything he'd eaten for dinner onto the floor. Henry stepped forward, covering his nose. Even with his fingers pinched tight, the smell burned. His flashlight cut into the cooler. Inside was a liquefied mess of human remains, hair swirling in a foul soup, skeletal fragments drifting alongside patches of greenish-black flesh clinging where skin used to be.

"Fuck!" Henry shouted before bolting outside and vomiting into the dirt.

Calvin tried to breathe, but every inhale brought another wave of rot. His body retched repeatedly, stomach cramping violently.

"Calvin," Henry said between heaves, "we need to get away from the cabin."

Calvin tried to move, but another spasm doubled him over. Henry grabbed his arm and dragged him back. "Come on. Move."

"Fuck, Henry. What did we just find?"

"No fucking clue. We need to call the chief medical examiner and get him on this. I think this may be one of our victims."

Calvin and Henry stood by their cruiser, watching the cabin and making sure no one went near it. They finally saw the medical examiner show up. He had his crew with him, and they quickly moved to the cabin, taking pictures and writing notes. After the evidence was carefully tagged and documented, the coolers were taken to the morgue. The chief medical examiner walked over to Calvin and Henry. "Hey, guys. This is quite the scene," he said, shaking his head.

Calvin stood up. "I got one question for you, Hank. How do you guys handle the smell?"

Hank pulled up his mask, revealing a gleam of paste on his nose. "Vicks and a mask can do wonders for smells."

Calvin and Henry laughed. "Damn," Calvin said. "Wish we could have had that."

"Damn straight," Hank chuckled, shaking his head. "Alright, guys. We'll examine the body and let you know who that poor person was." He shook their hands and walked to his car.

"Damn, Henry. What if this is Jenny?"

"I really hope you're wrong."

"Me too. Let's go back to the precinct. We have a lot of paperwork to do."

They waved to Larry and got in the car. Calvin knew this might be their first big break in figuring out who was murdering these girls.

Chapter 48 Calvin

A full week had passed, and with every day that dragged by, Calvin's hope thinned to a fragile thread. He had told himself that today would be the day. Today, the lab would finally call. Today, they would put a name to the body or what little was left of it that was sealed inside those coolers.

By midmorning, his patience had evaporated. Calvin dialed the DNA analyst lab again, his fingers tapping anxiously against his desk as the line rang. These murders were high priority. They needed answers. The town needed answers.

"Hey, Jan," Calvin said when the familiar voice answered. He tried to sound casual, but the strain bled through. "I'm really hoping you've got something for me."

There was a brief pause on the other end before Jan spoke again. "I was actually just about to call you," she said. "We just got the results back on the person in the coolers."

Calvin leaned back in his chair, the old springs creaking under his weight. After hounding Jan all week, the moment he had been waiting for suddenly felt like one he didn't want to hear at all.

"I'll fax the full report over," Jan continued, her voice softer now, "but I wanted you to know first. The two coolers only held one person. It came back as Jenny… Jenny McGrath."

The words landed like a punch to the chest.

"Damn," Calvin said quietly. "Thank you, Jan."

He hung up the phone and stayed there, reclined in his chair, staring at the ceiling. Somewhere deep down, a part of him had still clung to the hope that Jenny had simply vanished, that she would turn up exhausted and shaken, but alive. That hope died right there. Jenny had been in the coolers. He exhaled slowly, dread settling into his bones. Now he had to do the part of the job he hated most, telling a family their daughter was never coming home. Telling a town they had lost one of their own in the worst way imaginable.

Calvin dragged a hand down his face and thought about Jenny. She was not just a doctor. She was *the* doctor. The one who volunteered at free clinics, who donated her time to charities, who showed up for people when no one else would. She had stitched up kids who couldn't afford insurance and quietly paid bills for patients who were too proud to ask for help. This town was going to break when the news got out.

He stood abruptly, knowing the longer he waited, the worse it would get. But before he could take two steps from his desk, the phone rang again.

"Calvin Walters," he answered.

"Hey, Calvin. It's Fred from forensics."

Fred hesitated, then added, "We're faxing the results now, but there's something I wanted to tell you. We got a hit on the fingerprints from the knife."

Calvin stopped moving. "Good," he said. "That was fast. Who is it?"

Silence stretched across the line, long enough that Calvin thought the call had dropped. Then Fred cleared his throat.

"It's Chuck Braider."

Calvin's grip tightened on the phone. "Chuck… as in Chief Detective Chuck Braider?"

"Yes," Fred said carefully. "We ran it multiple times. Thought there had to be a mistake."

"Fuck," Calvin breathed.

"I know."

"Thanks for calling, Fred."

He hung up the phone and sat back down. How could it be Chuck's prints? What had that fucker done? Then it hit him, what Chuck had said about Jenny. He had said that he had been watching her closely, and Jenny had come in here months ago stating a dark-colored car was stalking her. Chuck had a dark-colored car. Chuck had told the girls to go to the campsite where they were murdered. Chuck was trying so hard to blame Nick. Everything linked back to Chuck, including his own fingerprint.

Calvin hurled the pen he had been fidgeting with across the room. "Fuck!"

Henry stepped into the doorway just as the shout echoed. "What's going on?"

Calvin looked up, his eyes dark. "Results came back. It's Jenny."

Henry's shoulders slumped. "Damn," he muttered. "That's… that's rough."

"That's not even the worst part."

Henry frowned. "What could be worse than that?"

Calvin met his eyes. "Chuck's fingerprints were on the knife."

"What?" Henry snapped. "How the hell—"

Calvin ran through everything aloud, the stalking report, the campsite, the obsession with Nick, the way Chuck had positioned himself at every turn. Henry raked a hand through his hair. "Fuck."

"Exactly."

They sat in stunned silence, staring at the wall, neither of them ready to fully accept what they now knew. Parker walked in and took one look at their faces.

"Let me guess," he said slowly. "The results came back."

Calvin filled him in, every detail heavier than the last. Parker sank into a chair, his eyes unfocused, his jaw clenched as he absorbed it all. The room felt suffocating.

Finally, Henry broke the silence. "Well," he said grimly, standing up, "guess it's time we find Chuck… and bring his ass in."

***

Calvin barely heard the chatter of the precinct as he and the other detectives stepped inside. Phones rang. Printers whirred. Someone laughed too loudly near the coffee pot. It all felt wrong… too normal.

"Where's Officer Braider?" Calvin asked, his voice cutting through the noise.

Darla looked up from her desk, her fingers still frozen over her keyboard. "Mail room," she said after a beat. "Saw him head that way a few minutes ago."

That was all Calvin needed. He moved fast, his boots striking tile with purpose. The closer he got, the quieter the hallway became, as if the building itself knew something was wrong. He slowed at the mail room door when voices drifted through the thin metal. Calvin peered through the narrow window.

Chuck had Holly backed into the far corner, her shoulders pressed flat against the wall. His hands were planted above her head, blocking any escape, his body close enough that she had nowhere to look but down.

Calvin felt heat rush to his face. He eased the door open just enough to hear.

"Chuck… I'm sorry," Holly said, her voice shaking. "I just… I don't feel that way. I never did."

Chuck laughed softly, the sound low and intimate, like they were sharing a secret. "You will," he said. "You just don't know it yet." He leaned closer. "When I'm done with you… you'll be thankful you gave in."

Calvin didn't think. The door slammed open against the wall. "Get the fuck away from her."

Chuck barely had time to turn before Calvin crossed the room and grabbed him by the collar, yanking him backward with brutal force. Chuck stumbled, crashing into a metal filing cabinet. Drawers rattled, one popping open as he barely caught himself from falling. He spun around, fury flashing across his face.

"What the fuck, Calvin?!"

Calvin stared at him, his jaw tight, his eyes burning. "Oh, this is rich," he said quietly. "You're standing here like I'm the problem."

"Relax," Chuck scoffed. "Holly wanted—"

The punch landed hard. There was a sickening crunch as Calvin's fist connected with Chuck's face. Blood sprayed instantly, streaking down Chuck's lip and chin. Calvin hit him again before Chuck could react, then again, each blow fueled by weeks of doubt, missed signs, and the look on Holly's face.

Hands grabbed Calvin from behind, pulling him back. "Get him off!" someone shouted.

Calvin strained against them, breathing hard. "You disgusting fucking piece of shit," he snarled, spitting onto Chuck's cheek.

"Calvin! Corner… Now!" Henry barked.

Chuck staggered backward, wiping at his nose, his eyes wide and wild. Henry grabbed him, spun him around, and slammed him against the wall.

"You are under arrest," Henry said sharply. "You have the right to remain silent. Anything you say can and will be used against you in a court of law—"

Handcuffs snapped shut around Chuck's wrists.

Chuck laughed, breathless and unhinged. "You're kidding me. This is a joke, right?" He looked around. "For what?"

Parker stepped forward. "For the murders of Carly, Tina, and Jenny."

The laughter died instantly. Chuck's face went pale. His mouth opened, then closed. It took a moment before sound came out. "You're serious?" he said finally. "Parker… come on. You know me. I would never—"

"The evidence says you would," Parker replied flatly.

"This is bullshit!" Chuck shouted, pulling against the cuffs. "I didn't do anything!"

Calvin stepped into his space, his eyes locked on his. "Say another word," he said quietly, "and harassing Holly becomes part of the charge."

Parker and Henry dragged Chuck down the hallway as he continued to protest, his voice echoing off the walls. Calvin watched until the interrogation room door slammed shut. He turned back to the bullpen.

"Darla," he said. "Go check on Holly. Stay with her."

Darla's face had gone white. "What's happening?"

"You'll be briefed later," Calvin said. "Go."

Inside the interrogation room, Chuck slammed his cuffed hands onto the table. "I didn't do what you think I did."

Calvin dropped the evidence folder in front of him, the sound sharp and final. Photos spilled across the table, crime scenes, evidence bags, lab reports.

"Then explain this," Calvin said. "Your prints on the knife. On the necklace we found in your truck. And why you told those girls exactly where to go and definitely had time to stage the scene."

Chuck flipped through the photos, faster and faster, his breathing shallow. "This doesn't make sense," he muttered. "I didn't do this." Then he stopped. His head lifted slowly. "The knife," he said. "That's Nick's. He showed it to me."

Calvin slammed his hands on the table. "Here we go. What is it with you trying to shove this onto Nick?"

"I'm not lying," Chuck said, shaking his head. "He showed it to me."

Parker leaned forward. "Then where are Nick's prints?"

Chuck scoffed. "If he framed someone, don't you think he'd wipe it clean?"

"Jenny reported a dark-colored vehicle stalking her," Calvin snapped. "Guess who owns one."

"A lot of people do!" Chuck yelled. "You're reaching!"

"We have witnesses," Calvin shouted back. "They saw you parked outside her house at night. And guess who the last call to Jenny was the night she went missing?"

"I was doing my job! I told her I'd keep an eye on her!"

Henry laughed darkly. "You did more than that."

"Fuck you!" Chuck yelled. "I didn't do this!"

Calvin stared at him for a long moment, then nodded slowly. "And Holly?" He pointed toward the observation glass. "Cornered and scared as you kept her locked in front of you."

"That was role play," Chuck said quickly. "She liked it."

Something inside Calvin snapped clean in half. He lunged forward and drove his fist into Chuck's face. Skin split. Blood spilled onto the table, dripping between scattered photographs.

"You are a pathetic excuse for a man," Calvin growled. "And you're done."

He turned sharply. "Take him."

Calvin stormed out of the room, slamming the door so hard the glass rattled. The room got quiet as the officers turned and stared. "Get back to work!" He barked.

He paced to the detective area and grabbed his phone. His hands shook as he dialed. *Nick needed to answer.*

Chapter 49 Nick

Nick had just finished his shift and couldn't wait to get home. Danielle had agreed to move in with him, and today was their first day living together. The thought of having her with him whenever he wanted excited him in a way he didn't understand. He had never wanted to be with someone, had never wanted to be tied down, and he liked to kill his girls. All those things had gone out the window when he met Danielle, and he still didn't know why.

He wasn't sure if it was her submission, her willingness to let him handle her with his claws out, never showing fear and never backing down no matter what he wanted to try. Either way, for some reason, he was very happy and felt normal. That was something he never thought he would say. She made him realize he could have a family, enjoy the rest of his life, and not have to deal with hiding evidence and lying all the time.

He pulled into the driveway and smiled. Danielle stood in the window, laughing as she danced with their new dog. Henry's front paws were clasped in her hands while his back legs awkwardly tried to keep up, turning their living room into a clumsy little waltz. When the pound had called to say Jenny's family couldn't keep the dog, that it hurt too much because he reminded them of her, Nick hadn't hesitated. They weren't ready to adopt him out yet, he just needed a temporary home. Nick had said yes instantly. Watching Danielle with Henry now, he was even more glad he had.

He had the family he never thought he would have. His dad had been the last family he knew, and when he passed, he never thought anyone could fix that hole in his life. Then Danielle had walked into his path and flipped his world upside down.

He stepped into the cabin and was immediately greeted by two very happy members of his new household. Henry rushed him first, tail wagging wildly. Nick scratched behind his ears before pulling Danielle into his arms. The quick kiss he had meant to give her turned deeper as his lips met hers. She tasted of white wine and strawberries, and he couldn't get enough. He swirled his tongue around hers, bruising her lips with the force of his kiss, his body reacting to her, his jeans becoming very tight.

"Bedroom. Now."

He watched her flushed face smirk, then turn and walk toward the bedroom. His phone rang, and he glanced at the name. He was going to drop the phone on the counter, but Calvin's name popped up. They had just gotten some pretty heavy news, and he knew he needed to hear out whatever Calvin might need to get off his chest.

"Calvin. What's up?"

"We found more evidence. Searched Chuck's truck. There was a girl's necklace in there. After searching through pictures and posting the necklace on social media, a mom from out west called us stating her missing daughter had the same one. Stated she had come to New Hampshire for a skiing trip. We're pretty sure there's another victim."

"Shit. Sorry, Calvin. I know this isn't easy for you."

"Thanks, bud. We took him into custody. His face already felt like part of his punishment. Judge won't let him out on bail. He's in here until his court date. Hope he burns for this."

"Damn. Good. Those were great people he took away." Nick was surprised at himself; the statement came out even more sincere than he had tried for.

"I know. But at least these families now have justice."

There was a beat of silence before Calvin spoke up again. "Alright, bud. I'll talk to you later. Have a good night."

"You too, Cal. Let's get a beer some night."

"That'd be great."

Nick closed the phone and smirked. Everything was working out exactly as he had intended it. He had been the one to call Larry, casually mentioning raccoons running in and out of an old cabin. Nick knew Larry couldn't resist that. Larry loved raccoons. Loved cooking them. Loved investigating anything that might lead to one. It would have been an innocent enough call if the police had asked him how he had found the coolers, but he knew it was drunk Larry. They would just assume he drunkenly wandered into the cabin.

He also knew they would find his knife with Chuck's hand prints on it from the other day. And that necklace from the nosy bitch that he had chipped into a million pieces, which he had placed in Chuck's truck a few days before all of this. He knew it would come back as the girl's; it was a unique necklace that most people wouldn't have had. And now he no longer had to worry. Chuck was taking the fall, and he no longer had to kill because, for some odd reason, Danielle had cured that insatiable need to feel their last breath.

Nick slipped his phone into his pocket and headed down the hallway, anticipation coiling tight inside him. He slipped the nipple clamps out of his pocket that he had bought earlier. He was going to wrap his hand around her throat, while he pulled lightly on the clamps, feel her give herself to him completely, and make her beg, like the good girl she was.

Chapter 50 Nick

A year later, Nick sat beside Danielle on the hard wooden bench, his body composed, his expression carefully neutral. The courtroom was packed, every seat filled, people lining the walls, the low hum of whispered speculation buzzing like static in the air. The jury had sent word they had reached a verdict, and now the entire room seemed to be holding its breath.

Danielle's hand trembled as she tightened her grip around his. He could feel the panic in the way her fingers clung to his, hear it in the shallow rise and fall of her breath. Chuck had been a fixture in her life for years, and the truth revealed over the last several days had shattered that image beyond repair. Nick gave her hand a slow, reassuring squeeze and glanced down at the princess-cut diamond on her ring finger, catching the light just the way he had imagined when he chose it.

His thoughts drifted back to the night he had asked her. She had come home from the community center to find roses covering the kitchen counters and spilling into the living room, candles glowing softly across the coffee table beside chocolates, strawberries, and her favorite red wine. The smile that broke across her face had nearly buckled his knees. He had been so nervous he could hardly speak, every time he opened his mouth, his stomach fluttered and the words vanished. So instead, he pulled her into his arms and kissed her, and when he finally let her go, his head was clear again. She always had that effect on him. He dropped to one knee and pulled the ring box from his pocket, but before he could even form the words, tears were already streaking down her cheeks. She had taken the ring herself, sliding it onto her finger with shaking hands before dropping to her knees to kiss him.

The rest of that night was mostly a blur, but he smirked, knowing it might be hurting her to sit down right now.

Nick's memory was interrupted by the side door opening. The judge entered first, her face impassive. The jury followed, filing into their box with solemn expressions, eyes fixed straight ahead. A hush rolled through the room, conversations dying instantly, the silence so thick it pressed against Nick's ears.

"Juror Number One," the judge said, her voice sharp and measured. "Please stand and state your verdict."

The juror rose, clearing his throat. His hands shook just slightly as he gripped the edge of the rail. "In the charge of first-degree murder in the death of Jenny McGrath," he said, pausing briefly, "we find the defendant… guilty."

A wave of sound rippled through the courtroom. gasps, stifled cries, and murmurs of disbelief. Nick didn't flinch. Chuck's head dropped forward, his shoulders folding in on themselves as if the weight of the word had physically crushed him. His hands clenched in his lap, his breathing visibly uneven.

The juror continued, his voice steady now, as though repetition had hardened him. Guilty for the murders of Carly and Tina. Guilty for the death of Kylie London. Each verdict landed like a nail being driven deeper into a coffin.

The judge adjusted her glasses and looked down at Chuck. "Based on the unanimous verdict of this jury," she said, "this court sentences the defendant to life imprisonment without the possibility of parole."

The room erupted. Family members sobbed openly, others shook their heads in disbelief, a few murmuring prayers under their breath. Deputies moved in swiftly, gripping Chuck by the arms as they led him toward the exit. His family reached for him, crying out his name, their grief raw and unfiltered.

Nick watched it all with quiet interest.

Danielle turned to him, tears spilling freely now. "I just… I don't understand," she whispered. "He was a good man. He wouldn't hurt anyone."

Nick brushed his thumb across her knuckles. "I know," he said softly. "I never thought it would end like this either. His family… God, I feel for them."

Danielle shook her head and blotted her face with a tissue. "I'm going to go talk to the family."

"Okay. I'm going to be over with Calvin. Come get me when you're ready."

She stood and walked away, her shoulders hunched under the weight of it all.

Nick crossed the aisle to where Calvin stood frozen, staring at the door Chuck had disappeared through. "Still shocking, huh?"

Calvin turned to Nick, his face a mask of shock. "I still can't believe he did it. I wonder what snapped in his mind?"

"That's the thing about guys like that. You'll never know."

Calvin shook his head in disgust. "God. Those poor families. What a fucking bastard."

Nick patted Calvin's shoulder. "We just need to make sure we're there for them as much as they need."

"Absolutely, man."

Nick turned his gaze back to the courtroom. People clustered together now, whispering, crying, shaking their heads. The scent of fear and grief hung in the air, sharp and familiar. A thought crept through him, cold and exhilarating. If he had not planned everything so carefully… that could have been him standing there. Instead, he felt a slow, unsettling thrill coil through his chest. He had ended lives with his own hands and had gotten away with it. That exhilaration made goosebumps form on his arms as he thought about killing again, about the feeling of hearing their last breath on his cheek as they begged with their eyes for relief.

Then he noticed Mrs. Johnson across the room. She caught his eye and smiled, her tongue flicking briefly over her lips before she turned away. Her husband stood beside her, oblivious, speaking quietly to another man.

Nick's jaw tightened. She was inviting attention she didn't deserve. She needed to be put in her place, and clearly, her husband was not going to do it. He felt this strong urge to be the one to do it.

Nick looked away before anyone could read his thoughts. He had everything he could possibly need, a life he never thought he would have, but the hunger was stirring again. The urge to fix the women of this world, and make them respect their man the way Danielle did. Mrs. Johnson was a prime example, she was careless and sloppy. She would never learn if someone didn't teach her a lesson she could not forget. Danielle would never see this side of him, but the craving had become a physical ache now, a relentless hunger gnawing at him, a thirst that demanded to be answered.

He had hid it from everyone once; he could hide it again.

The one he kept

Thank you to my readers

When I first started writing *The one he kept*, I knew I wanted to create a story that felt unsettling, addictive, emotional, and impossible to look away from. Nick and Danielle's world became one I lived in for a long time, and every chapter pulled me deeper into their darkness, obsession, and complicated connection.

Writing this book challenged me in the best ways possible, and I truly cannot thank you enough for taking the time to read it. Whether you stayed up too late finishing "just one more chapter," screamed at the characters, or questioned every decision they made, I'm incredibly grateful you went on this journey with me.

As an independent author, reader reviews make a massive difference and help more people discover my books. If you enjoyed *The one he kept*, I would be very thankful if you left a quick review on Amazon or Goodreads.

Thank you again for supporting my writing, my stories, and these characters that completely consumed my mind while creating them.

Until next time…

Follow your fear.

- Jill Norris

About the Author

Jill Norris is a horror and thriller author with a passion for creating dark, emotionally charged stories filled with obsession, tension, and horror that linger long after the final page.

When she isn't writing unsettling fiction, she co-hosts the paranormal podcast Bantering Banshees, where she explores haunted locations, paranormal history, and eerie legends alongside her best friend, Steph.

Outside of writing and podcasting, Jill can usually be found cosplaying Star Wars characters or planning her next paranormal adventure.

The one he kept is one of her darkest stories yet, but if you like this one check out her other book, Room 1210.

Made in the USA
Coppell, TX
09 June 2026

79657337R00194